7 MINUTES

J.D.
WRIGHT

7 Minutes

Jessica Wright

Woodhall Press
Norwalk, CT

woodhall press

Woodhall Press, 81 Old Saugatuck Road, Norwalk, CT 06855
WoodhallPress.com

Library of Congress Cataloging-in-Publication Data available

ISBN 978-1-949116-89-2   (paper: alk paper)
ISBN 978-1-949116-90-8   (electronic)

First Edition
Distributed by Independent Publishers Group
(800) 888-4741

Printed in the United States of America

This is a work of fiction. Names, characters, business, events and incidents are the products of the author's imagination. Any resemblance to actual persons, living or dead, or actual events is purely coincidental.

CONTENTS

To those who can't let go
and those who love too hard

CHAPTER ONE

The Night Before

Her body was the first to be found. Facedown on the kitchen floor. Blood pooled around her stiff and pale frame like a dropped glass of milk, staining the light yellow flowers of the flooring she hated, to where the worn-down petals now looked orange. The only thing she hated more than that flooring was the color orange.

Brain matter and skull fragments littered the floor around the discarded meat tenderizer, and one single clotted footprint could be seen walking toward the living room. The crime-scene photos showed her to be at peace, her expression that of a woman who knew death was coming and there was nothing to be done about it.

I wondered if that's what my face would look like tomorrow when I faced my death.

The detective would find her wedding ring still perched on the windowsill over the kitchen sink, exactly where she'd always forget it after washing the dinner dishes.

My son's body was the second to be found. Not yet dead, but close. His lips were blowing bubbles in the thick fluid draining from his head wound, not quite deep enough to snuff out his breath. The tiny sliver of life left in his body was an oversight, an egotistical mistake made by the man who had lifted the fireplace poker and struck his hard, angry head; a mistake that would haunt both of them for the rest of their lives.

Unlike his mother, he was not at peace. Slumped down on the couch, his face pulled into a scowl as his mind urged him to fight, to wake up and keep living. He had never appreciated his life to begin with, never understood the gift of existing. For his mind to fight so hard to not give up was as out of character as a firefighter staying in bed through a five-alarm blaze. The poor boy would struggle with his newfound will to embrace life once he was able to recognize his thoughts and tame his consciousness again. The body fighting beneath him would never be the same, nor would his mind. He'd struggle to move, struggle to remember, and struggle to close his eyes without terror seeping through every receptor in his body. It'd be years before he could walk unaided, and even then, he preferred to keep a cane around in case a loud sound or sudden movement pushed him over the edge. Ahead of him lay years of anguish, frustration, and wondering why he hadn't accepted the gift of death when he'd had the opportunity.

My body would be the third. Years would pass in between her physical death, his mental death, and mine. My body wouldn't be found after the fact but observed, and my last breath would be welcomed by thousands of people around the world. I planned to go happily tomorrow with the knowledge that I was off to the life I'd always wanted: eternity, next to her.

Unlike Trudy and Christopher, my body wouldn't be inspected and fussed over, but wheeled out of a cold sterile room, zipped up in a body bag, and quickly burned. There would be no plaque left on a wall for people to remember me by, no headstone in a lush green field. I would go quietly to an anonymous forever.

If my death was to give this world one thing, though, I wanted it to be for my kids to finally find peace—peace between this mad situation, and within all of us, whether we were here on Earth in the whole, the half, or in spirit only.

I knew Trudy was still here. I could feel her around me every day. She taunted me. She blamed me. She thanked me. She scolded me. Sometimes her breath on my neck was welcoming and sensual. Sometimes her slap on my face reminded me of why she had to die in the first place. But even in death, she still hung around to watch over me, waiting, counting down the days until our souls would be able to meet again.

Tomorrow is the day I will die.

A strong statement, yes, I know. But we must accept that there are people walking this Earth who know exactly when their life will be over. There are people who see signs their time has come. People who know the disease sitting within will soon take them. Those who know death is coming will prepare a five-course meal for the Reaper, waiting for him to ring their doorbell and take them home.

There are other people who wake up with a feeling deep in their soul that this will be their last day on Earth. Those lucky ones will make the choice to slam the door in Life's face once they've been dropped off from what they consider a horrible date with their last breath. They take matters into their own hands, breaking the hearts of unsuspecting people around them.

But none of those lucky people are me.

3

My death has been calculated down to the minute by a higher power. August 2, 2025. My time of death made headlines years before I found myself lying on this twin-size metal bed for the last night of my life, snuggling into a scratchy cotton sheet and threadbare waffle-weave blanket. My night won't be spent in deep sleep, though; rather, I'll spend it imagining how it might feel to stare into my executioner's frigid, disconnected, soulless eyes when we meet tomorrow. When we meet at the time they've scheduled for me to die.

Like other Death Row inmates, I had my last checkup today. A trial run, if you will, to make sure I was familiar with the gurney, and what to expect. The warden also said the walkthrough was done to help me be relaxed during the coming process. Truthfully, that takes an absurd amount of power to think you can tell someone they will die and you want them to feel comfortable with the process. What happened earlier today was nothing more than a Band-Aid for their conscience—not stitches for my well-controlled fear.

No matter how hard they tried, I wasn't prepared feel the executioner's nimble fingers tighten the thick, wide belts put in place to hold me down. The leather smelled like autumn but the smoothness felt too pure, too unmarred for this occasion. I wondered how many other wrists had been bound by these same brown straps, how many ankles had been kept from kicking by the same. And if the lack of scars in the leather meant they all went peacefully without a fight.

I hoped to go softly, just like the brochure given to me by the prison nurse said I should. I want to think I've had enough pain in this life, although I know others would disagree. Many people feel I deserve more.

Some days I feel that I do as well. Pain has a way of healing you, but I'm fairly confident that my soul could be shredded a few more times, my flesh torn open at least once more, and my blood shed from a few deep wounds for the others out in the world who hate me—those who will always hate me. There are people who would rejoice to hear I was hurting. They'd say the monster was being given a dose of his own medicine. And I would relish the intensity and agony of the injuries bestowed upon my body, knowing that the pain meant I was still alive.

The doctors and their support staff came to introduce themselves. I felt sorry for them, with their dead eyes and firm demeanors. Disconnected and detached. I wondered how they ended up here. Did they wake up one day and decide they wanted to legally kill people? Had they wanted to be something else when they were children, like an astronaut, a lawyer, or a fireman, but instead they wound up tightening the straps to end a man's life instead? At what point in medical school does a doctor decide to work for a jail and administer what is required to take a soul from our world? Surely no one truly wants to be an executioner. Or do they? I suppose for some people the thought of being a legal murderer might be appealing.

The very idea of a child being born with a desire to kill terrified me— even more so than the thought of my death creeping closer with each tick of the clock hanging on the wall. My fate had come to meet me.

I was strangely comforted by the fact that I would soon be reunited with my love. My one. My only. The very soul that marked me for death when she took her last gasps of air.

The doctor placed the cold stethoscope against my back and asked me to breathe.

I took a long, slow breath, hoping the sound was clear and gave them zero reasons for concern. I needed to be healthy, to pass the qualifications for someone allowed to die. I focused on making sure there was no rattle, no slight hitch to any of the breaths I took in, nice and slow. My life was over and I was ready. I wouldn't fight anymore.

Warden Stanfield was there, watching over the proceedings.

"What would you like for your last meal, James?" he asked.

"I'd like a bowl of hot tomato soup, a grilled cheese sandwich, a side of hash browns, and a strawberry milkshake," I said. "But if I could be so bold as to ask for real cheddar cheese, Campbell's soup mixed with heavy cream, and a real strawberry milkshake—not the bagged-mix kind from McDonald's. I don't want to be too imposing or an inconvenience, but this would mean a lot to me."

"Interesting. You may be our cheapest last meal ever. Maybe even the country's." Warden Stanfield laughed. "You've always been an easy one, James. Just a heart of gold."

He paused and set his pen down against his clipboard.

I expected him to have one of those expensive pens where you refill the ink and keep the casing in your breast pocket as a sign of prestige, but instead he laid down a cheap plastic one, its barrel full of the ink that leaves globs along the pages.

"I don't understand. Why'd you do it?" the warden said. "If I can be honest, and maybe a little out of line, if it weren't for the evidence, I wouldn't believe you were capable of such a heinous crime. Your wife? And your son? No, James. Dr. Peters and I agree. You just don't fit the profile."

I stayed silent, contemplating his words.

The question was so simple, and yet so complex. One I'd been asked over and over again. One I couldn't answer. The answer only existed between Trudy and myself. Maybe Christopher, one day, if he tried to remember the truth.

"Do you have to draw my blood, too?" I asked, dodging the question.

I'd never liked blood, but I'd never been squeamish about seeing something we all have, either.

Once they'd thrown Trudy's crime-scene photos in my face at the trial, a new phobia had developed. For some reason, the district attorney believed showing me the photos of my bludgeoned ex-wife would jog my memory, convince me to quit playing games and connect the dates and times they couldn't force to fit their theory. They screamed at me for being a liar, hiding details, wondering why my story about the day's events didn't match up with the evidence.

While I knew Trudy was dead, nothing can ever prepare you for seeing gruesome photos like this that would get locked inside of your head and forever change the way you see someone.

When I tried to sleep at night, I no longer dreamt of walking hand in hand with my sweet flaxen-haired love. Her lovely face was replaced with matted strands and fragments of skull stuck to dried pools of blood flooding from her temple. Red stains gushed and leaked from her chest and abdomen when she stumbled toward me, rage flowing in her eyes like electrical currents through a pool. I continuously had dreams where I made love to a zombie. In her madness and frustration she would reach inside of me and rip out my intestines, pulling every single foot of slimy pink bowel out with a smile, asking, "Why?" The question would come over and over and over again until I finally forced myself to wake, bolting upright in my bed, always back in the tiny cell.

I couldn't tell her ghost why this had happened to her. I couldn't tell her why she'd had to die in such a cruel fashion. I had no answers for her, dead or alive. I had no answers for the media. I had no answers for my children. And I had no answers for Warden Stanfield.

I did write my final thoughts in two letters and addressed them to the only two people who mattered. My children. One to Ava. One to Christopher. They may decide to open them to read my truth, or maybe they'll burn them in rage. I would understand both the curiosity and the anger. They hated me. They had hated me before Trudy's murder, but after she was lowered into the ground, there was no possible chance for forgiveness. I only hoped my death would give them at least a slight opportunity for relief from their pain.

"No blood today, James," Dr. Peters replied. "We took enough from you yesterday. And while you may not find this to be good news, given the circumstances, your results were clean. You, sir, are in perfect health."

I took a deep breath, this time without it being monitored. I felt the air shake down my esophagus like a pinball, bouncing from side to side as it journeyed to my lungs for a final score.

Yes, this was great news. I could legally be put to death by lethal injection at 10:17 a.m. tomorrow morning. One night and seven minutes were all that stood between me and once again being in the arms of the only girl I'd ever loved.

CHAPTER TWO

Trudy

I can't believe James said those things to me. Pushed me like that. Made me say those awful, awful things back. He sat there in that diner and acted like a self-righteous martyr. Like I owed him something. I owed him nothing. I'd already given him everything during our life together. Every single ounce of me. What more could he possibly want? There was nothing left to give.

Although I asked myself this silly question, I already knew the truth.

He was greedy. Even when I was depleted, completely out of anything left to give, he'd come up with some sliver of me to take and demand it on a silver platter. He repulsed me. Disgusted me. Infuriated me. And at the same time, he drove me crazy with a desire that never seemed to burn out. Even when I thought the flame was gone and I belonged elsewhere, the embers never ceased to glow. They'd rage until they found something to light aflame.

Did I love him? Of course. I loved both of them. We all needed each other and we always would. Our destiny had been written in the stars, and no matter how hard we wanted to fight fate, we couldn't. From childhood to now, it had never mattered what we'd said, how we acted, or the things we tried to hide from each other. We would always need each other. Denny, James, and me. The three of us would forever be intertwined.

But this.

Tonight was unforgivable. Lines were crossed. How dare Denny come at me like that because I was helping a friend? Our friend. Enough was enough, and I needed him to know I wouldn't accept this treatment anymore, and I was really done this time. I was tired. This time, that hardheaded son of a bitch would listen. I'd make him. He could have me, but he couldn't control me. Enough was enough. No more telling me how weak I was. No more laughing when I cried. No more empty threats of kicking me out because he knew I had nowhere else to go. Every bridge in my life was burnt to ash by my own hands; the kerosene used to ignite the towering flames spilt forth from my venom-laced tongue.

Truthfully, I didn't care about the trail of damage left in my wake. Everything could be rebuilt with time and care if a person was meant to be in your life. After all, how many times had we looked at each other and said those famous words: Enough is enough. We're done. This is the end, for real this time. We'd said it, and packed, moved out and left, blocked phone numbers, changed last names, and still wound up unpacking, moving back in, sharing numbers, and changing names again. The cycle was exhausting.

It was up to me to break the gears that kept my pitiful story running.

Soon, he would understand that this time, even though he'd think

I was joking, I meant it from the depths of my soul. Those three simple words slipped out last night when I crept into bed. No, I cried them out from the very core of my heart.

"Enough is enough!" I said, my threadbare cotton nightgown snagging against the corner of the bed.

He laughed, told me to stitch it up like a real woman, told me to stop complaining about not having any money. To stay at home, tend to the house—these were the greatest gifts a husband could give his wife, he said. My life was easy and I should be more grateful, bottom line.

I boiled over with combustible rage. This wasn't love. This wasn't life. This wasn't what I deserved, and I knew it. He didn't, clearly, but that wasn't my problem. Was it? No. But here I stood, in the center of the kitchen, reliving what had happened the night before and trying to figure out where I'd gone wrong.

After I'd told him to leave, to stop doing these things, he kept on pushing me to see exactly what I would let him get away with. And I let him, just like the women on afternoon TV, the women I'd yell at for being stupid.

His feelings were strong and obvious, loaded with the belief I wouldn't actually leave him again. That was my fault. I'd set myself up for this with all the years of leaving and coming back, of being in love and hate, of swearing this was the last time but still waking up next to him the following morning.

For some reason, I knew this time was different. There was no going back. Getting him to understand this fact was proving to be more difficult than I'd anticipated. I'd need more than words, but I wasn't exactly sure what that would be yet.

I was sure of a few things. First, I'm not a toy. My dreams are not toys. My emotions are not toys. I am a strong, independent, capable woman who deserves her time. I've raised two children. I've raised two men. I've paused my life and given all of them all of me. I have to stand up and claim time for myself. And they should let me—not because they love me, but because they understand how tied together we are. Like a weathered and frayed rope holding an anchor to a worn-out dinghy.

I pulled the meat tenderizer from the utensil drawer. Anger flooded over me, clouding my vision. I spread the plastic wrap over the top of the seasoned steak and readied the mallet in my hands. The first smack settled into the thick, fibrous meat. I couldn't help but smile as the muscle tissue started to split. It felt so good to release the years of frustration I had kept inside, the years of no one really caring how I felt, what I needed, or what I wanted.

What about my ambitions? What about my goals? I'd never mattered to any of them—not James, not Denny, not my own kids. I've always been part of a game, and yes, I know I let myself become the prize, and maybe I even liked being a small-town trophy. But when do I get to just be me?

There were days I felt he really loved me. Days I felt like we were getting closer to truly being the couple I wanted us to be. But his small, subconscious actions would show me he didn't know me at all. He would forget my favorite meal, even though I'd ordered that tomato soup and grilled cheese and hash browns at the diner for years. He'd forget that I hated mushrooms when we'd go out for dinner, ordering a filet masala and insisting that we split it.

Just once I'd like for him to ask me what I wanted, what I liked. To make me feel like I existed in this equation.

I slammed the mallet into the steak again. I watched the muscle fibers spread and the meat slowly bounce back. The elasticity was fascinating. I wondered if this was what our bodies did when we were smacked with a blunt object. If I hit him over the head, would he also be malleable? If I freed myself from him, would I feel the same relief I'm feeling with every slam as I prepare our dinner?

"Mom," Christopher yelled from the living room. "Keep it down, will ya? I'm trying to watch my show and I can't hear what they're saying over all the noise you're making."

I was tired of him, too. As a mother, that had to be the worst feeling in the world. But if I could just make some friends, hopefully women who had teenage kids, too, maybe they'd understand and I wouldn't feel so alone. Maybe we could talk about all the crazy things kids their age do instead of me being locked in this house, dusting shelf after empty shelf.

Christopher's spoiled teenager attitude was driving me up the wall. He didn't want anything we bought him, nothing was good enough, his time was too precious. I didn't understand him, and he didn't want to tell me what I didn't understand. I should just know. I was tired of cleaning piss off the bathroom floor, washing stiff socks full of who knows what, and trying to act like I didn't know about the magazines he kept under his bed—the same ones kept under our bed that I'd learned to stop crying over.

I gripped the mallet tighter and slammed it hard against the steak, putting a tear in the plastic wrap. The slight tear reminded me of skin. I pictured myself walking into the living room and bringing the mallet down hard on Christopher.

I shook my head. These were not the thoughts a mother should have about her own child.

"What the—?" Christopher yelled.

I heard him murmur something and I was sure he was cussing me under his breath. He gave a yelp that I took for bitchy frustration and I smacked the meat again and again to drown out his complaining. When

13

I stopped, he was silent.

This time I'd won, but I knew he'd hold it against me at the dinner table. His attitude would increase, no doubt, making what should be a delightful family meal I'd worked hard to create almost impossible to get through. There'd be snipes and comments under his breath, things we'd try to ignore until one of us blew up.

The most important question would be whether tonight's dinner would be the moment I'd finally lose my mind and do or say something I would later regret. In my life, there's always regret. Nothing stays on track. Nothing stays the course.

I heard heavy footsteps behind me. Steps too strong and clunky for Christopher. Too purposeful and driven.

My heart dropped when a man's heavy shadow fell over me, darkening the light I needed to continue working on dinner. My instinct for flight kicked in, when it should have been fight, and the mallet dropped to the counter.

I cringed when the linoleum countertop chipped. Denny would hold this against me. I could already hear him yelling at me for not respecting his property. I had to tiptoe around my own house every day, making sure I left no sign I lived here. This slight imperfection would not go unnoticed.

A heavy hand gripped my ponytail, yanking my head back. I tried to scream for Christopher when I saw his reflection in the window over the sink.

"What are you doing here?" I gasped. "You shouldn't be here."

The knife entered my chest easily, sliding between my ribs and plunging deep into a quickly spreading pool of red. I would be forced to watch him kill me in the reflection, see his face as he took his revenge on the woman he called the love of his life.

But I wasn't. He only loved himself, and he'd never admit it.

I saw the knife rise over my body again. He remained silent, a furious look plastered on his face. The knife plunged once more into the soft flesh of my abdomen. His actions were clear. He wanted to kill me slowly. He could have slit my throat, stabbed me in the heart, or disemboweled me. But no, he was using careful and methodical strikes to keep me alive, to continue the torture and to watch me suffer.

He'd already watched me suffer for years. To know that this wasn't enough for him was more painful than each strike of the knife. I tried to not give him any satisfaction, to not let a single grunt, groan, or gasp escape my lips. I tried to twist my mouth into a smile that would say "Thank you."

With each strike, silent on both of our parts, he became more aggressive. He'd give a little twist and I'd feel the blade scrape my bone. Finally I gave a squeak and his face spread into a crooked grin of satisfaction.

This was not how I'd let my story end. Not today, when I'd just given myself permission to be free.

The mallet was on the counter, just beyond my reach. I stretched my fingers, hoping to grab the wooden handle and give myself a fighting chance. This was a stupid plan, and looking at my reflection in the kitchen window, I could tell I'd already lost too much blood. Even if I hit him, got in one good strike, it wouldn't kill him. If he had even one mark, one bruise, one break on his skin, he could claim self-defense and my death would be justified.

No, if I was going to die, I wasn't giving anyone a viable excuse to not be held accountable. My fingers relaxed and I succumbed to my fate.

He laughed, a deep throaty chuckle that I'd never heard before: a bone-chilling, devilish, gleefully evil sound. Each staccato note released a heavy burst of whiskey on his breath. Another broken promise. Before the sweet saccharine scent hit my nostrils, I was hoping he'd realize the error of his choices and tell me he loved me, tell me he was sorry, and tell me this was an accident. But I knew there would be no love tonight when I bled out on the kitchen floor. No regrets. No apologies.

I glanced at his face in the window's reflection, silently declaring I'd wipe the malicious smile from his face by haunting him for the rest of his life.

"Christopher," I gurgled, even though the streaks of blood on his navy blue hoodie told me he'd already carried out the sick fantasy I myself had been considering while pounding away at a dinner we'd never eat.

At first I felt a pang of jealousy. He always took everything from me. I quickly shook those thoughts out of my head.

Christopher was my child. Had I brought this upon us? Had my frustration been so pure, so full, so hate-fueled, that I'd manifested our deaths? Was it possible that I was daydreaming right now, silently pounding out steak filets to please two men who couldn't care less about me?

The tenderizing mallet struck my right temple. I felt the grooves stick in my skin, my skull separating into small fragments when he pulled the heavy block out of my forehead. The sharp pain faded quickly into dense pleasure, like every ounce of stress and regret I carried inside of my busy mind had been set free. My worries exploded from my right temple, carried on waves of life. Waves that would soon give me freedom.

My blood flowed profusely, thick, heavy, dark, streaming over my cheeks and onto my lips. I inhaled as he struck me again, getting a taste of my own life, the last of my blood keeping me alive, before letting the darkness slip over me.

CHAPTER THREE

Childhood

I was only five years old the first time I saw Trudy Baker, and even then, I knew one day she would be Trudy Jackson.

I loved her immediately. Her skinned knees would shine in the sun with each kick of her slightly chubby legs when she pushed the swing higher. She didn't know it, but she made my heart flop. To me, she was as beautiful as a flower, with rosy cheeks covered in perfectly spaced freckles, and expertly plaited hair. But only those who paid close attention, like me, could tell she had a secret underbelly full of snips, snails, and puppy dog tails. She fought harder than the other girls. All of them said they were determined to one day circle around the top bar of the swing set. No one ever did, of course, but that girl sure did try.

The recess bell would ring every day at 11:35 a.m. One extended sharp trill of metal vibrating on metal. Our entire class would start to get antsy around 11:25, watching the second hand tick out six hundred painful seconds to freedom.

If you were out the door first, you'd get one of the four hard plastic swings with ridges that dug into the backs of your legs until each kick made you grimace. Trudy never showed any signs of pain. She only showed that she was a champion, intent on flying higher than anyone else, pumping her legs as hard as she could with an aerodynamically sound arch of her back.

There was an unwritten rule that the third swing from the left belonged to Trudy. She said the chain was well oiled and the squeaks minimal. Most importantly, the placement of the swing relative to the top bar and the pit worn through the mulch where feet consistently ran over the ground was just right. This was a fact, she had told us; she'd used her older brother's high school chemistry book to develop a formula calculating the requirements of a flawless swing.

I never had the heart to tell her that chemistry didn't have anything to do with her swing. Chemistry did, however, have everything to do with the way she made my heart flop over and settle into my stomach like a skipping stone carelessly tossed into a shallow pond.

I'd sit crisscross applesauce over the exact center of the merry-go-round, right where the spinning couldn't touch you. The only centrifugal force I felt was the weight of gravity on my heart as I fell more helplessly in love with the spry little girl who lived down the street from me. My idea of the perfect recess was to watch her furiously pump her body for the full half an hour we were released from class, to get our energy out. I was hopelessly in love before I even knew what love was, years before I'd get my first surging hormones that usually lead boys to contemplate whether or not girls had cooties.

Every day Trudy would fail at her quest. And every day she'd proudly proclaim that tomorrow would be her day. Each time that proclamation left her soft pink lips, I'd sink deeper into the spell she cast over every single boy on the playground. But while they sat and watched to see up her skirt, I sat and watched to see into her soul.

One crisp early autumn day, she came the closest to swinging over the top bar that any kindergarten student at George Washington Elementary had ever come. At the exact moment her swing lifted itself slightly higher than the precise right angle to the top bar, we all held our breath. She furiously kicked her legs, and then we gasped when the chain suddenly caught a bit of slack and threw her backwards.

She landed in the mulch with a thump, shooting up a cloud of dry dust, and lay perfectly still.

"Is she alive?" Denny asked.

He was my best friend. We'd grown up next door to each other and had been trading toys and testing the limits of our imagination since we'd figured out how to close our baby fists around whatever our parents put in our hands.

"I don't think she's moving, James."

But I saw her breathing. And I saw her eyes gently flutter open, focusing on the white clouds rolling overhead.

The magic spell surrounding Trudy Baker shattered into the mulch that day for every boy on the playground. Every boy, that is, except me.

I crawled next to her and lay down in the scratchy mulch, shoulder to shoulder, before gently grasping her hand. To me she was more beautiful than ever, even with layers of dust caked into the sweat surrounding her neck and pieces of wood chips sticking out of her normally impeccably crafted braids.

"It's okay, Trudy. You did your best," I said, trying to soothe her broken heart.

"My best? Didn't you see? I did it. I circled the bar. I simply went too fast and lost control on the second swing around. Don't you see, James? I'm a legend. Today, Trudy Baker is a legend."

She shook off my hand before sitting up with a grunt. Small patches of blood trickled down the backs of her arms and chunks of mulch stubbornly clung to the edges of her floral dress. Without looking back, she walked through the glass doors leading directly to our classroom.

Trudy Baker would never swing again.

"Hurry up," Mrs. Davis called over the eager chatter of thirty five-year-olds. "Pick your names for the Secret Santa giveaway. Remember—do not share your names. This is Secret Santa, not Everyone Knows Santa. And don't forget, you have a limit of only ten dollars for your present. If your parents have questions, tell them to call me."

She never should have trusted such important instructions to a hyped-up mob of children during one of the most exciting times of the year.

I crossed my fingers tight, knowing there were only two names in the entire class I would want to draw: my best friend Denny or the eternal love of my life, Trudy. I had nothing in common with any of the other kids in my class. I didn't sit around picking boogers, crying, pulling girls' ponytails, dumping out toy bins, or sticking the large Legos in the teacher's seat to see how loudly she'd squeal when she sat down. And at that age, I didn't have the energy to play kissing cootie games or to chase any girl except for the world's most magnificent creature.

One by one we lined up, and one by one, Denny and I were shoved to the back.

I cringed, thinking about the sticky and gooey fingers sliding into

Mrs. Davis's bag of names. I knew if I didn't slide my hand directly into the center of the bag, I would risk collecting boogers stuck to the sides after sliding off one of my classmates' grubby fingers.

As Denny and I approached the bag, we looked each other in the eyes. I took a step back to give him the first pull.

He unfolded the paper and rolled his eyes.

"Wonderful," he said. "Can I give someone a bar of soap, or is that against the rules, too?"

Mrs. Davis gasped. "Denny Lloyd! You grab your things and march your smart mouth right down to the principal's office. Now."

"Gladly," he replied.

I tried my best to stifle a giggle. I knew he had drawn Jimmy Barrett, the only kid in the class who didn't believe in soap, laundry detergent, and possibly toilet paper based on the last time I'd had to sit downwind from him in the library during story time.

Mrs. Davis turned to write the hall pass sending Denny to his doom. The bag of names was haphazardly perched on the corner of her desk. Slowly, the soft green velvet pouch with the tacky gold drawstring began to crumble, sliding over the side like a Slinky until it plopped to the ground.

Upon impact, one little piece of paper floated out and settled just under her desk.

My heart jumped. Only one name could cause a piece of paper to flutter like a perfectly painted butterfly.

"Mrs. Davis," I called, waiting patiently for a response. "Mrs. Davis? I didn't get to draw."

I stared at the paper, scared to move forward and grab it. My body jiggled in anticipation as I debated whether I should call out for her attention again. I didn't want to join Denny in the principal's office.

I'd never been in trouble in my life, and I sure wasn't going to start now. The days were already stressful enough at home with the holidays coming up. If Mrs. Davis decided I was being too much and I had to go to detention, too, I'd never live it down. I knew if my first big violation at school happened when I was five, it would be held against me for the rest of my life, every time I got in trouble. My dad already had a problem forgetting the time I'd left the scissors on the front porch overnight last year.

"Mrs. Davis?"

"James! I hear you. Just . . . just grab that piece there on the floor, under the desk. The one that fell out. Should be the last one anyway."

I jumped forward and scooped it up, tracing my fingers over the most beautiful set of letters I'd ever seen. Trudy.

Even the magic Christmas bag agreed we should be together.

I had exactly one week to come up with the world's most perfect Secret Santa gift to win Trudy's heart and seal our destiny. Our love story would start this year. I'd see to that with all of my heart and soul.

I was about to sweep Trudy Baker off her feet like no swing ever could.

On Secret Santa day, Mrs. Davis couldn't keep us focused. This was the first and only day I'd ever allowed myself to squirm in my seat, stare out the window, avoid my in-class work, and constantly check the clock to see if the minutes were even passing.

When the parent helpers finally started to arrive with their large plastic boxes stuffed with overbaked cookies and too-dry cakes with canned icing, I accidentally let out a squeal. My sharp alarm caught the attention of all the other students as well. In a split second, I'd single-handedly disrupted the painfully fought-for attention of my classmates, rendering

Mrs. Davis into a pile of frustration. She sank into her orange swivel chair and rubbed her temples.

My classmates and I jumped up and ran to the tree to find our sloppily written names on tags tacked to awkwardly wrapped boxes.

No one else saw Mrs. Davis pour something from a silver flask into her coffee. I did.

I figured it was some of the same amber liquid that poisoned my dad. Would she also call me a degenerate? Was she poisoning herself because of me, too?

I vowed then and there to never again speak out of turn in class.

"Kids, return to your seats. No! Chris, do not open your present yet. Kids, do not rip the paper. Return to your . . . Fine. Do whatever you want. Just clean up after yourselves," she yelled over the noise.

She nodded to the parent helpers, letting them know this was their time to fill us with enough sugar to make everyone regret letting us go to school today.

Paper flew everywhere. Cupcakes were gobbled. Cookies were dropped and stepped on. Kids screamed with joy when they got a present that was well over the ten-dollar limit and shrieked with frustration when they opened something clearly picked up at the grocery store on a last-minute grab-and-run.

I peered at Trudy, the only person still sitting in their seat.

I swallowed, trying to move the lump in my throat. Hopefully there would be some sign of approval, or disappointment—anything. But she just sat there. With one finger, she lightly pushed the small blue swing I'd cut from an old, shredded bicycle tire left behind our garage. The thin links of chain were made from a broken necklace and held the seat between a frame made from plastic straws, fortified with toothpicks and glue, and meticulously covered with metallic paints I'd found in Mom's craft drawer. The makeshift swing set sat on a cardboard base where I'd stuck tissue-paper flowers in between tissue-paper grass to spell out "Trudy."

Finally, she moved. She whipped around in her seat and narrowed her eyes, staring at all of our classmates.

"Who did this?" she yelled.

No one noticed.

Trudy jumped up on her seat and yelled louder, silencing the room with one furious sentence. "Who is my Secret Santa?"

No one moved. Everyone was too shocked at her outburst.

A chorus of giggles started to spread when people saw what sat on her desk. Some kids had new crayons and coloring books, or cheap bendable plastic dolls. Some had unwrapped the hottest action figure of the season thanks to parents who wanted to use this opportunity to solidify their social standing. But Trudy, poor Trudy, they thought. She had a pile of junk, glued together and slightly crooked.

Denny caught my eyes and he knew. Without missing a beat, he stood up, walked over to her desk, and offered his hand to help her down from her perch.

"It was me," he said. "I think you're the best swinger in the world, and you deserved a trophy."

I expected her to hit him in the face, right there in front of everyone.

Instead, she smiled the purest smile I'd ever seen, leaned in, and kissed him. Right there in the middle of the classroom, and right in front of me.

My heart broke to the chorus of my classmates once again giggling and cheering for something I'd done but hadn't been man enough to claim.

CHAPTER FOUR

The Walk

"It's time, James," Warden Stanfield said, lifting his palm and signaling for the guards to open my cell. He walked toward me with shackles in hand. "I'm sorry, son. It's protocol, you know. We have to do this."

"Do you apologize to everyone?" I asked, swallowing the last bit of grilled cheese sandwich drowned in tomato soup, the bite I'd tucked away in a piece of paper ripped from a book, hidden under my pillow for a little over a day. Taking my last walk was intimidating, but I hoped that one last bite of familiarity at the last minute would allow me to savor the past.

My last night had been wrapped in nostalgia, serenaded by the best of the 1980s and a meal fit for a child. Even though I was ready to go, and I'd accepted my fate long ago, nothing can ever truly prepare you to walk to your death. The little taste of the creamy soup and crunchy bread with cheese oozing from the center reminded me why I was happy to be leaving this body and this Earth behind. I knew she would be on the other side, waiting for me, just like I'd been waiting for her every day since the gavel had fallen, decreeing my fate.

This morning, each step would lead me to my death. Every second of this day would be calculated, scheduled, and expected. There would be no surprises, just precision. We would all find out how prepared we were.

Warden Stanfield bit his lip, torn between professionalism and letting me in on his thoughts. But what was professionalism, exactly, when you worked at a jail, a dark world where typically very little goes as planned, where your life is on the line every day—when you choose to not call out sick, that is.

The warden and I had become friendly, exchanging jokes and quips about how the world used to be after he'd tell me about what it was like now. The state of the world scared me, for my children's sake.

He hesitated quite a while before answering my question, but decided today was as good a day as any to let that final guard down.

"Well, honestly, no. Some people don't deserve apologies. They get exactly what they deserve. I've worked with guys so dark they'd melt your soul and make you ask for an exorcist after sitting near them. There are times I don't even want to enter their cell—like I can feel my breath leaving my body."

He paused and shook his head.

"It's no joke, James. We walk guys down this hallway that would scare you shitless, you know? You've met them in the yard. Big guys. Even with the shackles on, your body is naturally in fight-or-flight mode. Every hair on your body is standing on end, warning you that you're in danger. They've done awful things—not that you haven't, but they're proud of what they've done. They're oh so proud," he explained, locking heavy metal cuffs around my ankles, then my wrists. He made sure they were snug but not so tight that they'd cause me pain. The chains hung just loose enough to allow movement but not loose enough to where I'd be able to take out the warden or the guards if I was one of those guys who terrified him so deeply. "I'd walk next to you even without this iron, though. You've never scared me."

"That's a shame," I replied. After all he'd said to me, a fear I understood because I'd felt the evil of these men drifting over the yard, I inadvertently rejected the last person on Earth who was still trying to be friendly.

His face twisted in shock. "A shame? Why?"

"Well, wouldn't it be easier to believe I was a monster? To slip the needle in my arm today and send me to my death with a sigh of relief?"

"Ah." He let out a nervous laugh. "Perhaps. I suppose that, yes, on the surface it'd seem easier. At least I wouldn't have so many questions, and possibly doubts."

"Doubts are a devil of a thing, aren't they?"

"They are, James. They are." He sighed, his thick shoulders rolling under the weight of his curiosity.

"You shouldn't have any doubts about me, Warden. Not a single one."

"That's what you keep saying, but I'm not sure you're any more convincing today than you were on any other day."

He nodded head toward the door, indicating we should be moving. The sharp twist of his neck sent another pop through the room. His tight skin couldn't disguise the aging that had started to creep in more rapidly the past few years. There were a few stray gray hairs poking around his ears, the hair on his crown was getting thin, and when he furrowed his brow, the wrinkles set in his forehead weren't as menacing because they never really left.

Suddenly my heart fell. Throughout this entire process, I never would have imagined that longing to grow old—to feel the pop and pain of arthritis, to stress over my thinning hair—would be what finally made me feel sad about dying. I should realize I'm lucky; I'll never have to worry about my body failing as I struggle to stay alive.

I looked at the gray walls that had provided me with a home, and eventually, some comfort over the years. I'd forgotten how big the world was and what existed outside of the gates, barbed wire, and heavy, reinforced stone walls that kept me in this place.

Even if a miracle had happened and I was to be set free today, I don't think I'd be able to exist out there again. I'd try; without a doubt I'd try. But that world had never been kind to me. I was always too weak in the face of temptation. There was no denying that I just wasn't meant for this world, especially when she wasn't here.

"How long do you think the hallway is, Warden?" I asked, flicking my eyes toward the open cell door.

I looked at the other two guards, marveling at their size. No doubt they put the most imposing guards on Death Row to handle the more-vicious prisoners. I couldn't help but chuckle, as this certainly wasn't necessary with me. Their necks were larger than my biceps, which was something, as I was actually quite proud of the body I'd sculpted in my tiny cell. With nothing else to do, I'd spent my final six months exercising, for once in my life.

"About a hundred feet," said the warden, trying to hide his confusion with a yawn.

He didn't fool me. I saw him wince when I let the chuckle slip, no doubt sending a small shiver of panic through him. Prisoners come up with crazy last-minute ploys all the time. His eyebrows furrowed and I watched his muddy green eyes twitch.

"Having second thoughts, James? You've been extremely calm during this whole process. Calmer than most. You've barely asked a question or shown the slightest anxiety. I don't think I've ever met someone so at peace with their fate. Even the guys who ask for the death penalty show a little stress when the day approaches."

"I'm not most people," I replied without hesitation.

I reeled myself back in. I wasn't ready to deliver a confession or say anything that didn't need to be said, to anyone but two very specific people. My secrets would go to the grave, and stay there, until Ava and Christopher were ready for the truth. Their truth, if they were willing to hear it.

"No second thoughts, Warden. I hoped it would be just a little shorter. I'm ready, sir. I'm extremely ready for the next steps of my life."

I didn't realize what I'd said could be taken in multiple ways, but it ended up being true. I was ready for each and every little step we would take as we moved toward the injection room. I was ready for each and every step that needed to be taken to end my life. I was ready for the proverbial steps that would take me to the next stage of my existence, even if that next stage was death.

My heart rate started to quicken, driven by the excitement of knowing I was just a few minutes away from never breathing again. The concept of death didn't scare me at all, but wondering if she'd be waiting for me on the other side drove me mad.

Truthfully, if I had my entire life to do over, as long as my days ended with Trudy, I'd live every single painful moment again. Maybe I'd fight a little harder, convince her to stay, do whatever it was that she thought I didn't do to show her how much I cared. Even if I knew it would still end the same way, I'd at least try harder if there was even the smallest chance of a different outcome.

"Hey, Warden," I said, interrupting the silence. "Can I ask you a silly question?"

Warden Stanfield paused. The guards followed suit. No one looked concerned, but they all looked confused. This probably wasn't the time to throw a wrench in the plans, which I'm sure many people before me have tried. And to be fair, any questions I had should have been asked when we were still in my cell, before I was shackled and being led down this cold and soulless hallway.

"Go ahead, James. I suppose no question is silly at this point."

I took a deep breath. I wasn't sure why this was suddenly important to me, but it felt right. And I'd learned the hard way that I had to welcome what my soul wanted instead of waiting for a different outcome.

"Could I walk barefoot? I just keep looking at the floor. I want to feel it—that cold hardness."

The warden looked down at my feet, currently adorned with flimsy disposable slippers and those socks with the rubber nubs on them. He chuckled, something he probably always felt like doing when he saw what folks like me had to wear during our ridiculous final walk, but hadn't, out of respect.

"You know what? I should tell you no, but I'm feeling rebellious today. And you're a good one, James, no matter what they say, and no matter what you won't say. If you can get those socks off by yourself, then of course."

The slippers flew off easily and hit the wall with a soft thud. I was able to wiggle the right sock off with little effort, followed by the left.

A deep breath filled my lungs and the icy cold concrete floor shocked the withering roots holding me to the Earth. Truthfully, it felt divine. So simple. So smooth. I just wanted to remind myself of what the real world felt like.

WRIGHT

CHAPTER FIVE

Ava

The phone rang, shrill and angry, echoing through my dorm room. Anger coursed through my body, furious curse words flying without a second thought.

My friends knew I was studying for my GRE and shouldn't be bothered. I had made my needs very clear to my boyfriend Chad, to my friends, to my mom. In today's world, if I wanted a real chance at stepping away from my past, a bachelor's degree simply wasn't enough. I wanted more. I needed more. I deserved more. Getting into a quality MBA program was my best chance at shedding the ties of my previous life and stepping into a new one as a strong, driven, successful woman. The woman my mother never was. The woman she doubted I could be.

I let the call go to the machine, smirking when the message started to play.

My whole life, I'd been a pushover. Caving in to what other people wanted, letting them call the shots, telling me who and what I should be. I'd spent years listening to my mother, to Denny, to James—all worthless now that I was getting older, realizing I could not be manipulated.

I would no longer fall prey to Mom's depressed cries that I was abandoning her, nor would I pacify her need to be saved. I would no longer feel guilty over James's fall from grace, going from the only respectable figure in my life to a wasted human blob on the side of the street. And I would absolutely no longer acknowledge Denny, who tried to be my father only when it suited his games. He had made so many attempts to convince me I belonged in a small town. I could never understand why he wanted me to fail so badly; not even the worst soap opera on television had such a manipulative character.

"Thank you for calling Ava. Also, thank you for forgetting that I'm studying for my GRE. If your call is important enough to interrupt my future, leave a message and I'll be the judge. If it's not, hang up."

Harsh? Maybe. But if I'd learned anything from my screwed-up home life and my pushover of a mother, it was that you must fiercely guard your goals and dreams. You must move toward them without apology. You should never give up your time for other people's avoidable emergencies, especially when they aren't invested in your future. I refused to wither away, to turn into a dull shell of my already pathetic self, spending all day waxing poetic about my choice to put other people first.

I was not fragile. I was not weak. I was not my mother.

The machine didn't register a message but was left beeping with anger.

Pride soared through my body. I was grateful something good had come from the challenges of my youth. Not everyone who grows up in a fucked-up family escapes or makes something out of their disaster. But I wasn't everybody. I was somebody, and I wouldn't stop until every single person from my past understood this, without a shred of doubt.

The phone rang again.

I slammed my pencil down, cracking it in half. With a deep and full breath in, I planned my verbal attack on whoever this idiot was with the nerve to interrupt me.

I snatched the cordless phone from the cradle, knocking the base to the floor with a hollow thud.

Before I could utter a single word, I found myself on the receiving end of a very frantic greeting. Words flowed through the phone at a fierce speed, slurring into each other.

I could feel my anxiety rising immediately. My body and mind fed off the energy being transmitted over hundreds of miles. A pulse-pounding fear coursed through my veins, kicking my brain into action. No matter how hard I tried to fight, Mother Nature took over and my body obeyed.

I'd never be able to return to studying now. Today was ruined. All hope for a last-minute cram session had just gone down the drain because I was too stupid to let the phone go to voicemail one more time. Driven by anger, by the need to prove my strength and place in my own life, I'd done exactly what I knew I shouldn't when I picked up the phone.

Maybe Denny was right during his drunken rants: I'd always be reactive, unable to use logic, living on false strength in hopes of fooling those around me, desperate to prove that I was different—even though deep down I knew I'd always be a part of them, and therefore, just like them.

It was in our blood.

"Dad?" I paused, trying to recognize the voice. "Slow down, Denny. What's going on?" I rolled my eyes. I couldn't believe I'd just called him Dad.

Of course it couldn't have been James calling. Who knew what street corner he was on now, or how he'd even get a quarter for a pay phone. Not to mention the fact that James quit caring about me years ago, when he'd let that monster take over. He was no better than the coward who'd abandoned me in the first place. I'm sure I'd set some kind of record in my short life: daughter abandoned the most times by both her father and stepfather.

That simple slip, that one single word, would cost me. For years to come, he'd use this title that should hold love against me, putting extra emphasis on each letter just to climb under my skin. He'd only give up once he noticed I refused to break. The frustration over my slip would feed my aggression as long as it fed his pride.

I quickly changed my tone and went into protection mode. The only information I needed to absorb was the important key words: nouns and verbs.

But the tone and nature of the call threw me almost immediately. I was used to Mom being manic and frustrated, but Denny? The man was naturally cold and always scarily composed.

"What did Mom do now?" I asked, without a hint of sympathy. I knew if Denny was calling, she was up to no good—either manic, or getting on his nerves. My job was always to talk her off ledges, cool her down, and make his life easy. There was never any consideration as to how difficult they both made my life by assuming I knew how to parent my parents.

Part of me expected to hear something silly, like she'd run over Waffles, who I'm shocked is still alive. Maybe she'd taken too many pills in the bath again, or threatened him with divorce. Again. The usual every-other-week crisis I had to deal with and extinguish because two adults in a legal relationship couldn't seem to figure it out for themselves, the type of crises that children shouldn't have to resolve on behalf of adults.

Granted, their health and well-being were things I should care about, but the farther I pulled away from my family, the less I cared about their drama getting in the way of my flight.

But then I heard him say the one word I wasn't prepared for.

Dead.

"I'm sorry, Denny. You need to slow down. Like, way down, because I can't deal with this right now. You know I'm studying for my GRE—it's so typical of you to bust in without any consideration."

I paused, feeling that surge of power he always teased me about, saying I craved it.

He was right. I didn't care.

"Who's dead? Waffles? We knew that was coming. That dog is as old as dirt."

"No, Ava. Not Waffles," he said. "Your mother. Trudy. She's dead. Murdered."

Denny drew in a deep breath. Stumbling over his words, he repeated himself more slowly. It sounded like he was crying, but I shuddered at the undeniable coldness underneath his words.

"Dead, Ava. Your mother is dead."

All of my power slipped out on the wings of my next breath. I went from being a woman in charge of my day to a child again.

Instantly I was five years old and sitting in her lap reading a book. On the next breath I was twelve, sipping milkshakes and promising her I wouldn't tell James we'd had dinner with Denny. With the next blink I was packing my room up and moving out, living on the promise that we'd have a better life and family if I lived with my real dad.

The way Denny's voice dropped with pain and fear filled me with guilt. Guilt for ignoring the phone call. Guilt for being abrasive. Guilt for valuing my time over his, and hers. Guilt for not being home when my family was falling apart and they needed me. Guilt for even caring, and starting to feel emotions well up when I realized I'd never see her again, when just a second ago I was hoping for that very thing.

Each word out of his lips was deliberate, even through the panic. I could feel his fear of being alone. His doubt over what comes next. His inability to understand that this time she was really gone, and under no circumstances would she come back like she had so many times before.

I wallowed in the guilt that started to constrict my throat, realizing I was more of my mother than I'd ever willfully admit. How quickly one could lose their strength when tested. The universe had just delivered exactly what I'd wanted, tied up with a bow.

And I rejected the gift.

"Dead . . ."

I wanted him to fill in the pause with an explanation, or details, or comfort. I knew he wasn't capable of comforting me. He wasn't even capable of accepting me as his daughter when I was at my cutest stage: a tiny baby incapable of speaking, with the venom-laced tongue I would develop over time.

"When?"

"Last night. Dinnertime. I came home and, oh my God, Ava, it was just awful. I found her in the kitchen."

He paused and sobbed, a rare, sober sob without the crackles of phlegm from alcohol-encouraged smoking.

"I had no choice but to start the investigation once backup arrived. Oh, Ava, it's just awful. I wish you were here, but I'm . . . well, I'm glad you're not . . ."

Another pause.

"What about Christopher. Is he . . ."

"No. Well, he's not dead, yet, but he's close. He was also attacked, and his injuries are severe. He could go at any time. Ava, I know you're busy and I don't want to ask—"

"Yes," I interrupted. "Yes, Dad. I'm coming home. I'll leave right now. I have to know . . . was it . . . was it him?"

We both knew who I meant.

"Yes, Ava. Yes, I think it was. I mean, I don't know. I shouldn't tell you since it's still under investigation. But we have evidence. I think he did it. He murdered your mother. Oh my God, Ava. What am I going to do without her?"

The next sob he released was deep; I could tell that it came from his gut. And without a doubt, his heart.

I sobbed. I wasn't sure how I'd drive home in this state.

Maybe that was part of his plan—to kill me with grief by making me drive off the road on my way home.

"Is he in custody? Do they have that piece of shit?" I screamed, my voice echoing through the phone. "How could he do this? It doesn't seem right. Not him."

"I know it's hard. We'll talk when you get here. Just, please, come as soon as you can. James is locked up right now. They arrested him on a bus to New Mexico. On a ticket he bought with her stolen credit card. I shouldn't be telling you any of this. You don't need to hear it. I'm saying too much—I really need to go."

He was frantic. I could hear the fear in his voice. The town's strongest detective reduced to a pile of bumbling idiocy.

What was he so afraid of? Facing James? Living without Trudy? Having to finally be a father? Or for once in his life, the fact that he was truly alone and left to his own devices?

"I'm on my way. I'll see you soon."

I didn't even hang up the phone. It slipped through my fingers, the

38

battery flying out when the slim black handset crashed to the hard tile floor of my dorm room.

That man should be happy he's already locked away. If they release him while I'm back, I'll kill him myself.

CHAPTER SIX

Later Childhood

The three of us were thick as thieves. Seeing just two of us together was enough of a rarity that members of our small town would immediately fly into a panic. Questions like, "Where's the other one?" "Did something happen?" "Did that evil man do something to that precious child?" would flow until the missing wheel suddenly showed up and set questioning minds to rest.

The one thing we never did as friends was talk about our home life, even though we all knew what happened behind closed doors, and the entire town knew the secrets our parents tried to keep from curious minds and prying eyes. As an adult, it's easy to recognize that finding peace from the things we never discussed probably bonded us; the things that happened in our homes, where we should have been safe. As children, we only knew that together, we had peace for a little part of each day.

My dad was a good man. He put food on the table for breakfast and dinner. He kept my mom in nice clothes. He made sure I had shoes and never got cold in the winter. And in return he expected certain services from all members in our household. Sometimes we knew what he wanted, sometimes we didn't. It was always when we didn't know, when we couldn't read his mind, when the whiskey had set in too deeply, that we realized while he was still a good man, he wasn't a nice man. When he wasn't nice, we'd tolerate his anger because this meant the next day would be full of hugs, apologies, and, depending on how mean he got, presents.

One time he shoved Mom because the meatloaf was missing the finely diced carrots that added a hint of sweetness, and he didn't like the flavor without them. She fell hard, cracking her head against the corner of the outdated light blue refrigerator with the handle that looked like the back of Grandma's Cadillac. The blood that slipped from her hairline was softly pushed away and she went back to mashing more potatoes and standing by until she was given permission to eat her own dinner: a salad of only vegetables with some lemon juice. Dad said she had to keep her figure. "The best way for a wife to show gratitude to her husband for his hard work was by staying tight in body and in bed," he'd say. He'd also say we ruined one of those for him, but we never knew what that meant.

The next day, Mom got a shiny new Cadillac of her own. I couldn't help but notice her tremble when the heavy metal keys clinked into her hand.

Denny's dad was not a nice man any time of the day. The first time he stayed the night at my house and we changed into our pajamas, I saw the ochre, violet, and indigo traces peppering his body. They were so deep, so intertwined, and oddly beautiful.

The rare time my dad got mean with me instead of my mom, my skin would get hard and red. The welts would burn for a few hours but slip

41

back into my flesh within a day, not a single mark to be seen. I'd never seen the beautiful shades that Denny had on my own body. I couldn't help but be oddly jealous over the way he looked, like one of the exotic peacocks at the zoo, even though this made me feel wrong all the way down to the pit of my stomach.

"Did you fall off your bike?" I asked, even though we both knew his bike had a broken rim from the time his dad tried to back over him in the driveway one night, in a fit of rage.

"I've told you to stop going down the big hill so fast. You can't control yourself when you hit those big rocks at the bottom," I said.

"You know I like to live dangerously," he replied, trying not to wince when he pulled his superhero pajamas back over his battered body. "Maybe we should go sweep those rocks up so they don't create problems for anyone else."

"Maybe we should. Do you think we're big enough?"

He shrugged his shoulders.

We both knew we weren't. And we both knew we weren't talking about the rocks.

Trudy's father was a stand-up man. He worked hard, never raised a hand in anger or to lift a bottle.

Her older brother was the one who had the town worried. He lived fast, lived hard, and rumors circulated for years that he had eyes for those too young to understand what having eyes for someone meant. When he took Trudy to the playground, kids would be pulled away. Mothers would grasp tightly to the sticky, pudgy hands of their babies while shuffling away as fast as their wedged feet could carry them.

Trudy always thought it was something she did, and deep down, I always thought that's why she tried so hard to swing over that top bar. If she could achieve that task, be the self-proclaimed queen of the playground, maybe the kids wouldn't scatter when she came near. Instead, they would line up to see what she'd accomplish each day and beg their mothers to stay. But after she fell from the swing and watched her dreams disappear into the mulch of the George Washington Elementary schoolyard, Trudy would never again attempt another great playground feat.

When the three of us were together, we felt unstoppable. There were no monsters under our beds, no hands around our throats, no mysteriously opening bathroom doors when we were showering, and no need to be anything except what we were: kids.

We did what kids should do. Instead of hiding behind the access panel in the corner of the coat closet, we walked to the diner for strawberry milkshakes. Instead of cowering behind the couch, we stocked up on sweets and snuck into movie theaters. To this day, if you asked any one of us about our childhood, we'd still tell you we had the best summers, the prettiest springs, and the naughtiest of autumns.

But winter? We would never talk about winter. Bad things came out when the nights were too long.

The fall of 1988 was one of the best years of our lives, one we'd always circle back to in later years. This was the year the Jamaican bobsled team went to the Olympics; when the original Globe Theater was uncovered (and our English teacher never shut up about it); the year the space shuttle program restarted after a post-Challenger hiatus, and the Dodgers won the World Series. Notre Dame topped the NCAA, George Bush promised, "No new taxes," and boys around the world fell in love with a cartoon redhead married to a rabbit.

Most boys, anyway. I still only had eyes for Trudy.

When the leaves turned to fiery reds and yellows, falling from the trees in a storm of crunchy beauty, we knew it was almost time. Halloween was our favorite holiday, more important to us than Christmas. Now that we were eleven, we were allowed to stay out past curfew without supervision, and we got free candy. Satisfaction on Halloween was guaranteed, unlike any other holiday, or our birthdays.

Due to Halloween falling on a Monday that year, our neighborhood decided Saturday would be the safest day for trick-or-treating, and most importantly, it would not interrupt our studies. The three of us agreed to meet at seven p.m. under the old oak tree by the park gates.

I arrived first at exactly fifteen minutes before the hour, sneaking out the back door of my house the moment I heard the first crisp pop of a fresh beer can. I'm sure I didn't have to sneak out—both of my parents knew it was the night for trick-or-treating—but I didn't want to take any chances.

Denny showed up next, two minutes past seven, in his typical fashion: on time but still late. We waited there, Mario and Luigi, looking for our Princess.

"Do you think we should go pick her up?" Denny asked, at 7:08.

"No. You know Trudy will get upset if we even try to take away a sliver of her independence. She'll be here."

At 7:13 I tapped on the face of my three-tone rubber watch with the cool straps you could switch out when you got bored with the design. "I think we should go pick her up."

"I suggested that five minutes ago," Denny replied.

As much as Trudy loved her independence, Denny loved his dominance. Truthfully, the three of us were a powder keg and should have been kept far apart. We were dangerously close to finding the spark that would blow us up every time we got together. Everyone knew this but us. So when we finally combusted decades later, no one was surprised. No one but us.

We had just turned around to start for Trudy's when time stopped.

The basic rules of the universe dissipated when my eyes connected with the most beautiful princess in either the Mushroom Kingdom or on planet Earth. Her pink dress floated over the sidewalk, making each step look like she was gliding on air. Her blonde tresses were tied up in a perfect ballerina bun and a peeling aluminum crown with large plastic gems was precariously perched on top, held down by a pink ribbon tied under her chin.

"Sorry, guys," she greeted us, with a crooked smile. "My mom insisted she should try to get my hair perfect, but every time she put this darn crown on my head, all she did was pull my hair right back out. I thought I'd never get out of the house. And don't even get me started on the photos. We're going to have to pay a small fortune to develop them next week."

"You make a pretty decent princess," Denny said. "Except the pink is wrong, and you definitely shouldn't be wearing sneakers."

"You look perfect," I butted in, not allowing him to continue.

And she did. I would never forget the way this one innocent Halloween jump-started my body's descent into puberty.

"Well, all right then. Let's go before all the good candy is gone and we're left with licorice and pennies," she said, ignoring our comments.

Even though Denny liked having the last word, we never made an attempt to overtake Trudy. In keeping with tradition, we fell in line, arms linked like we belonged in a happy movie from the 1950s, and took off skipping down the sidewalk. We laughed, we bounced, and we kicked our way through piles of leaves, greedily filling up our plastic pumpkin-shaped buckets that still smelled like Happy Meals. It didn't matter how much soap you used, the salt and grease from what McDonald's called French fries would never really wash out.

"This is fantastic!" I screamed. I clutched a king-size Snickers bar in my right hand and threw it up in the air before catching it again and galloping down a perfectly manicured brick path and through the gate of a white picket fence. "I wish every day was Halloween!"

"We could try to make that happen!" Trudy said. She proudly displayed her Butterfinger with a laugh, already starting to chew off the corner of the wrapper to get to the prize inside.

A wailing siren loudly pierced the happy chatter of trick-or-treaters, interrupting our joy. You never truly realize how loud a siren is until the emergency vehicle has to slowly pass by to avoid taking out the town's entire population of kids.

Another police car followed slowly, and suddenly, everyone decided trick-or-treating was over. We settled into our own parade of costumed oglers, placing bets on what we'd find when we reached the destination.

Arm in arm we continued, comforted by each other's presence in the face of the unknown. We walked in unison, as we always did. We never had to try; we just synced up in perfect rhythm. We could walk together, finish each other's sentences, complete the perfect little white lies, providing each other with on-the-spot alibis.

"Do you think it's a body?" Denny asked, a little too excited for my liking.

"Eww, gross. I don't want to see a body," Trudy gasped.

I couldn't help but smile when she linked her arm a little tighter into mine, closing the distance between our two bodies.

"It's not gross. One day I'm going to be the best sheriff in this entire town. Maybe even a detective. I'll solve all the tough cases and lock all the bad guys away."

"Yeah, with all the horrible crime that happens here in Parker Point, I'm sure you'll be real busy." I laughed, and then laughed even harder when I saw the daggers shooting from Denny's eyes. Eventually he let up and laughed back, knowing I wasn't picking on him or his dreams but stating the cold, hard facts about our small Pennsylvania town.

We didn't say anything else about what we thought would be at the end of this street, just followed the two squad cars, lights twisting wildly, to the cul-de-sac at the northern end of our subdivision.

The crowd continued to grow. No longer limited to curious costumed children, the candy givers had since joined our ranks, some lining up with bowls of candy in hand.

Trudy snuck her hand into one such green bowl and pulled out a few more yellow-wrapped candy bars with a smile. I watched her contemplate whether she could grab a few more before anyone noticed.

We dodged and dipped between the mob until we were front and center. Squinting into the darkness, we had difficulty making out what the fuss was at first. But slowly, a scene emerged that chilled me to the bone. Through a perfectly suitable pre–All Hallows' Eve mist, on the edge of the tree line, emerged two police officers flanking the sides of their newest prisoner.

"I told you," Denny cheered. "The only reason anyone goes in the woods here is to dump a body. They must have caught him in the act. Can we get any closer?"

"You're crazy, Denny," I said. I squinted, trying to get my eyes to focus in the darkness. "Who do you think it is?"

With a gasp, Trudy answered for us.

"It's freedom. That right there, my friends, is freedom."

In a few seconds, I understood exactly what she meant. The prisoner being escorted to the squad cars was none other than Trudy's brother.

With a huge smile, Trudy grabbed us and pushed back through the crowd. We didn't have time to ask her where we were going before she started skipping. Trudy didn't say another word, but led us up to every porch where bowls of candy had been left out to serve the children who hadn't followed the sirens to the action. We emptied every single one, a decision we would come to regret later that night when we were groaning in pain on the worn-down mustard-yellow couch in Denny's garage.

For all three of us, this Halloween would be one of the best nights of our lives.

For Trudy, the night would come to represent the start of her rejoining life as a fearless young girl.

If we had stayed just a few minutes more, we would have seen why the ambulance had also joined the scene. Denny would have gotten to see his first body bag emerge from the woods.

Trudy may have been set free from her brother's tyranny, but another girl from our class had been set free from this world altogether.

We wouldn't learn what really happened that day until our high school graduation. Being a child in the eighties came with the privilege of being blissfully unaware.

CHAPTER SEVEN

Christopher

My body was stiff. I'd had hangovers before, but this one already topped any I'd ever had by a level I'd never imagined.

My eyes didn't want to open. My fingers wouldn't move. I had a pounding headache, and when I squeezed my eyes shut in response to the first sliver of light, a shooting pain ran from the back of my skull to my temple. I tried to talk but my tongue wouldn't move. It sat in my mouth, heavy, dry, and swollen.

The position I'd fallen asleep in was awkward—slightly raised in the back, my legs propped up on something stiff. I must have fallen asleep on someone's couch, most likely a broken-down throwaway recovered from a dumpster in a garage or basement. My right leg almost felt like it was trapped, and something cool was on my left hand. This must have been one wild party.

My mind was foggy. I didn't remember going out. I didn't even remember school. After the last time I'd come home hungover, when I thought Denny was going to break my arm after slamming me into the wall and calling me an embarrassment, I had said, No more. No more parties, no more drugs, no more skipping school. I was going to clean up my act.

There'd be no way to explain this when I got home. Mom was going to be pissed, and I didn't even want to think about what Denny would do. He didn't have any more patience for me. There was nowhere else for me to go, not with Dad being on the street. If Dad wasn't on the street, maybe I wouldn't be here, giving up on life, and myself, in pursuit of a good time. He had promised Mom he'd never abandon her, or me, and I'd heard that time and time again when Mom would get into one of her moods. But he did. Too easily. And I'd never forgive him.

Someone had left their alarm on. No doubt Jack, who always tried to be responsible and go to work, but would likely be fired from his seventh job for partying too hard and missing his wake-up call. I couldn't get my mouth to work to yell at him to turn the beeping off, but inside I chuckled. He and I were two peas in a pod. We could talk about wanting to change until we were blue in the face, but down to our core we were nothing but worthless party monsters.

I tried to push my eyes open again, but they were stuck solid. The corners were full of dried goop, and between the pain of tearing them open and the blindingly bright light, all I could do was groan. Every inch of energy in my body went to trying to move my right hand so I could clean the corners of my eyes. It refused to move, shooting pain down my spine. This was bad.

I heard a voice I didn't recognize call out, "He's awake!"

The laughter I'd expect to come from my friends didn't follow.

Instead, I felt a soft hand on my shoulder, and I winced in pain. I tried to speak, but all I could do was groan.

Jack really needed to turn that alarm off. The steady beeping was too much to handle.

"Take it slow. Easy there, Christopher," a firm female voice said. "Easy. Nice and slow."

She called for ice chips and I heard someone shuffle out of the room.

A cool cloth hit the corner of my eyes. I winced as the hard goop was removed.

Something was really wrong here. The pounding in my head was too intense, and my body wouldn't work. My left eye opened first, fighting to adjust to the lighting. The room was blurry and I couldn't seem to focus, no matter where I tried to look. One thing was obvious: I wasn't in someone's garage. I could smell alcohol, but not my typical poison of beer or whiskey. This was stronger, more stringent. This was clean.

I was in the hospital.

Now I was really in trouble. I must have gotten behind the wheel. Why would I do something so stupid? I knew better. All of my friends knew Denny and would never let me drive if I was even mildly intoxicated. How did I get out? What car did I drive?

I hoped I hadn't wrecked Mom's car. She had saved for years, skimping on things for herself that she really needed in order to buy that car. Behind Denny's back she called it Freedom. That name was an inside understanding between us, our own private joke. One of the very few things we shared. Otherwise we barely talked.

Mom would let me borrow Freedom sometimes. She knew I also needed to roll down the windows, feel the wind in my hair, and just be a carefree teenager. I needed to escape the rules and the yelling, the strict military order that he imposed on everyone except himself.

If I'd taken Freedom away from her, I'd never forgive myself. Never.

But I couldn't dwell on that yet. It had just dawned on me that there could be even worse news. Had I killed any of my friends? Or a stranger? How intense was the accident? Would I recover only to go to jail for vehicular manslaughter?

My eyes shot open, finally driven by adrenaline. The light burned, but I didn't care. I had too many questions. I needed answers. The room buzzed with doctors, shining lights in my eyes, asking me questions, checking the machines that were sending annoying beeps through the room—not Jack's alarm clock after all.

"Christopher, how many fingers am I holding up?" a male doctor asked as a nurse took my blood pressure.

I tried to answer three, but I couldn't. All that came out was a groan.

"It's okay. Stay calm. Christopher, you're in the hospital. There's been an accident."

I did my best to brace myself for the truth, no matter how hard it might be.

It suddenly occurred to me what was missing—why the room felt so odd.

No one was here with me. I couldn't see Mom, Denny, or God forbid, Dad. I must have really done something bad if they couldn't even bear to be here when I woke up.

Even darker thoughts started to settle in.

What if I'd hurt them? What if they weren't here not because they're upset with me, but because I had killed them?

No. That's not what happened. They probably went to the cafeteria. I didn't even know how long I'd been here. Surely not long.

When I touched my cheek I didn't feel anything, not even the slightest prickle of stubble. If I'd been in here longer than two days I'd have that annoying itch from where the whiskers start to peek through the skin. This was a relief.

Cool bits of broken ice hit my lips, the water trickling over my tongue. I needed more. The first drop of liquid created an intense craving, stronger than any I'd ever had for any drug or drink. While those substances felt crucial for my mind, this was a new carnal desire springing up from the very core of my body, an intense craving for survival.

Another groan escaped as I tried to talk. I didn't know what I wanted to say, but it wasn't coming out. Everything was so heavy. My head, my arms, my legs, my eyes. I didn't understand why I was here, or why my family wasn't here, either.

"Christopher, it's okay. There's been an accident," the doctor said again.

Yes, I know. You keep saying that, but it doesn't mean anything, I thought to myself, wishing I could say it out loud.

Intense pain shot through my head. I gasped and let out a light scream. My right eye faded out again, and soon I was under a shroud of black, slipping back into unconsciousness.

Twenty days later I was released to go home. That's what they called the bare walls and empty rooms enveloping me when I arrived back at Denny's.

Those stale and lifeless slabs of drywall had never felt like home, and now, knowing Mom wouldn't be there, it never would. The colorless confines felt smaller than I remembered, and I couldn't help but notice that all traces of Mom were gone, like she'd never existed.

My short-term memory had been affected, but slowly, little pieces started coming back.

I recognized the leathery smell of Denny's Jeep seats. He cleaned them twice a week with a damp microfiber cloth and always made sure to treat the soft brown cloth monthly with a conditioner. His wood-paneled Wagoneer was a source of great pride for Denny. I couldn't help but feel shocked when he chose to drive me home in it. There were clear rules in the house, and number one was to never sit in, touch, or even look at his chair too long.

On the ride back to what would never be home for me, I realized there were no seat belts. As I was thrown around in the front seat on sharp turns made slightly too fast, it felt like he knew exactly what he was doing. I tried my best not to touch anything lest I leave a fingerprint, a lesson I learned as a child on one of my extremely rare rides in his precious toy. A lesson that today would likely be bloody, as I felt a stitch on my head pop when I furrowed my brow too hard.

Here, in the living room, as I looked around for something to remind me of Mom, anything that might feel comforting, all that came back to my memory was how there was never anything comforting here to begin with. I'd rather be back in the hospital. At least people there wanted to make sure my heart was still beating. Not even Ava had stayed to see me home, although that didn't surprise me too much either.

The plaster walls in the living room were devoid of humanity and care. What little bit my mother had tried to inject was gone with the wind. There was no heartbeat in this house.

When I looked again, however, I was surprised to see that the walls had been freshly repainted. And the kitchen had a new tiled floor, which was ironic. Mom had always wanted tile, but Denny had said we couldn't afford it, that the godawful aged linoleum was good enough. Now she's gone, and he suddenly has money to make her dreams come true.

It broke my heart that she didn't get what she wanted while she was here. Even the flooring in this dead old house was symbolic of the way she'd lived. Or the way she'd never gotten to live. Walked on, walked over, seen as just good enough to get by.

"Where is everything?" I asked, looking around.

"Everything that needs to be here is here," Denny replied, walking off to the kitchen.

He didn't stop to give me a hand. He didn't ask if I needed anything. He didn't even look at me. I couldn't help but wonder if the everything he was talking about included me, or if he meant everything but me.

"I mean Mom's stuff. It's all gone."

He sighed, or maybe he laughed. I couldn't help but think the slight shimmy of his shoulders was hiding a chuckle. He kept pouring his beer, keeping the frozen mug tilted at the perfect angle to reduce the foamy head. The action was clean and crisp, something he'd done multiple times before—a clear priority over me as I stood there on crutches, with shaky feet and weak arms.

My head throbbed. The room tilted.

To my left was the couch, and a deep brown stain on the far cushion caught my eye.

Blood. My blood. Why wouldn't he get a new couch, too?

I felt bile rise in my throat looking at the expansive stain.

"Yeah, you're a real bleeder," he said, smacking my back.

I gasped and coughed. I felt another tiny burst of blood squeak out of the slowly healing wound on my head. This was no friendly smack in jest, no familiar pat. There was no father–son connection between us. This blow had underlying currents that left a handprint of rage between my shoulder blades.

I fell forward, my hands landing just south of the blood that used to flow through me. The blood that barely kept me alive that day.

Memories came flooding into my pulsing brain of a man in a black hoodie. The scraping of metal against brick. Confusion. Pain. Wetness from my head. Wetness from my pants.

"Denny," I said. I was gasping. "I need to move."

"Then move," he said, his eyes carrying a dark twinkle.

He scared me.

"My room . . ."

"You're free to go."

He smirked.

I recoiled in fear.

He smirked some more.

Standing to my shaky feet, I put my weight against the crutches. Confusion settled in as I tried to process the moves my weak and limited body was making, fast and strenuous, falling and getting back up. Every single twitch of a muscle, voluntary or not, taxed what little life I could feel remaining inside of my battered frame. The flesh lining my skull under my shorn head threatened to explode; my knees promised to fail if I pushed too quickly. My entire body, once youthful and full of potential, was crumbling beneath me.

My eyes met Denny's as his stocky frame settled easily into the new oversized, deep blue recliner dominating the corner of the living room, where Mom once kept her records. He'd bought himself a new chair but hadn't bothered to replace the couch covered in bits of me.

Had he wanted me to see the blood when I finally got released from the hospital? Was he teasing me?

"Go on, boy. Don't be such a pussy," he said, pulling on the wooden handle of the recliner and leaning back comfortably. "You'll never get back on your own if you don't start getting your shit together."

He flicked on the TV and raised the volume before I could say anything.

I tapped into all the strength I had left in my body, steadied myself against the crutches, and hobbled down the hallway toward what I hoped was still my room.

CHAPTER EIGHT

Strapping In

The door to the execution chamber opened after a few turns to the right, with a single key, jingling impatiently from Warden Stanfield's oversized ring. I couldn't help but be shocked, given that the cells, bathrooms, and other walkways required at least two keys and sometimes a fingerprint scan or swipe of an ID card.

"Is it harder to get in when you've got the mean guys, Warden?" I asked, catching him by surprise. I chuckled. "Don't worry. I'm not going to make a break for it or anything. I just assumed the room would be a little tougher to get into."

"I suppose if someone is at this point in the process, everyone in their way is already gone," he said.

I couldn't help but notice his voice was shaking, betraying a formerly hidden layer of insecurity.

"We've brought that up in a few budget meetings, but they keep saying next year," he added.

The next breath to rattle out of his lips told me he felt he'd said too much.

"Don't worry. I'll take that secret to my grave." I winked, but he didn't notice.

His shoulders were stiff, his limbs rigid. Any trace of the familiarity we'd built between us was gone.

To my surprise, I realized that all of the fancy directors had somehow managed to nail the emotion and process of a prisoner's death walk in their movies. I couldn't help but wonder if they'd ever sat in a gallery and taken notes, watching while someone actually died. Maybe they'd watched scores of videos snatched from hidden ceiling cameras, or interviewed the dark and barren souls who strapped people down and sent them to Hell.

Hollywood wasn't real life, however, no matter how hard they tried to convince us it was. There wasn't a big-shot lawyer who took on your case, overthrew your conviction, and saved your life, or, more importantly, convinced the outside world you were the victim. Without the superhero in a suit screaming in the headlines, your innocence didn't matter. The court of public opinion was always more important than the private court of law.

Secretly, I'd hoped everything I'd been taught about Death Row through pop culture or crime novels would be wrong. I held on to the hope that the execution chamber wouldn't be as sterile, as cold, or as empty as those on the outside made them out to be.

Or maybe part of me wanted that room to be harsher, rougher, and more full of despair, to tear any last strings of hope from the final beats of my heart.

I knew the large mirror to my left concealed the gallery full of people waiting to watch me die, some with smiles on their faces, no doubt. There would be media, people from human rights organizations in case the injections were botched, and maybe, they would be sitting there. Hidden. Saying the final words they would never say to me under their breath, cursing each final blink of my eyes, hoping my spirit was sent straight to Hell.

I wasn't sure if they'd ever understand exactly what had happened. Their mother had died. She'd been murdered. That's all they understood. And as their father, birth or not, I couldn't argue with that, or invalidate their emotions. The actions of my life had caused them enough pain, and I knew better than to take this away from them, too.

If Ava and Chris were strong enough to face all of the demons circling around our lives, and if they had decided to come today, hiding behind the confidentiality that the mirror provided, I hoped they could tell I still loved them both dearly.

Still, I hoped they wouldn't come. This wasn't what I wished for them. I didn't want them to remember me this way. When the gallery window was opened, I didn't want their final memory to be of my chicken legs sticking out of a too-short prison pants in a sterile room while drugs were pumped into my system. But like so many of the days that pieced together my final years, this was out of my control. If they chose to come, they'd do so knowing they'd have to digest my memory, chewing off bits and pieces of what they would watch while their insides decided if the morsels were nourishment or poison.

I didn't know if Denny would come. Could he watch me die? Could he sit there and see his best friend, the one convicted of murdering the woman we both loved, take his last breath? Would the memories of our childhood come swirling back, surrounding him with nostalgic thoughts of the good old days, or would his eyes stay as cold as they'd been during my trial, shooting dark rays of hate my way in the courtroom?

When I'd glanced at him during my sentencing, his eyes looked like whatever remained of his soul had been sucked out and pulled from his body. They were empty, cavernous sinkholes. He scared me; there was something about him that had changed, an intense anger or rage that he'd fed now taking over his body and mind, whatever remained inside his fleshy exterior.

Giles, the large guard who towered over even my six-foot-two frame, and who always snuck me gummy bears and playing cards, guided me toward the black table. The vinyl covering smelled of ammonia and stuck to my legs when I slid into place. My legs were quickly strapped down just below the knee and under my hips. Thick leather cuffs were tightened around each ankle, the metal clasps cool where they grazed my skin before being carefully taped in place to make sure nothing came undone.

Warden Stanfield put a comforting hand on my shoulder and then tightened the chest straps.

"Are you okay?" he asked, genuine concern in his voice. The steely demeanor that overshadowed our walk was gone, at least for now. "They don't have the microphones on yet. Is there anything you want to say?"

I knew he meant well, and I knew he wanted answers. Everyone wanted answers, even people I'd never met.

But Warden Stanfield had lied to me. The microphones were on. I could see the red light blinking next to the ceiling camera above my head. They hadn't placed the external backup microphone on my shirt yet, but the standard room microphone attached to the camera was already on.

Giles had slipped me some newspapers, and I'd made no attempt to hide the fact that I had read every article ever written about my case. Close attention was paid to all of the theories developed by people with no clue as to what I'd been through, and I read about all of their "educated" guesses as to why I'd spared my son and slowly tortured my ex-wife.

I knew what Warden Stanfield was really asking. But there would be no deathbed confession today, no solving the mystery of why I'd murdered my wife, no sobbing apology for almost murdering my own son. No. There would be none of this from me.

"Yes, sir. I'm just fine. We're too late to be too concerned now, aren't we?" I finally replied. I tried to respond as nicely as possible, but truth be told, I was exhausted from years of the circus surrounding Trudy's murder.

My arms were pulled out to my sides and strapped down on independent boards, my body forming the semblance of a holy crucifix. I wondered if this was a sign I should have prayed more, or at least taken the prayers I did send up more seriously.

Each wrist was tightened in a set of cuffs matching the heavy leather wrapped around my ankles. The amount of straps on my body was concerning. I hoped these were not a sign that I would be experiencing horrible pain or symptoms that necessitated having my body so tightly secured, and instead, merely a precaution against dangerous inmates.

Perhaps they were both. We'd all find out very shortly.

Four stickers were placed along my chest to monitor my heart rate. The cold latex of the executioner's gloves sent a chill through my body. His touch was emotionless, calloused. I hoped this was him simply disconnecting himself from his job. I prayed his wife, if he had one, didn't have to endure a heartless touch, too.

One thing my mind would never be able to understand is how a man could just turn off his feelings, his compassion, and his desire to connect with other humans. Does it become easier when someone disgusts you? Sure, I'd told Trudy that I hated her. I'd told her I didn't love her. We both knew I didn't mean either of these things. In all of my life up until now, though, I'd never met a human so vile as to be able to shut off their own humanity—to knowingly prepare another person to die.

"What did you want to be when you were growing up?" I asked the executioner.

"Excuse me?" he responded, shock spreading over his face.

"Was this what you thought you'd be doing? As a kid?"

"Oh . . . Well, no. Does anyone ever say they want to kill people for a living?"

He paused, realizing the weight of his words, and knowing they'd been caught on the recording.

"I mean, you know . . ."

"I know. That's why I asked. What did you want to be as a child?"

The executioner tore open the small square package holding alcohol swabs and began to clean the surface of my right arm.

"Depends on the year. Sometimes I wanted to be a chef. Other times, an astronaut. After a vacation to the Caribbean, I wanted to be a deep sea diver." He chuckled. "I was too scared of the ocean, though, and spent the entire boat ride throwing up over the side. Never got my sea legs."

I laughed in response.

"And here you are. Did you go to medical school, then?" I asked. "Drop the wide-eyed little-kid dreams and go for a big adult job?"

I felt the snap and tightening of a rubber tourniquet as it cut off circulation to my arm. I hoped that finding a vein was easy. A good vein meant good flow, and hopefully, according to what I'd read, less struggle for me; less chance for something to go wrong.

"No. Actually, I don't really have any medical training. I mean, I went through a certification to do this, which makes me a medical aide. Initially, I went to school to be a teacher. But unless I move or someone quits, there's nothing for me here in Parker Point. My mom's too sick for me to go anywhere else right now. Maybe one day."

"I bet you'd make a good history teacher." I winced, feeling the sharp sting of the first needle slide into my arm.

"The main line is in," he said to the room, documenting his process.

The warmth he had previously shown while talking about his past and childhood dreams was once again gone, shut off with the flick of a switch.

"We'll move to the other arm now for the second line."

This needle went in easily as well, and I was thankful. I hoped this was a sign of an easy, by-the-books, no-surprises death for me today.

CHAPTER NINE

Denny

I couldn't look away from her body. She lay there in the kitchen, covered in crimson waves of someone's anger—an anger that was all-encompassing, built from the deepest layers of betrayal. Each slice of her soft flesh was smooth and nothing less than methodical. Every puncture was precise and meant to inflict pain, not death. But together, when the strokes of an artisanal madman were added together, death was the only possible outcome.

This had not been quick. The murder was not driven by a sudden need for revenge. The process of taking her life had been planned, calculated, and studied. Only one word could describe the scene before me: premeditated. This was certainly not a crime of passion.

Trudy had always hated the color red. She said it was an angry color, a mean color, a forceful color meant to show power by hiding the wearer's insecurities. Seeing her lifeless body lying in what looked like every drop of the crimson fluid her body once held, I started to understand her hatred for the shade. I felt mad just looking at it, the thick river forming a stain on my floor that would be impossible to remove, and tinting the golden strands of her hair the color of muddy bricks made from Deep South river clay.

The scene was odd. On one hand she looked extremely peaceful, unmoving, almost like she was sleeping in the utmost layer of nirvana. On the other, Trudy had been a fighter when she'd wanted to be, which explained the meat tenderizer and the need for her killer to make sure their mission had been completed.

The person who took her out knew her well; they knew she shouldn't survive the knife wounds, but they also knew she'd play games. In the last minutes of her life, if they had simply trusted her to die, she would have waited as patiently as possible before spending her last bits of energy to crawl to the phone and contact the authorities, whereupon she'd name her killer. To put it simply, that couldn't be allowed, and the only possible choice was to bash her head in.

Such a waste. Those hopeless thoughts, shining through the fiery light of her eyes, no doubt cost her the last seconds of her life. To see her lying facedown on the kitchen floor, something that was once so soft, so sweet, and so harmless, but was now rigid and monstrous, was a moment I wouldn't be able to rinse from my memory anytime soon. At least not without the help of a man named Jack, gently poured over ice cubes each night.

My childhood best friend, lover, mother of my children, and truthfully, thorn in my side, had finally met her match and was now lifeless because of another person's anger and uncontrollable power.

Common sense evaded me as I fell down next to her body, my knees sticking to the remnants of her life with a gut-wrenching squelch.

I knew I should have considered the crime scene before I lifted her lifeless flesh, but the evidence didn't matter to me. The boys in my department were on their way to inspect the scene. They'd understand when they found me down here with her. If this was one of their wives, I'd expect to find them in the same way. Not a single soul would have expected me to just let my wife lay on our floor untouched, alone, and dead.

This town knew our history. They knew our story. They knew we were destined for each other from a young age, had questioned why she'd walked down the aisle with him, and told me she was where she belonged when she had walked down the aisle with me.

This was my town. My home. James was nothing more than a blight on our lives, and he always had been. And now, he would be my suspect zero. I'd make him pay. There could be no one else; he'd gone downhill, from golden boy to a life of violence, lockups, and now, homelessness. The entire town wanted him gone, off the streets, and put someplace where he couldn't be a menace. They'd always said he needed to be taken care of before he became dangerous.

Too late.

I held Trudy's lifeless hand in mine and swore on every memory we had made together that I'd make him pay. I'd promise the entire country that Trudy's death would not go unanswered.

Her body felt lighter, no doubt from the loss of blood, but I could tell that the weight of senseless worries she'd duct-taped to her soul had also slipped away. Trudy was always worrying, always stressed; she was always concerned with small issues she would inevitably turn into a mountain of trouble. A mountain she was never ready to climb. Now she could be at peace.

Now I could be at peace, as well, freed from the chains her burdens had unknowingly placed on my life. The angry morning phone calls, the nights without dinner as she sat in her reading chair, nearly comatose, staring out the window. I always wanted to know what she was thinking but never cared enough to ask. The conversation would be too long, aimed at making me into a horrible husband. They would be laced with undertones, like maybe she'd made a mistake coming back to me, and full of the unspoken understanding that deep down, she hated me, maybe more than she loved me.

"No, not now," I whispered. This was not the time to be thinking about her death setting me free. "Compose yourself," I said.

"It's okay, Detective," Ted Sullivan said, placing his hand on my shoulder.

I startled. I hadn't heard him enter the house.

"You don't have to be in work mode right now," he said. "Take your time."

Sullivan was one of my best juniors, always at the top of his game. Even as a rookie, he'd caught mistakes and inconsistencies others didn't, and was able to read between the lines in ways you couldn't train someone to do.

I didn't want him here right now, seeing me like this. His presence was meant to be comforting, but to me, he was threatening, ready to strike at any opportunity to crack a case. Tonight's events, as tantalizing as they might seem, had to be kept from him if I wanted my reputation as the town's ace detective to remain in place. A murder in Parker Point was a rare occasion, and could either make someone's career soar, or sour.

Blue and red lights flashed against the walls, slipping in through the blood-splattered kitchen window. They reflected off the stainless-steel refrigerator, magnifying their impact on the horrific scene and casting an eerie red glow that highlighted all of the blood. So much blood.

"Detective Lloyd?" a voice called out.

I was able to place the nasally squeak of my second in command.

"In here, Hardy. In the kitchen."

I tried to keep my voice steady, to not betray my fear. I still had to appear strong, able to lead my department through even the most personal of tragedies. I had to show everyone that Ted was not the dominant force in this room. Control was everything, and weakness would not be allowed.

"Oh my sweet Jesus," Hardy said, stepping into the kitchen.

"Careful—don't come in here until we've photographed everything. We need to preserve the scene."

I paused for dramatic effect and looked at my bloodied hands, at the spatter covering my pants from where I'd fallen to my knees.

"As much as we can, anyway. My DNA is all over this house, but we can't risk anyone else's getting mixed in."

"Yes, sir. I'll stay right here."

Hardy picked up his radio and sent another call for backup. "We're going to need major help here, guys. It's serious. It's Trudy." He lowered his voice but I still heard him. "I don't think Detective Lloyd was able to process the scene when he called it in. And I don't know what to do. He's sitting in it . . . in her . . . well, blood. With her."

I expected beginners to go green around the gills, to struggle. Be weak. The fact that Hardy was still standing surprised me and let me know he wasn't the average rookie. We weren't Chicago or New York. We weren't constantly called to large crime scenes and dead bodies. Our force was called to rescue cats, unlock cars, and put out grease fires when someone's grandma tried to cook too much bacon.

The lights bouncing through the kitchen multiplied and I knew the ambulance had arrived. The front door burst open, banging against the porch siding, no doubt leaving a dent that I'd have to pop out at a later date.

"Guys," a female called. "There's another one. In here."

"A . . . another one?" I stammered. "Christopher. Oh my God. I didn't know he was home! Christopher," I shouted, refusing to drop my wife's dead body. "Christopher! Answer me, buddy. Answer me."

A paramedic yelled loud enough for me to hear where I sat in the pool of blood.

"This one's alive. I feel a pulse. Get him on the board and call this in: male, around six-foot-three, sixteen to seventeen years old, severe blunt force trauma to the head. He'll have to go to Philadelphia's trauma unit if he's going to survive this. Get me a helicopter. Now!"

"He's alive?" I asked, shaking. "Christopher is alive?"

"Sir," Hardy interrupted. "I think we need to ask you to stand up. I know it's hard, but we have to work this scene."

"I'll work this scene, Hardy. No one runs it but me," I replied, the aggression in my voice growing to levels he was not familiar with.

Pulling together the sternest look I could muster, the very look Ava always said was disturbing and evil, I turned to my two juniors.

"This is my scene, do you understand me? Send someone to the back to get me a change of clothes. I don't care what you pull, but document the removal. Nothing in this house, in my house, is touched, moved, or even looked at without a photograph, writing it down, and following every inch of proper protocol. Do you understand me?"

"Yes, sir," Ted stammered. "Yes."

From the back I heard someone shout.

"In here, in the bathtub. There's clothing, covered in blood."

"Get me my damn change of clothes so I can do my job," I yelled, rejoicing as my powerful voice echoed through the crowded house.

CHAPTER TEN

High School

For some kids, high school is the best time of their life. Those four sweet years of careless bliss are where they peak and enjoy being on top of the world. For others, it's the worst.

And then there are the rare ducks who don't care if they're good or bad, they simply keep on walking with their heads down, knowing life will keep moving either way when all is said and done.

When the three of us walked into the hallowed halls of Parker Point High School, we were still thick as thieves. The town still expected us to be together at all times, and the teachers made a point of trying to keep us apart, right from the get-go. They said their decision would be better for us in the long run. We needed to meet other people, make new friends, get out of our comfort zones in order to progress in our lives, to grow as our own individual people.

We disagreed, feverishly, from the moment we got our schedules until we crossed the threshold and officially became freshmen. No amount of begging, pleading, or showing up to the administrator's office with homemade chocolate chip cookies made a difference. The schedules were set and we'd just have to get through six and a half hours a day without being glued to each other.

Somehow we made it through, hanging out in the cafeteria before classes began, meeting up in the hallways between periods, and walking home together each day when the weather allowed, riding the bus when it didn't. Together, in whatever free time we managed to squeeze out of our days, grand plans were orchestrated for when the first member of our group finally got their driver's license.

We'd come up with a unique plan. All of our parents thought it was crazy, but we thought that if we worked together and pooled the money we made at our summer jobs, we could buy a group car together. We'd have no limits as to what we could do and where we could go. Together, we might even be able to leave this town and find new horizons full of promise.

Over pizza, we also vowed to keep the very serious three-way pinkie promise we'd made: to attend every dance as a trio, or not at all. No other dates. No interference. Just the three of us for the next four years.

To be honest, if Denny had come up to our group one day and said he wanted to bring a date, I wouldn't have objected. That would have given me an excuse to spend the night with Trudy, to find a way to woo her without violating our friendship pact. We could apologize by saying it just happened while Denny was busy living his life outside of our circle. Silently, I prayed for this to happen every time a new dance was announced.

It never did.

Instead, every day that rolled past, I couldn't help but notice we were changing from the inside. Our group was shifting, and I couldn't figure out why, no matter how hard I tried.

There were moments of laughter when Denny and Trudy suddenly apologized for an inside joke. A silent piece of trust I wasn't meant to know about. And in their trust was the unspoken truth that they were somehow spending extra time together. Private time.

My jealousy started to build around this mystery, my mind consumed by watching and trying to figure out where, when, and how. More importantly, why. Why were they excluding me? What had I done to get pushed to the outside of the circle? Why wouldn't they want to invite me to these secret meetings, the ones they inadvertently threw in my face, and were obviously full of fun?

I found my answers thanks to a hall pass during a calculus test. I had faked diarrhea so I could use a bathroom break for a locker run, where I'd have time to double-check an important formula I had forgotten.

Conveniently, Trudy's class was across the hall from my locker. I figured a quick glance might soothe my nerves and get my head back in the game. Math was not my strong suit, and I needed to keep my GPA up in order to retain academic scholarship opportunities. Parker Point was nice and all, but I wanted to see what I could do out in the real world. I wanted to be the one who got out of this one-horse town, and if I returned, I wanted it to be because I wanted to, not because I had to. I certainly wouldn't remain in Parker Point because I was stuck.

With each step closer to her classroom, I could feel her. She was the current to my battery, the magnetic force driving my compass, the North Star to my lost soul. My body automatically directed itself to her, like the course had already been set for thousands of years.

The door to her classroom was open, which was strange. I saw a substitute, wringing his hands and stuttering through lesson plans left by the absentee teacher.

I caught a glimpse of Trudy through the open door, attracted by the aura emanating from her blonde hair and glowing face. Trudy was one of the only girls at school who refused to perm and tease her hair, or to cover the natural shine with layers of hairspray. This defiance elevated her radiance in my eyes, driving me even deeper into my lovesick ways.

I couldn't help but smile as I traced her slender limbs with my eyes.

But something wasn't right. Her cheeks were flushed. She was laughing, covering her mouth with delicate fingers, her nails adorned with chipped bubblegum-pink nail polish. And someone's hand was on her knee. Someone she was leaning toward, opening herself up in a way I'd opened myself to her for years. A hand I knew very well but couldn't place.

"Can I help you?" the substitute teacher asked loudly, breaking the whispers and secretive chatter in the room.

I shook my head no. I couldn't get any words to come out. Especially after the whole class turned to see who the teacher was speaking to and I noticed that the stray hand belonged to Denny.

When our eyes met, he smirked. Not a friendly hello, but a challenging glare that sent a chill down my spine. The little things I'd been noticing were more than hidden moments. They were covering an entire hidden relationship, violating our friendship at the deepest level. Denny's smirk turned into a full smile, the twisted grin of a comic book villain as he knocks out the hero.

Trudy's face went blank. She realized she'd been caught, our pact ruined. There was no apology on the face I loved. No shame. No guilt. Just a blank stare. She didn't care.

I felt like I'd been punched in the stomach, and my heart began to pound. I felt their betrayal more deeply than I'd ever felt any emotion before.

"So you're trying out for the football team, D?" Trudy asked, leaning closer to Denny. The light caught her chocolate eyes, but he was the only thing swimming in their depths.

Even though it was just a single letter, the nickname infuriated me. "D." So stupid and impersonal.

Today was pizza day, her favorite. Trudy would normally load her tray up with red French dressing, meticulously peel off the cheese in perfect strips, and then lap up every drop of dressing with the crust. The way she ate pizza may have been the only part of her I ever found to be utterly disgusting. She hadn't even put the dressing on her tray today.

Denny interlaced his fingers with hers, lightly pushing a stray piece of hair from her cheek. A soft rose spread over her skin, following the pattern drawn by his fingertips.

"I am. Coach pulled me aside last month after we played dodgeball in gym class. Said I'd be a good running back with my size and agility. I figured I might as well; If I'm good enough, it might open another opportunity for college, you know? Speaking of college," he said, breaking his concentration and turning to me, "how's Calc?"

"Horrible." I groaned. "I need to get my grade up but I just don't understand all of these formulas. And if I don't pass, I'm screwed. My entire college plan is off. I'll be pushed down into easier math courses and my transcripts will be a mess."

"Why don't you try out for football with me, J? I bet you'd make a good kicker."

75

That single letter. I hoped this wasn't something that would follow us for life. Trudy called him "D", her chosen nickname as they moved to lovers; Denny used "J" for me because he could tell everything they did as a couple got under my skin. He could read me like a well-worn book.

"You get one big idea from your gym teacher and suddenly you know all of the positions on the field well enough to place people?" The words snaked out effortlessly. Now my cheeks were flushed from embarrassment, not passion like Trudy's.

"Easy there, tiger," Trudy said. "I know you're frustrated because of school, but Denny is just trying to help you out. I think he's on to something. Why not give it a try?"

"Are you going to eat your pizza, T? You forgot your dressing," I replied. I emphasized the T, drew it out with venom in hopes of making the one letter nickname sound as stupid as I thought it was. Honey, baby, sugar, those made my stomach turn, but their choice was just plain lazy.

My insides were burning.

Sports had never been part of our plan. We'd always made fun of the oversized buffoons slamming their fists on the tables during lunch and having soda-chugging contests, revving their car engines in the parking lot after school, and getting out of everything because they were needed for the game on Friday night.

"Listen, James, just stop by tomorrow. You never know. Sometimes we need to try new things. Isn't that what high school is all about? Trying new things?"

"Thank you for letting me know what high school is all about now, after we've already made plans for the next four years. I didn't know there was room for negotiation when we said, 'I promise.' I thought everything we agreed on would stand."

Denny said something else but I zoned out and didn't catch his words.

The first semester of high school wasn't even over yet and he'd already betrayed me.

Twice.

CHAPTER ELEVEN

The Vein

The door to the execution chamber opened.

As I watched Father Frederick walk into the frigid room, for some reason I expected his presence to blanket me with peace. It didn't. His billowing robe created a black hole in the void surrounding me, ready to swallow my soul whole. His head was bowed, Bible in hand, impeccably starched collar proudly in place. The prison priest was a Reaper, an omen of death, a bringer of shadow and night. While I'd never been a religious man, I'd never feared religious men. Today, that had changed. Where I'd hoped to feel warmth I found a wall of ice, a man forced to face those who had violated every principle he stood for and doing his best to save their souls.

"Would you like to pray today, James?" the priest asked, his voice gentle and unassuming, the exact opposite of the glare that splintered his steely eyes. He wasn't forcing me to bow my head, and I knew if I said no, he'd still pray under his breath for God to take my soul home. I knew he would feel more solace if he could speak the words aloud. The prayer to come had nothing to do with me, and everything to do with his comfort.

I softly replied, "Yes."

He cocked his head, and a childlike glee set in. I wondered what he was thinking. Did he believe that on my deathbed he would convert the unconverted? Was I secretly a child of God all along? Maybe I was.

I can remember my mother saying she'd rather pray and end up finding God on the other side than to walk up to the pearly gates having shunned him during her mortal life. While I'd found this profound, many times I also felt like it was the same as, "I'd rather jump off a bridge and break both legs than never jump and not know the feeling of flying." I always played it safe. I never liked to jump, or fly, at all.

The lights in the gallery came on, revealing the faces of those here to watch me die. We were no longer alone. This was no longer a personal moment, and I regretted telling him that yes, we could pray. I didn't want to share this intimate baring of my soul with anyone else, even if the purpose was slathered in false motives. The headlines would run that I was repentant, apologetic, that I welcomed redemption. I felt none of those things.

Most of the faces peering out of the gallery were unfamiliar. I recognized a few from local TV news programs, or from their photos next to the newspaper columns they write. With pen and paper in hand, there was no denying their purpose. Reporters had to take notes now, since mobile phones and electronic devices had recently been prohibited after another execution was videotaped and leaked. I knew that every last breath, muscle spasm, sigh, or uttered word would be documented and presented to the hungry wolves salivating for the gory details of my final moments.

The prosecuting attorney was sitting up front, no doubt representing Trudy and her family. His suit was just as posh as the ones he'd worn during the trial, his demeanor as powerful as when I'd first met him in that courtroom. The only difference was a few more white hairs peeking through the black dye he used in an attempt to still feel young. I wondered how many executions he'd attended over the years, how many men had been sent to their deaths by his hands. Did he feel proud when their bodies were zipped into cold black bags and wheeled away from the living?

Trudy's family wasn't here. They'd already had their hearts broken by one child long before their only daughter had been found facedown on a kitchen floor only three blocks away, a kitchen floor they'd never even seen. I imagine they carried the burden of her lost childhood and bad decisions as an adult long after her brother was found dead in the jail yard, shanked through the heart with a sharpened toothbrush. Both siblings dead, victims of their bad decisions and inability to control their natural impulses. Both siblings led by a craving for danger and things they knew they shouldn't use to quench their thirst.

My heart dropped when I looked to the right, behind the stern-faced lawyer who had convinced the judge to put me here today.

Ava.

She sat there, red-nosed, her eyes swollen. I hoped to see her tightly holding hands with Christopher, but she wasn't. My eyes rolled over the row of chairs until I saw him sitting tight and rigid like a stone. He didn't avert his glance when our eyes met. The quiet show of dominance made me proud. Deep down, even though he didn't know it, he was a strong boy, and with a little bit of time, some healing, and a damn good therapist, he would get his life back. Step by step, he could keep moving and make something of himself, if he'd only try. But first, he had to want it.

80

I couldn't tell from their expressions if they'd read my letters. I didn't know if the warden had mailed them yet. Maybe he was holding them until I was gone, or maybe he'd decided the better option would be to not send them at all.

Warden Stanfield was my last hope of connecting with my kids. He had seemed to agree with my decision to write the letters. I'd agonized over each carefully selected word, each painfully written sentence, wondering if they would matter in the long run. Would it make a difference that I'd poured everything out on college-ruled paper, or would it be better to just leave Christopher and Ava in peace? Would the truth shake them—or ruin them? I couldn't say.

In my heart of hearts, though, I felt I should try, and let them figure out the rest. They were adults now, and free to make their own choices. I would love them regardless of their beliefs about who they thought I was. I would love them regardless of anything.

"Today, in this execution chamber belonging to the great state of Pennsylvania," Father Frederick began, turning toward the gallery, "we will put James Jackson to death. Mr. Jackson will be executed for crimes he committed, namely murder. Violence, vengeance, hate, anger—we all find ourselves complicit in these emotions from time to time. Greed, jealousy, and wrath are all known to show themselves in even the most pious person's life. Even if someone has taken a life, they are still one of God's children.

"As we are all God's children, today we stand with Mr. James Jackson, to offer words of kindness, blessing, and assurance as he leaves this mortal world and moves toward judgment, and his eternal life."

My throat clenched, unwillingly spasming. I bit down on my bottom lip, drawing blood in an effort to silence my thoughts.

This was my death. He shouldn't be addressing the gallery. They couldn't care less about saying a true prayer for me. Some of the watchers, rubbernecking from their comfortable seats, might be clutching their gold and diamond-encrusted crosses. We all knew they were here for one reason: to watch a man take another man's life, justifying their presence here on the wings of a prayer. They'd talk about God, how he should have my soul, how he has me in his thoughts. They'd walk away from here with a high they'll forever be seeking after watching me take my last breath. I didn't think God would be present with them on their drive home or in the bottom of the whiskey they'd use to drown out their thoughts in a few hours.

"Let us bow our heads and pray. O Heavenly Father, God of pure and never-ending love, who keeps a watchful eye over our sinful bodies— we claim to want peace, but we act against His love. We come to you today with heavy hearts. We ask that you have mercy on us, and have mercy on Mr. Jackson, who will shortly receive final judgment upon his soul. We pray that you will ease the pain laid upon the hearts of those in the gallery—that you will stand beside those who watch Mr. Jackson take his final breaths here on Earth.

"Let your loving arms wrap around everyone as they leave here today. Let them speak to you in their own time, in their own way. I humbly ask that you fill us with your love so that we can flood the world with hope, peace, and understanding. Father, I ask for you to grant us peace on this day of great challenges for many. Amen."

"Thank you, Father," I said. "That was a beautiful prayer."

Warden Stanfield moved toward my right shoulder, once again laying his stocky and muscular hand on my body. For a big man, his touch was gentle and comforting.

I knew what was coming before he looked me in the eyes. I'd rehearsed this moment over and over again. When he opened his mouth, he'd ask me a very important question, and I'd have to decide my very last, most important words.

Every possible scenario had played through my mind in the days leading up to this moment. What would I say if the kids were brave and decided to come? What would I say if they didn't? What should I say regardless of who was in the gallery?

The only person I wanted to be present to watch me die was Denny, and he hadn't come. I wondered if it's because he couldn't handle the pain, fear, and frustration that would arise from watching his childhood best friend put to death for killing his other childhood best friend. Maybe his love for Trudy was pure after all. Maybe the memories of that night would be too fresh. Maybe, at his core, he was a coward, just like the rest of us.

The microphone was clipped onto my top, a backup in case the ceiling microphone wasn't able to pick up the audio, or in case the technology quit working. The last words of a Death Row inmate were important. These statements were studied by psychologists and detectives, mulled over by families, and reported in the news to indicate how big of a psychopath someone was.

I didn't want to give any famous last words; I just needed to say a few. But with Denny's absence, I knew I'd have to be a little more creative. I wanted my last words to haunt him, to tear into him, to show him how he'd betrayed me in my life. I wanted his soul to be just as tortured as mine was, so he'd never forget this day.

Warden Stanfield looked at me. He lowered his voice, and with the patience of a father teaching his firstborn to ride a bicycle, he said, "Any last words, James?"

"Yes, Warden Stanfield. I do have a few."

What I'd practiced, of course, was quickly forgotten, gone out the window, lost to the black abyss that formed in my mind. I was overwhelmed by seeing the bloodshot eyes of my daughter and the steely stare of my son. I made the mistake of moving my eyes to their faces, the pain and anger piercing my lungs, making each breath more difficult to produce.

"I . . . I practiced this. But practice can't prepare you for actually being here. I hoped you two wouldn't come. You've been through enough and don't need to see this, to let this be how you remember me. Know that I'm going in peace, and I hope one day you will understand why. I love you. I always have. I always will. And one day, may peace find you, too."

I paused, thinking about how to say what I needed to say next, the key piece to get them to understand the truth behind Trudy's murder.

There was only one statement powerful enough to break through to everyone. One phrase the media would latch on to, that people would talk about and analyze, and one statement capable of hitting Denny deep in his soul. But I knew saying those two words would only cause confusion and pain for my children.

I turned to them again, and with deep pain in my heart for the reaction I knew was coming, I said what I had to say.

"I won," I said.

"Excuse me?" Warden Stanfield said, slightly taken aback.

"All that matters with my death is that I won."

An icy coldness settled over everyone in the room. With this phrase, I'd sucked the life out of them. These final words would be seen as my confession. Trudy's murder was a game, one I had taken to the extreme on my deathbed.

I had played well. I had taken extreme measures. But I had not played the game they thought I was playing, and one day, they'd know exactly who had played who.

Looking into the gallery, I knew that day would not be today.

I knew what would come next: sodium thiopental, a barbiturate. If this worked as it should, I would be unconscious within three minutes.

Supposedly, I wouldn't feel a thing coming my way. I wouldn't feel the burning pain of the other drugs coursing through my body, forcing it to shut down. At least, that's what it said in the informational materials. I always do my own research, however, and in the prison library I was able to find out that sometimes the necessary drugs aren't available, and substitutions are made. Untested, unregulated substitutions that have failed in some cases and led to excruciatingly long deaths in others.

Warden Stanfield set his palm back on my shoulder.

"Thank you for that clarification, James," he said. His hand was firm this time, not soft and caring like before.

"I'm not sure that was a clarification, Warden. One day. Just not today."

He looked at me quizzically, but I couldn't give him anything else. The truth was between me and three other people: one was dead, one couldn't remember, and one was absent. The truth needed to stay within the circle of four until someone decided to step outside the lines and speak up.

One by one everyone left the room. The support guards. Father Frederick. Warden Stanfield. I watched them go, wondering what they were thinking, what they would do after they watched me die. I looked out to the gallery, to the reporters frantically scribbling their notes. Here I was, strapped to a gurney, about to die, and I was looking at complete strangers and judging their lives.

My eyes moved to my children. I didn't want to see their anger, their confusion, or their pain, but I wanted to leave this world looking at two of the best parts of my life.

"I want you to leave here today in peace," I said, not sure if they could hear me. "I love you."

I heard the call come over the speaker in the room, letting me know the first round of drugs had been administered from the control room. The executioner wasn't allowed to be in the room with me. He hid in anonymity and safety behind a wall, where the clear plastic tubes of my IVs ran through two small holes. When he stepped in to check my vitals in a few minutes, he would wear a hood like mask, concealing his identity from the gallery. For his safety, they never would never see the person I talked to moments ago

If my research was correct, I'd be asleep very soon, anywhere from thirty seconds to three minutes from now. I wasn't sure if my eyelids were feeling heavy from the drugs or from conceding to my fate.

CHAPTER TWELVE

Christopher

Mom didn't know I saw her go back to pick him up after she dropped me off at school. I'd walked up the stairs and waved good-bye like I always did. Then, instead of going inside the imposing building that threatened to steal my hopes and dreams, I walked back toward the street and watched her drive away. I hid in the shadows of the large oak tree, crouched down behind the brick pillar at the front of the school's steps. The deep red reflections of her brake lights were still illuminating her path of deception, slowly snaking down the misty early-morning street.

I saw the way she'd looked at him that morning, sitting outside of the café, feeling sorry for him. It was impossible for her to hide her thoughts. They were glints behind cloudy eyes, revealed through tiny twitches when she said his name, and "What a shame" when talking about "his path."

I saw the longing, the curiosity, and knew those would be followed by her desire to be his savior. As often as she talked about him, clicking her tongue with a tsk as we drove by, the way the fine lines twisted around her eyes—it always betrayed her true thoughts. And if the fissures on her forehead deepened too far, she was lost in nostalgia, what could have been, and what she'd call the "good ol' days." I find it hard to believe she ever had any of those in her life. But when it came to James, Mom always felt she'd be able to lift him up, get him back on his feet, and with enough effort, change the way the town saw him.

I hoped she'd never succeed. I didn't think he deserved redemption.

The elephant in the room was always the part she played in paving that road. Everyone in this family was just as guilty as the other for every challenge, dark moment, or curse laid upon us. We were a chemistry experiment gone wrong; a pool of undefined elements giving false positive reactions before combusting in flames.

I knew today would be the day she crossed the proverbial line in the sand. We could look at Dad, drowning in his bad decisions on the street corner, but we couldn't talk to him. His presence was meant to be ignored, to serve as a reminder that in our own twisted beliefs, we were the good ones. We could lift up even our worst decisions by saying, "At least we aren't James."

But today, she would betray us all at a level beyond comprehension. One simple action would put us back into a cycle of moving to a new place, manic episodes, and exposed lies. Who knows what else would come out of Pandora's box when it was opened.

I saw her brake lights glow brighter as she slowed down next to the café. My suspicions were confirmed. When I saw him climb into her car, I decided she was dead to me, too. I just needed to figure out my exit plan and what level of collateral damage I'd be willing to endure in order to get away.

First, I needed to talk to Ava. She was smart. She'd left this twisted town as soon as she could. Her GPA, SAT scores, and school résumé would have allowed her to study anywhere, but the East Coast Ivy Leagues didn't put enough miles in between our family and her dreams. Anything within a day's drive was too close, she had said when fiercely arguing her reasoning for refusing to attend any of the colleges Mom had applied to on her behalf. Mom would scream about the wasted application fees and how far that money could have gone. Ava would rightfully argue back that she couldn't be held responsible for the decisions of others.

But that was our life; somehow we would always be blamed when adult logic ran short. Who cares about the decisions you made? Just blame the young ones, because without them, you wouldn't have had to even think about certain situations to begin with, right?

When UC Berkeley offered Ava a full academic scholarship, she accepted, packed up, and left without so much as a note. The letter came on a Wednesday and she was gone by the following Monday, her room completely cleared out. Anything that wouldn't fit in her car was discarded, right down to her bedsheets. She left no trace to prove that she'd ever existed under the roof we tried to call home.

We all knew she'd be okay, and she'd check in when she wanted to, if she ever wanted to. I think I was the only one who'd miss her. Even though we chose to keep a steady distance between us, seeing each other as symbols of destruction, halfblooded dragons of despair in what could have been a perfect family, there was a silent understanding that we needed each other in order to keep going. I always knew she would leave even though I'd tried to tell myself she wouldn't do that to me. And when the day came, when I woke up at 6:30 a.m. and she was already gone like a mist in the middle of the night, I felt abandoned, lost, like an open wound after the Band-Aid has been ripped off too soon.

That choice to leave would show me who she really was. Ava took the sharpest pair of scissors one could find and sliced the cords of our relationship. She became cold, distant, and forgetful.

My situation was different. We all knew it. After Ava left, Denny took every opportunity to remind me that I'd never be able to run like she did. I was chained to our family, chained to them for my basic needs, tied to generations of bad choices. It was in my DNA. I'd inherited the worst parts of each of them, tied into the core of my genetic makeup, and I could never escape the destiny written in my blood.

I'd fucked around in school. I didn't play any sports because I didn't want to be like the stories Dad had told us about Denny. The way Dad told it, football had turned Denny into a monster. Their friendship was destroyed over bonfires, booze, and bimbos. Promises were broken, lives shattered in his hands as he took on the "King of the School" crown too proudly. And no one stopped him. Everyone had turned a blind eye then, and they still did.

Denny didn't know that I had found his collection of tapes, the ones he'd pulled out of his cruiser so people couldn't question what he did with his badge. I'd seen everything: the women forced to pay off their traffic violations over the trunks of their cars, the men beaten and wallets emptied, and the first fight with Dad. I knew all of his dark secrets, and there was nothing I could do with any of them. Not if I wanted to stay alive.

When I saw Mom's brake lights, I felt the veins in my head pop, crackling with anger. Waves of pain started to rush over my forehead. I'd never felt such intense frustration and disgust. When James stood up from the curb and ambled over to the car, facing the ground like the disgusting, unworthy coward that he was, electricity shot through my brain. The edges of my vision started to go black. Irrational thoughts began to fill my head, thoughts of revenge, of ending the two of them and exposing Denny, of ending myself to expose all of them.

I needed to move. If I'd stayed there, hiding in the shadows and seething, I may have made a bad choice. Already, my rationality and ability to hold on to reality was slipping. This was how it felt when I'd tipped back a few too many shots, and now, without a touch of alcohol on my tongue, a blackout was just a few steps away.

I walked off the school grounds, not caring if anyone saw me go. What's the worst that could have happened? They knew Denny's wrath. Reporting that I'd left would have only landed them in hot water for not doing their jobs. He'd go public, he'd shame them, jobs would be lost, the school system would be under intense public scrutiny, and mob mentality would settle in like a small-town virus as parents started blaming the administration for all of their kids' problems, as well. As his legal son, I was untouchable to everyone except him.

I'd been through Denny's rage too many times to care. I knew his limits, and this time, I'd have the trump card. I wasn't skipping to smoke behind the school, prank my teachers, or raise hell in town. Today was about making sure my mother didn't fuck everything up. If the school did call, when I told Denny I'd been watching Mom pick up James, with the intention of telling him what they did together, maybe for once he'd see me as a real son, not just on paper. He'd see that I could be on his side, we could work together, and if we tried, we could find common ground as we searched for some semblance of quality in our lives.

Mom's red SUV pulled off before I was able to get too close. The fact that they'd left together was evidence enough that she had no plans to stay with us for much longer. Her track record of leaving and switching sides when things got rough was long, and almost anyone in town could recite the when, where, and why of each time she'd flipped sides.

If what I was watching was an innocent conversation, if she was just checking in on him after seeing his pitiful face every morning outside the café, then they'd still be sitting there. I'd see her in the back window, wildly waving her hands as she tried to make a point that no one else understood. But they had driven off, and I knew this meant it wouldn't be long before Mom was telling us to be patient with him, to give him a chance, to forgive him, and to welcome him back into whatever new home she would drag us off to in order to make a new start on what she thought would be a better life.

Right now, my plan was to follow them, to confront them together, to get the truth, and let them know that their choices had completely shattered my life. Without a doubt, this hidden rendezvous wasn't an innocent "How are you doing," or "I'm very worried about you." He had climbed into her car, street grime and liquored breath and all, and they were gone.

I pulled up the GPS app on my phone. Denny wasn't very slick with his tricks. He'd put the tracker on the car to monitor my mom, and hacking his phone to get access to the app was ridiculously easy. When she betrayed his wishes and let me borrow the car, which she did frequently, he liked to send a notification to his buddies to pull me over if I was even slightly speeding. Sometimes I'd gun it just for fun, kicking the speed up just enough to set the alert off on his phone. He'd call the nearest patrol car, tell them to get ready, and then I'd pass their position, making sure I was just slightly under the speed limit. If he wanted to play games with me, trying to keep us like caged animals in a derelict zoo, I'd play twice as hard.

The blue blinking dot showed they were at the Twin Pumps Truck Stop. Mom always stopped there before a long road trip. "Cheaper gas and cheaper snacks," she'd say. She always joked that if she was going to run away and start a new life, she'd start the journey there to load up on supplies.

My stomach knotted into a tight cramp of rejection. I was right. She was leaving. My fear that I'd wake up one day and she'd be gone was justified. I wanted her to break out of her self-imposed prison of regret, pain, and neglect, but I wanted her to take me with her. Once again, though, she'd made her choice, and it didn't involve me.

I entered the place meant to be our home, our sanctuary, our safe place. The empty walls and precise placement of each item made the rooms feel like cells. Today the house felt exceptionally barren, cold, devoid of any heartbeat.

I ran into the kitchen, ripping open the drawers under the built-in desk Mom used to write the novels she'd never publish. The spare keys were gone. Her emergency stash of cash she'd thought was well hidden in the bottom of her pencil can was missing.

I took off down the hallway, pushing into their room. I didn't mind that I was breaking rule number one—to never go into the master bedroom without an adult present, and without an invitation. In all the years I'd lived in this house, I'd only been in this room once.

I wasn't even sure what to look for or where to start. I tore open the closet and began looking for important pieces that were missing. I looked for gaps in the perfectly lined up shoes. I tried to see if any luggage was missing. I realized I knew very little about my mother—what she owned, what she wore, what she'd take with her. Obviously I didn't know what she could live without, either. Most children would assume they'd fall into that category, but then, I'd always been the exception to every rule.

I really didn't need to find any evidence; her GPS and the way all the good had been sucked out of the house told me she was gone. I did the only thing I knew to do—to try and stop her, to bring her back. She wasn't going to get off this easy, and she sure as hell wasn't going to uproot my life again for him.

I pulled my phone from my pocket and sent Denny a text, advising him to track his wife's GPS.

While he was stalking her, stopping her, I'd be busy packing. Tonight, when they were fighting and screaming, when she tried to justify why what she'd done wasn't bad, and that he was overreacting, they'd practically push me out the door just to get one more thing off their plate.

Whenever they were upset with each other, if I even walked into the room I'd get yelled at to leave. I would be reminded that my presence wasn't wanted, and they'd accuse me of trying to start extra drama just by showing my face.

I'd bait them tonight and tell them that I'd leave for good. They'd dare me to try to make it on my own without them; they'd laugh at me, mock me, challenge me. But I'd go, and never turn back.

Once I was free and clear, they could do whatever they wanted with their twisted, codependent, toxic lives.

All I needed was one bag and enough money for a bus ticket. When they kicked me out, I'd head off to the station and buy the first ticket out of town. The door would slam behind me and they'd be congratulating themselves for showing me who was boss, but I'd show them.

Thoughts of freedom, of what was to come, took over. I couldn't control myself any longer. I couldn't hold back the oncoming dark wave. My mind was flooded and I surrendered to the blackout, hoping I'd take the right path and come out of this alive.

CHAPTER THIRTEEN

Homecoming

Homecoming became a big deal with our trio after Denny made the football team, and it became a religious event after he transitioned to star quarterback. When senior year started, Trudy still worshipped the ground he walked on, never seeing the way he worshipped the ground every other girl walked on. Or maybe she chose not to. She was head-strong, and sometimes I wondered if breaking up with Denny would be considered defeat in her relationship playbook.

I had to straddle the delicate lines of our changing and unplanned dynamic on a daily basis, in an effort to hold our group together. We were supposed to be the three amigos until the end. We used to chat over milkshakes about our kids playing together, group vacations, and even buying a big farm where we would build three houses separated only by golf cart paths. This was the plan I tightly clung to under our friendship pact. I learned to accept the possibility that we would only be building two houses now and not three on our friends-forever compound.

Or maybe we shouldn't build any and instead think about getting away from each other.

When the college scouts started showing up, Denny started talking about California, Georgia, and Texas. Pennsylvania was not part of his future.

I was okay with this because I realized I wanted to get out, too. Slowly, the chats about our group farm changed to chats about his future high-rise penthouses and mansions with multiple pools and twenty-car two-story garages. He wasn't even out of high school and his reality was quickly becoming tainted by pipe dreams. In his mind, he was already throwing the winning points in a down to the buzzer Super Bowl between archrivals.

Trudy never noticed that when Denny talked about the future he only talked about what he wanted. His house. His car. His pool. His parties. His game room. He never talked about what they could build together.

Would Denny know Trudy wanted a grand piano, preferably white, to write her songs? Would he know she wanted a kitchen large enough to entertain even though she only had two friends? She loved to bake bread on Sunday mornings and only drank fresh-squeezed orange juice out of highball glasses. Her dream car was an International Scout, bought in rough condition and restored to a shimmering metallic cherry red with white leather seats. She wanted three dogs: one blue merle Great Dane, one elderly rescue mutt who needed a good place to call home for a few more years, and a Poodle. She'd always been fascinated with flowers and wanted a rose garden. Most of all, Trudy wanted an art studio with floor-to-ceiling windows overlooking either a forest or mountains.

She deserved all of these dreams, and if Denny's plans came to fruition, he would be able to fulfill them for her. But that would require Denny to realize she was a person with dreams of her own. That would require him to listen and invest his energy into someone else.

"So the game starts at seven-thirty," Denny was saying. "Big game, you two. I need you both on point to cheer us on. You have a royal blue sweater, J, yeah? I need you out of that red trash and to join our space. Be part of the team."

I rolled my eyes.

"You know you want to," he said, punching me on the shoulder.

"You know I don't."

"Imagine all the tail you'd pull if you were, though. Trust me, J. Trust. Me," he said, before shifting awkwardly in his seat. "According to the boys, of course. They score chicks from every city. Doesn't matter where we pull in, they pull out. Well, sometimes they do. Sometimes they don't. We may have our own statewide football team in eighteen years."

He laughed.

We didn't.

"So, Trudy, how are your ceramics classes coming along?" I asked.

The anger I felt over what Denny was really saying, what Trudy surely understood but chose to ignore, slowly dissipated when she smiled, and the radiance returned to her eyes.

"Really great. Thank you for—"

"Focus, you two. This is serious," Denny cut in. "What time does the game start?"

"Seven-thirty," we replied in unison.

"And what time will you get there?"

"Seven o'clock, so we can sit in the front row where you can hear us."

"And what will you wear?"

"Royal fucking blue," I said, perhaps a little too full of spite.

"Exactly. All right. See you then. I have to run and do some pregame ritual. Don't be late. You understand?"

He didn't wait for our response, just stood up from the table, pointed at us, and jogged away.

The cafeteria monitor watched but didn't dare tell him to slow down or try to reinforce the "no running in the hallways" rule that the rest of us had to obey.

"Why do you stay with him, Trudy? Must be exhausting."

I couldn't hold back my frustration any longer. For three and a half years, I'd stomached my feelings of betrayal. I had played the quiet third wheel, the supportive best friend, the shoulder to cry on, and many times, the chauffeur in the car we didn't buy together after all. Denny never even offered to pay for gas or clean his vomit off the backseat when I picked him up from a kegger he'd never bothered to tell me he was going to.

He never told Trudy, either.

Denny and I had secrets. Secrets that could bury his relationship with Trudy and take him down under the cold musty earth, too.

"Can you believe that final pass?" Denny hooted, smacking his fists on the red Formica tabletop, hard enough to make our silverware rattle and the ice angrily shift in our lemon water. "I mean, we were going to win anyway, but when you can slam some more points in the face of your mortal enemies, who would deny that? No one. That's who."

Trudy eyed him suspiciously. She wasn't wondering if he was drunk; the vodka on his breath made it obvious.

"Denny," she began, choosing her words carefully. "At what point during the postgame dance did you, well, have some extra fun?"

He winced. His mouth opened but nothing came out.

Trudy rolled her eyes. "Oh, don't be daft. I know you're drunk. Who gave you the booze, Denny? How did you even get alcohol into the dance?"

I watched his shoulders relax to their normal position. A gust of vodka-laced breath smacked me in the face.

"You want to know how we got the liquor in? We're rock stars, that's how. No one cares what we do. We own this town. We can do what we want."

"Denny," she began, in the most forceful way I'd ever heard her speak to him.

I could tell she'd probably never spoken to him this strongly before.

Their low-volume bickering ranged from his broken promise to slow down on his drinking and focus on his studies to what it does to a relationship when you break a promise.

I bit my tongue.

I knew that drinking was not the worst offense Denny committed on any given day, and certainly not during the homecoming dance. While he was slow-dancing with Trudy, one hand firmly gripping her ass, his eyes were taking in the bodies of every other girl moving around him. He was considered a prize, and almost every girl at Parker Point wanted to be the one to replace the girl standing in their way.

The quarterback should be with a cheerleader, they felt, or the potential prom queen, or the daughter of a steel magnate, not some simpleton who everyone knew was still a virgin. A man like Denny deserved to be spoiled by a woman's touch, to enjoy her body and walk with pride, they'd say. And they'd try. And he wouldn't stop them.

Jennifer Stewart worked especially hard to catch his attention. The slinky silver dress she wore made me wonder whether her parents had even seen her before the dance, if they'd taken the typical pre-dance photos moms normally went gaga over. The hemline was a bit too high and the neckline, too low—certainly groundbreaking for the early nineties. What should have been a halter instead crisscrossed in front of her neck before being tied behind, leaving a large keyhole opening in the front, a picture frame for the ample bosom most boys in our class longed to see.

She'd walk a little too close to Denny and brush against his back. I noticed his free hand run slightly under the hem of her dress when she passed by. From the other side of the room, she'd adjust her arms in ways that made her chest pop, displaying a little more flesh than her dress code–busting monstrosity already revealed.

And when she reached behind her swanlike neck to loosen the tie to where it barely hung together before turning and walking through a set of side doors that led to the locker rooms, I watched Denny whisper something in Trudy's ear, gingerly kiss her on the lips, and excuse himself—to go to the restroom, I guessed.

Trudy sat down next to me at our table and started to strike up a conversation. I apologized and excused myself, saying I had to go to the restroom, too. The look on her face pierced me to the core. I didn't dare try to explain.

Slipping through the same set of side doors was easy. No one noticed me. No one cared what I was up to. Every male in the room was eyeing the girls, even the teachers. Every female chaperone was busy guarding the punchbowl from stray flasks or pulling dancing couples apart until there was a full body width between them. The tall silent kid who only had two friends could easily move through the shadows and never be missed.

The locker-room door let out a soft creak. At first I cringed, but the sound of moaning covered up any sign of my intrusion.

I slid along the locker bay edges, stopping when I came to the opening of the shower room. One silver stiletto lay in the doorway next to a pair of patent leather men's dress shoes and the edge of a pant leg.

"Does she do this to you?" Jennifer asked.

"If I beg," Denny replied, a soft moan slipping out. "But not nearly enough."

"If I was your girl, you wouldn't have to beg."

Denny let out a louder groan and murmured something I couldn't quite make out.

She giggled.

I wanted to hear what he was saying but I couldn't risk getting any closer.

"If I was your girl, Mr. Quarterback, then I'd let you. But I'm not, and I don't let anyone in this temple."

She was teasing him, trying to entice him into breaking up with Trudy by offering sex in a mildewed, ammonia-soaked shower.

"Denny, what are you doing?" she gasped. "I said no."

"You didn't say no. You said if you were my girl you'd let me fuck you," he said, his voice forceful and harsh.

I started to take a step forward, but what would I do? What could I do? Denny was solid muscle. He was unpredictable at best when he was sober. Now he was not only drunk but I knew how much he hated to be challenged. I had no doubts he would take out his rage on me in a heart-beat if I walked in, or if I told Trudy.

Jennifer let out a sharp yelp of pain.

"Am I your girl, then?" she asked, her voice strained and broken.

"I don't date whores," he replied.

I didn't want to hear any more. I started to make my way back toward the exit, shutting out her sobs and pleading. Jennifer didn't deserve this, and the monster in that room was not my best friend. Someone else had taken over his body, violating everyone and everything in his path.

I turned back around.

"Denny," I shouted, letting my voice echo through the locker room. "We're waiting on you outside."

"Yeah?" he replied. "Don't worry, I'm coming. Like right," he groaned, "now."

I'll never forget the laugh that echoed through the cavernous room, bouncing off the concrete block walls, echoing without a sign of stopping.

"You might want to straighten your hair and reapply your lipstick," Denny said. "Let your friends know you conquered this mountain, and that they're welcome to try."

"Fuck you, Denny!" she screamed.

"Again? I don't know. I don't usually get hard for sloppy seconds, but if you ask nicely . . ."

I heard a slap and then a scuffle of feet.

Enough was enough. If Denny beat me up, then so be it. He was turning into a beast, barely human. The fame of small town football had gone to his head. I couldn't let my fear of him get in the way of what was right.

I barreled into the shower room, appalled to see Jennifer in shambles, her hair flattened, some of it pulled out, a chunk lying on the blue mosaic floor. Shoes, socks, pants, and other random pieces of clothing were scattered over the soap-coated floor that would turn to sludge with the slightest drop of water.

"Denny,. You're done. Get your pants on and get back out there." I paused. I'd have to be smart. I needed to get him out of the room and then help Jennifer before he turned on either of us, or both of us. He was unpredictable. "Trudy is outside waiting. She shouldn't be sitting at our table alone."

"Shove it, J," he slurred. "You only care about that boring dried-up prude because you've been obsessed with her since kindergarten. News-flash: She swings off these nuts and always will. No one wants a loser like you. She'll sit at that table all night if she thinks I'll be coming back."

"Denny . . ."

"Oh, can it, Professor Perfect."

He picked up his pants and slid them on, leaving his boxers behind. He was too drunk to notice. I secretly wished he'd zip his cheating penis up in his tuxedo pants and take himself out of commission for a while.

"I'm on my way. And not a word of this to anyone, buddy. I'll kill you."

I pushed Denny to the door. My hand stayed firmly on the small of his back for guidance. He stumbled forward and I watched him disappear into the dancing crowd.

"Jennifer?" I called and briskly walked back towards the shower. "Jen?" My voice was shaky. I turned the corner to see her straightening her dress. Her lipstick had been wiped off but the smeared eyeliner would be hard to fix. "Can I help you?"

"Can you help me?" she scoffed and repeated the same phrase louder. "How long were you there? Were you guarding the door for him like a good boy? Fuck you, James. This is as much your fault as his."

She placed both hands on my shoulders and shoved. I stumbled over my feet, barely keeping myself upright. I closed my eyes and let her push me again. She was wrong. This wasn't as much my fault as Denny's; it was more.

"Jennifer, I'm sorry. Denny is, just–"

"Save it. He may be a jerk but you're a coward. You're pathetic."

She spit and I grimaced as it hit my face.

I waited a few minutes after she left the locker room before I made my exit. I wasn't surprised to see Denny on the dance floor. I could only assume he hadn't made it back to our table yet.

"Denny, let's go sit down," I said and grabbed his upper arm.

He didn't fight back but laughed. "Not a word. I'll kill you," he whispered into my ear.

I wished he would.

Trudy breathed a sigh of relief when she saw us coming, but she couldn't mask the anxiety in her doe eyes.

"There you are," she said. "I was worried you forgot about me over here."

Denny didn't answer, but turned to me instead. "Told you." The smile that crept over his face shook me to my core.

"What's he talking about?"

"Nothing. Just an inside joke."

"How drunk is he?"

"I don't know," I lied. "I think he got hit a little hard in the game tonight. Might have a concussion. I noticed him wobble off and was worried. Sure enough, vomiting in the bathroom. We'll need to keep an eye on him tonight."

"Yes, we will," she replied.

We both knew this was not the case. We had a different reason to keep him in our sights at all times.

I wish I would have told her the truth, even though it would have broken her heart into a million tiny pieces. She would have been strong enough to report Denny, at least I think she would. Women protect women. Men like me, cowards, we protect ourselves.

The only thing I did do right that night was start to distance myself from Denny, finally letting go of our plans for a perfect lifelong friendship.

CHAPTER FOURTEEN

Minute One

I could feel my fingers tingle. I wasn't sure if my arms felt heavy from being forced out to my sides in a way that didn't allow for much blood flow, or if the medicine was settling into my veins. My eyelids would droop and I'd snap back awake, like a bored office employee trying to make it through a pre-holiday shift after spiking my coffee. I chocked this up to the past few restless nights. My mind had been consumed with making sure everything was done and in place, my fees and bills settled so my children would not be left with any burdens.

What a sad state of affairs—going from potential lawyer with a savings account, able to provide a beautiful life for a future family, to down and out, flat broke, and on Death Row. When I was putting together my twenty-year life plan on the first night in my dorm room, filled with pride for getting out and breaking bonds I felt had become toxic, celebrating my bravery in leaving Parker Point, nowhere on my list did I write "Kill your future wife and sit on Death Row for years while leaving no positive legacy for your children."

Shit happens.

Maybe the fear of what would come next had finally settled in as the medicine coursed through the major arteries of my body, trying to find the right places to settle. What if I felt everything that came next? How badly would it hurt, to feel my body become chemically paralyzed and my ability to breathe stifled? Would I know I was suffocating? I had so many last-minute questions. So many questions I should have asked in the days leading up to today, the questions I thought the pamphlets had answered but probably should have heard coming from someone's mouth.

Over time I had convinced myself that I didn't need to know all the answers. Knowing would only make the inevitable worse. And asking would be worthless, take my focus away from remaining calm.

Staying calm was the most important thing. I didn't want people to leap to conclusions about whether or not I would be giving any deathbed confessions, if I had regrets, if I showed signs of remorse. All I wanted to do was to fade away into oblivion and not be picked apart.

I had chosen this exit strategy on purpose, because of the way everything started. At the beginning of my jail time, I had fought. Hard. I appealed. I asked for new counsel. I tried to refute evidence, find fault in the trials, and prove my innocence. Days were spent in the prison library reading every textbook, every court case I could find, every true-crime book, every detective novel, and every newspaper, hoping I'd find a glimmer of hope, a potential exit strategy, a loophole. I did everything I could to cast doubt, but doubt could not be cast when the wife of a police officer winds up dead and the main suspect is a discarded part of a love triangle and seen as a street urchin. In reality, the evidence was just too heavily stacked against me.

The night Trudy was murdered is now foggy in my mind. Sometimes I question if I do remember what happened, or if I remember what I want to have happened. I was there. That's never been denied. But the body of evidence puts me inside of the house, and that's what I can't remember. Am I choosing to forget, or am I trying to remember based on what they said at my trial? The hardest question for me to understand is which path is right? The trail of support, or the story I've told myself time and time again over the past few years?

When Trudy left me for Denny, I was angry. Furious. I felt betrayal at a level I never thought was humanly possible. Emotions were roused I didn't even know I was capable of having; extreme levels of anger followed by intense pinnacles of sadness that consumed me from the inside out, like a leech. Deep down, though, I always knew it would happen. In the depths of my brain, the nagging bits of self-doubt always made me spoil her beyond sensible limits in order to keep her close. If she wanted a new purse, I'd buy her four in an effort to show her I would always provide what Denny so proudly refused to give her. My actions forced her to stay with me against her will by holding her a prisoner of need. There was never love exchanged in our house, just fear for both of us, over what might come next.

My veins burned with the incoming anesthetic, and from recognizing the truth—that while she lay next to me and gladly suckled from my willing energy, she never really loved me as much as she would love him.

Without a doubt, those feelings of betrayal needed to be aimed at myself. Not her. She was a victim from the time she was claimed by her brother, always looking for the definition of love and never understanding that the world's most beautiful emotion could exist without pain and force.

After she left, I thought I needed to learn how to tap into whatever it was Trudy was actually looking for. To toughen up, to shed my soft and caring exterior. There were a few nights I tried to master my need to find this dark and uncontrollable side by getting blackout drunk. I'd wake up in the morning in a strange woman's bed, or in the park, or even in my car, with absolutely no recollection of what had happened in the previous hours. Those nights were absolutely terrifying. Watching as life slowly seemed to dissolve from the edges, seeing the fissures develop in my perfectly manicured life. She was a drug and I was an addict, willing to go to the depths of Hell for one more hit.

But I was on that bus to New Mexico, and I was sober. Wasn't I? Or did I get drunk and do something awful that I've chosen to forget? Surely that would be impossible.

I'm confident I know what happened that day. I'm fairly confident I know what I didn't do that night. But in the back of my mind, questions remain. Anything is possible.

No matter how mad she made me, I had a hard time convincing myself I ever would have taken out my anger on Trudy. She infuriated me at levels a human shouldn't feel, levels that consume your every thought and drive you down a path you know you shouldn't take.

Everyone seemed to overlook the fact that her death was a direct consequence of her decisions. How dare she show up on the street that day, whisking me away like she was my savior? Feeding me and giving me clothes and acting like she was doing me a favor, when she'd been the one to put me on the sidewalk in the first place.

Rage started to build up inside of me again, and my eyes pulsed as my brain furiously tried to pump out adrenaline, fighting against the oncoming drugs.

I tried to calm myself by taking a deep breath and beginning a slow backwards count from twenty. I would not die with anger on my mind, following me into the next life. I'd found my peace by working hard to accept the future chosen for me by the people in a jury box. I'd settled my mind, telling myself what was done was done.

The door creaked open, and I heard footsteps. I knew the executioner was checking to see if I was asleep yet. My vitals were affected, I was sure of that. I didn't need a machine beeping to let me know my heart was slowing and my temperature was dropping.

The executioner stopped next to me, checking the machine, feeling for my pulse, and then looking me in the eyes. Even with his hood on, I knew who he was. I'd seen his face.

"Administer a higher dose," he said to those in control behind the glass. "Did you guys even give the right dose? Both vials? He's going down too slowly. Don't mess this up. I don't want to be on the news."

He turned to the gallery, shaking his finger.

"Don't you dare put that in your papers, either. James," he said, turning to me, "looks like we went a little light. Another minute or so and you'll be out."

I felt something hit the vein in my left arm.

"There it is," I said to no one in particular. "Nice and cold." Just like when I was ten, having my tonsils out. Growing up, I constantly had a sore throat, one after the other after the other, until finally a doctor had said I'd need surgery to get my tonsils removed.

That was the first time I'd ever felt true terror. I'll never forget the stiffness of the nurse's overly starched blue dress when she sat next to me, explaining what to expect. She called the surgery a "procedure," which made it sound even more terrifying. I pictured a mad scientist in a haunted house. I was confident the doctor would enter the room with a hacksaw, blood splattered all over his green scrubs and a large reflective light strapped to his forehead, turned on to blind me and make sure I couldn't identify him if he botched my surgery.

The tears started instantly, my little body shaking as I choked on the thick strands of spittle that clogged the back of my already swollen throat.

When the nurse tried to hug me, I scooted to the edge of the table as quickly as possible. The thin paper used to keep the table sanitary scrunched under my body and ripped. I cried harder, thinking I'd done something unforgivable.

Dad came over and scooped me up, his arms soft in what looked like a loving hug. I knew the grip would tighten once we got closer to the parking lot and out of view of anyone who might judge him.

When we got to our gold station wagon he dropped me into the backseat and told me to grow up before walking back inside and scheduling my surgery for the first possible day.

On the way home he huffed and puffed about the inconvenience of having to take a day off. When we pulled in the driveway, ten minutes quicker than we should have, the pop and fizz of a freshly opened beer echoed through the car before he'd even taken the key from the ignition.

I felt really sorry for Mom that night. I swore to try my best to never get sick again. I was beyond ashamed that my inability to control my tonsils had led to Mom walking with a limp the next morning.

Surgery day came and went. I realized I'd cried for nothing.

Mom was the only one who had a reason for crying, but she never did. At least someone in our family had strength.

I had to restart my backwards counting, as I'd lost my place. This time, however, I didn't have a doctor standing over me making funny faces to put me at ease. I only had the blurring faces of those who hated me with a passion fading out in the background.

With one final blink, I surveyed the room and the gallery. My eyes flitted over the heavy glass pane separating me from the observers just in time to see a tall dark-haired man in a cheap suit slide in next to Ava.

Denny had arrived.

CHAPTER FIFTEEN

Denny

I crept into the gallery, sliding between the chairs with care. The timing of my entry was crucial and planned down to the second. I needed James to worry about whether or not I'd show up today, to think about me, to wait to see my face and spend his last seconds wondering what I could possibly be doing if I wasn't here to watch him die for his crimes. I wanted his heart to race with anger and sadness, to force his emotions to twist around the red flesh of his heart while it slowed down to nothing more than a faint flicker.

To be completely honest, I wanted nothing more than to see him die in front of me. Watching his chest slowly and painstakingly rise and then quake on the way down from the terror of knowing another breath wouldn't follow would be a massive relief. I could rest easy knowing all of my problems were over and nothing could get in the way of my future. With James gone, I could move on with life. I could put this darkchapter behind me, do the healing I needed to do, and step up as a father to my children.

If I had one regret in life, which I normally wouldn't even allow myself to entertain as a thought, it would probably be the years I lost ignoring Ava and Christopher. I gave too much time to other relationship struggles, holding that frustration and angst against them.

But if I could get Christopher to see himself as my son now, with James out of the picture, then that would definitely work in my favor. We all knew he was too helpless, a broken shell from his injuries and in need of too much guidance to turn his back on me. He'd been incapable of living on his own, and he knew I had gone above and beyond my legal duties to help him. Eventually, he'd have no choice but to suck up the foolish pride he wore like a badge of honor and come to me.

Getting a job that paid a living wage would be difficult given his physical challenges. I'd make him think I was bending over backwards to help him, to be there for him, and to remind him of every seemingly heartfelt thing I did. In order to finally and completely erase James, he had to see that I was the better man of the two he considered father figures during the course of his pathetic life. I'd destroy every ounce of positive memory or thought he might still have for the waste of flesh quickly expiring on the other side of the glass partition.

With James gone I'd also be able to atone for the time I walked away from Ava—make this right with the God I wasn't sure I believed in but found myself starting to fear with each mistake I made. I'd never wanted to walk away from her, but sometimes we do things we can't explain.

Becoming a father when you have a chance to get back on top can make you scared. I was afraid a child would force me to be tied down, to lose touch with everything that made me great. I was more concerned with holding on to the dream that I would make my big comeback. There were many nights I would lie awake, alone, wondering how different my life would have been if I had never listened to my gym teacher and picked up that football. The fame, the girls, the taste of a life I was raised to believe I would never be capable of living sat on my taste buds like a curse.

But when I realized stepping back on the field meant stepping away from the power I wielded here in Parker Point, starting from zero, I knew I just couldn't give up the years of work I'd put into asserting my dominance over an entire town. And when Trudy said she'd marry James, with my child growing inside of her, and my future being written under a different name, I couldn't let that go so easily. My resentment over how easily they wrote me out of her life fueled my need to destroy them. I just had to take my time. Slowly, Trudy came back to me, and James ruined himself.

I hate that we had to end this way. We were best friends who promised to be everything to each other forever, but those promises turned into a recipe for disaster. When we were kids, just innocent, simple beings, before we were in the black hole of this moment, I wanted to be exactly where I was now: solving crimes and protecting my city. In high school, when new doors opened, I had to test them out. So many of my choices were driven by a new desire, a reopened carnal desire I wasn't aware I possessed. Perhaps a part of me would always be defined as primitive, driven by competition and the need to dominate. I never imagined that this need would define my relationships with my two best friends, but it did, and here we are, watching the tragic conclusion to the battle royale of our miserable lives.

Pulling my elbows off my knees, I straightened my back.

James's eyes were fluttering, but it looked like he knew I was there, like he was fighting to look at me. I hoped he was. Every inch of the good and evil in my body hoped he'd seen me walking into the gallery—that this would be the last conscious thought his mind would be capable of forming. A soft giggle slipped out, which I quickly stifled when the reporter in front of me shifted uncomfortably. I'd need to be more careful to hide the enjoyment I felt in watching James die. I was a grieving widower, after all. I should be flooded with emotion, selling my story to the highest bidder.

I slid in next to Chris, avoiding eye contact. I would always struggle with the outward and obvious reminders of his recovery. My insistence on continuing to take care of him as an adult was the perfectchapter to end my tragic story and helped to capture the hearts of everyone watching the drama unroll with bated breath. But as I heard his breath rattle in his chest, heard the wheezing exhale that would always accompany him for the rest of his life, the sound that rattled through my house and my sanity, I couldn't help but wish that he'd died that night along with Trudy. I'd taken on the burden of his physical therapy for years, draining my retirement fund, even though every time our story hit the national news there'd be an influx of donations. The money was never enough, but that was the price of my choices.

We hadn't even made it to his mental therapy yet. In all the years he'd been sitting in his room and rotting within his ungratefulness and bad attitude, he had refused to go. He didn't want to remember that night or any more of the truth than he already did. For this, I was thankful. Reopening darkness can only lead to more darkness. At least that's what I believed. I kept my darkness locked away, reserved for only special occasions.

My eyes drifted back to James, lying on the gurney, strapped in tight.

The leather looked thick, heavy against the skin, uncomfortable. I swallowed my fear that his execution wouldn't happen and the case would be reopened. The first shot had already been administered, the second was being prepared; after that, there was no going back. James would be a dead man.

His eyes scanned the room. It looked like he was trying to take everything in, to understand his final seconds. I watched his eyes close, his body go still. The monitor continued to show his vital signs dropping, confirmed by the executioner's inability to rouse any form of response. I knew we weren't completely out of the woods, so to speak. Until the second drug was administered, technically, the execution could be stayed. The anesthetic wasn't a lethal dose, and he could be pulled from his current state.

"Breathe, Denny," Christopher said. He patted my knee gently, his hand shaking involuntarily, encouraging me to relax. "I know this is hard, but we deserve this. Yeah? Mom deserves this. We'll overcome. Rebuild."

His voice was shaky; his pain, hard to ignore. A twinge of guilt settled over my mind. I pushed it away. There was no room for guilt, for remorse, for doing what was right. James had made his choices, and so had Christopher. He chose to call me that day, to tell me she'd picked James up. Christopher admitted to knowing about the GPS tracker, unknowingly revealing more secrets than just Trudy's afternoon of lies. The pain he feels every day, the dreams that make him scream at night—these are his burden for his own wish to ruin his mother.

God, we were all fucked. All of us. Like the evil of our parents was written in our DNA and passed through the cells that made our bodies whole.

I flicked my eyes down the row to Ava, feeling my lips reflexively tweak into a grin when our eyes locked. Even on the worst of days, she couldn't be there for Christopher, choosing to sit far away. Surely she blamed him for her mother's death.

I'll never forget the look of shock on her face when he admitted to calling me during his testimony. I never told any of them I already knew; I wasn't stupid. I had to let them think Christopher had blown everything open. When they subpoenaed his cell-phone records, there was a call to me, a call to James, a call to Trudy, and a call to a blocked number. Maybe he had called James and yelled at him, sending him over the edge. Maybe he had called someone who threatened James and sent him into a murderous rage. Maybe his call to his mother had changed her mind about whatever she was about to do, and sent James into a jealous fit.

One thing was certain: Ava felt Christopher was to blame, and she hated him. And she hated me even more because she wasn't yet able to blame me for my part in Trudy's death.

Breaking her would be hard.

Ava sat like a stone. She was always cold. Bitter. Hard. A selfish, self-centered, uncaring bitch I wasn't sure I'd ever get to know, love, or be able to be around for more than five minutes at a time. I had to try, though. She couldn't be the victim in this story. I wouldn't let her take credit for the suffering we all felt. It made me so angry. Here I was, sitting here in this room solely to provide emotional support for the two of them. She could have at least acknowledged me.

I've often wished Ava had been home that day instead of Chris. Maybe if she'd been hit over the head, whatever kept her heart hardened would have been forced out. If she had been home that day instead of Chris, this would have been a double murder. I knew that for a fact.

As I looked at these two kids, I realized one thing: I didn't regret not spending time with them. Instead, I realized I hated both of them. I hoped I'd never see them again after we left this room.

CHAPTER SIXTEEN

College

With only one semester left until I received my bachelor's, I wanted to stay in Philadelphia and study over Christmas break, but she called. I could hear the urgency in her voice. Something was wrong. She swore there was nothing; she just needed her friends back together. Trudy was always a horrible liar, too pure-hearted to pull off deception, too sweet to hide her hurt.

I packed my car and left immediately. The day had been long: end-of-semester tests, study groups, and a little bit of kissing with one of my study mates on the walk home.

Jill had pulled me into a dark alley by the auditorium, gently placed her hands on the sides of my face, and guided me to her plush and eager lips. The kiss I'd always saved for Trudy was given away, and I was okay with this.

I laughed. In one intense moment that smelled like a back-lane dumpster, I realized I had given up my life waiting on the world's most hardheaded girl. For seventeen years I'd held off, swinging by a rope of hope that one day she might like me back. That rope had slowly twisted and turned until a perfect noose had been formed, by which I was slowly hanging myself.

But tonight, the rope broke.

"Would you like to come up?" Jill asked when we stopped at the entry to her sorority house.

I debated in my head. I stammered, and choked on my words. Every inch of my body wanted to go, but I didn't know what to do once I followed her. Just a second ago, I'd had my first real kiss. Should I tell her? If I did go up, would she agree to play Scrabble, or would she want more—something that I'm just not ready to give?

"I think I should go, Jill. But I'd like to take you on a proper date. If that's okay with you, of course. Dinner, a walk in the park, whatever you'd like," I said, babbling uncontrollably.

She stopped me by leaning in, giving me my second kiss, and introducing me to physical lust. I wanted to go upstairs so badly, but something told me I'd be a disappointment. I needed to study first, read some of those articles in the women's magazines, make sure I knew how to hide the fact I'd never touched a woman before.

"Sounds wonderful. How about tomorrow?"

My head spun with excitement. Tomorrow. I could do that. First dates are supposed to be sweet and innocent. Respect her, get to know her, set up the second date.

"Tomorrow is wonderful. I'll pick you up at seven?"

"Seven is wonderful. I'll see you then."

She smiled, gave me my third kiss, and entered the sorority house without looking back.

That woman had confidence.

Woman. The word amused me. I'd always seen Trudy as a girl, even now. My childhood friend. My first crush. But I didn't see her as a woman.

Dumbfounded, I walked back to my dorm wondering what this new realization meant. What had I missed out on? Why was I holding myself back? In what other areas of my life had I stunted my growth while waiting for Trudy?

My head was spinning as I made my way to my room. The answering machine light was blinking furiously next to a number thirteen. Unlucky, and as a slightly superstitious person, I debated whether I should hit delete or wait for a fourteenth message to arrive.

The phone rang again. The only time my phone ever rang was on Sunday to say a prayer with my parents before they ate their post-church dinner; or when a classmate called to schedule a study session; or when there was an emergency. Today was not Sunday, I just came from a study session, and this meant only one thing: there were thirteen messages about an emergency, and one ringing through right now.

I lifted the phone from the cradle, my heart beating like a scared horse running down a cobblestoned street.

"Hello?" I whispered, my voice cracking.

"J. Where have you been?" A familiar voice with frantic undertones. "I've been trying to reach you all day."

"Hi, Trudy. I'm so sorry. I was on a date," I replied. I don't know why I lied. I suppose it could be considered a half-truth.

"A date? Oh. Wow. Okay. Well, that's interesting." She paused.

I heard anger in her silence. She found my dating life interesting? Why was she shocked by how I spent my time? What I'd realized tonight was right. Trudy was a child. I deserved a woman. A strong, powerful, career-driven woman to stand by my side. And starting tomorrow night at seven o'clock, I would take the necessary steps to make one of these women my future bride.

"What are you doing this weekend? Wednesday is Christmas, after all. Are you coming home? James, please tell me you're coming home."

"Did something happen? You sound really bad, Trudy. Is this your anxiety again? Should I call Denny?"

"No. No. Don't call Denny. Please."

Those words stuck a knife into my soul.

Ever since Denny had suffered a severe knee injury his sophomore year in college, during a hard tackle, he hadn't been the same. His football career was over, which was understandably frustrating, but he also lost his scholarship and was kicked out of school. Turns out he wasn't going to class, and he hadn't been passing any of his courses, either. Once he was no longer an asset, there was no reason to keep him around and allow his antics to destroy the university's reputation.

With no other choice, he'd returned to Parker Point, back to his loyal girlfriend, and back to his parents' basement.

"I can't keep secrets between you two. That's not fair. If you want to continue this conversation, you will have to tell me what's going on."

"Nothing is going on. I just miss you. I want my friends back together. It's Christmas, you know? Hey, J, do you remember the year we went sledding down at the Troll's Stomach? Who named it that anyway? What a silly name."

I laughed. "Of course I remember. Denny showed up with trash-can lids, saying they'd go faster. Boy was he right. Can you imagine if we had started a business making saucer sleds, how rich we'd be today? Do you remember when I hit the bump they built to keep kids from flying into the cow pasture and it didn't stop me—just launched me right over the barbed wire?"

Her soft giggles burned my heart—the heart that had just turned against her with a first kiss.

"Who could forget?" she said, still laughing. "Your hand landed right in a massive pile of cow shit. You're lucky it wasn't your face."

We chuckled together and it felt like old times.

"Please come home, James. We can decorate the tree, sit by the fire drinking hot chocolate. Doesn't that sound great?"

It did.

"Okay, Trudy. Let me call my mother. We'll meet at the diner tomorrow evening. Eggnog milkshakes and gingerbread cheesecake?"

"Oh, yes. Absolutely. I'll be waiting."

So would I.

I phoned my mom. My dad was long gone, buried in a coffin probably soaked with whiskey. I was shocked the liquor store cashier hadn't shown up to mourn his most loyal customer.

Mom was excited to hear I was coming home, happy to not be alone for the holidays. For the first time, I let go of the anger I'd felt toward her, for loving my dad until he died. I never went home because I felt like she had betrayed me by staying with him. But hearing the sadness crackling over the phone line, the frail voice that once belonged to a warrior, told me it was time to let it go.

The next morning I filled a duffel bag with a week's worth of clothes, basic toiletries, and a few key textbooks for some holiday break studies. I took off with an eagerness to make things right with my mom, and to get to the bottom of what was troubling Trudy. I never called Jill to tell her I was leaving or to cancel our date.

I was ravenous when I pulled up to the diner.

I hadn't been home in two and a half years. Trudy and I usually spoke once or twice a week, but our conversations felt short and forced. I couldn't tell you what she was working on, if she was practicing on the free piano she'd found in an alleyway, if she'd rethought Denny's half-assed proposal, or if she wanted to finally do something for herself and start making some different decisions.

I noticed her hair immediately under the dull fluorescent lights. While not as bright as before, a slight halo still surrounded her face. She smiled when she saw me but her face didn't light up the way it once did. Her eyes looked sunken, her cheeks puffy, and her skin no longer held a radiant glow. She looked exhausted.

My assumptions were right. Something was very wrong.

"Hey, you," I said, greeting her but urging her to stay seated. I could see her clothes hung from her shoulders, the thin lines of her collarbone forming a slash across her upper chest.

"Welcome home, J. I already ordered you a milkshake. Are you hungry?"

"Starving. I haven't been eating much lately. Had a major lecture yesterday and then study group. Barely had time to sit down, let alone eat. And this morning, I was just in a hurry to get on the road."

"I thought you had a date last night? That's what you said on the phone," she said, catching the small inconsistency.

"I mean, yeah, I did. Jill. She's really sweet. She's also pre-law. We study and then grab a bite sometimes. We'll get more romantic when we have time. For now, it's our career and our future that get us all hot and bothered."

I sounded like an idiot. Hot and bothered? I've never spoken like this in my life. I always found statements like that to be crass, vulgar, and slightly uneducated. Probably because of my constant desire to fight against overly macho guys. The very person Denny had become.

"Interesting. Pre-law, huh? You're really doing this, J. I'm proud of you. What's your next step?"

"I'm trying for Harvard. I've applied, but I haven't heard back yet. It's probably too late. I have a list of backup schools, but who really likes their backup schools? I guess it's hard to settle for second best. You know me. I hold on to what I want, even if the universe is telling me I'll never get it."

Behind me the door chimed again.

"Oh, good. Denny's here! I wasn't sure he'd make it out."

I swear while she was talking, the very last sparkle she held in her eyes, the last drop of natural glow permeating her skin, faded. Every ounce of life left in her seemed to just disappear before my very eyes.

"What's up, you two?" Denny said, forcefully sliding over the red vinyl booth and pushing Trudy toward the wall. There was more than enough room for him to sit comfortably on the end, but no. He didn't care who he inconvenienced.

Neither of us answered.

I raised my hand to signal the waitress. She was a new face, not anyone I knew.

"Where's Betty?" I asked. "I was hoping to see her today. Been a while since I ordered my favorite grilled cheese from my favorite ball-buster."

"Oh, poor Betty. She passed away last year. Had a heart attack right after Thanksgiving," the waitress replied. I looked at her nametag: Betty. "Oh, it's not her tag. I'm also Betty. But I won't eat myself to an early grave."

She laughed.

We didn't.

"I'll take a cheeseburger, extra onion, no lettuce, no tomato," I replied. I don't know where that came from. I'd never ordered a cheese-burger here before.

Trudy cocked her head, looking at me like an alien suddenly occupied the other half of the booth.

"I'll take a cup of tomato soup and a side of hash browns," she stammered, not looking at the waitress while she ordered. I already knew this was what she'd get.

"I'll take what he's having. Sounds pretty good," Denny said. "And a Coke, but only half ice, and don't fill the coke up all the way, about three-quarters full. Okay?"

The waitress nodded, repeated the order, and scooted away.

I watched her go, rounding the pie case without any pie. She walked just like our old Betty, slightly stilted with a drag of the right foot, moving from her waist instead of her hips. If I didn't know better, I would have assumed I'd hit a time warp and gone back to our Betty's first days at our small-town diner.

"Welcome back to town," Denny said. "You've been a stranger. Too good for us now?"

I took a deep breath. "Of course not. Just busy with school."

"Always chasing that scholarship, huh?" he sniped.

I bit my tongue. I refused to ingest the venom.

"You just finished at the Academy, right? So you're an officer now?" I made an attempt to cycle the conversation back to his favorite topic: himself.

"Good news travels surprisingly fast," he replied, eyeing Trudy. "Correct. Going to keep pushing until I'm running this town. Same dream I had as a child. We're all making our dreams come true now, aren't we?"

"I guess we are."

Three tall glasses hit the table—two milkshakes and one coke, half ice, three-quarters full.

Denny reached into his shirt pocket and produced a silver flask, generously tipping in the contents to fill his glass to the top.

Trudy stayed silent.

"Have you set the date for your wedding?"

"No," Denny answered, preventing Trudy from saying anything. "We're not in any rush. Still young. All the time in the world to sign away our lives."

"Oh, okay. Well, what about locations? Have you thought about where you want to get married?"

Trudy cut in quickly. "I know this sounds silly, but I was thinking at the elementary school. In front of the swings."

"Why in the world would we get married there?" Denny said. "That makes no sense, Trudy."

"Come on, Denny. Don't you remember how it all started?" she asked, her voice soft, pleading for confirmation. "Don't you remember the swing set you gave me for Christmas, back in kindergarten? We may not be here right now if it wasn't for that Secret Santa gift."

My breath hitched, capturing the table's attention.

"Yes, I remember that. Of course I do," Denny said, looking at me.

I wanted to tell him not to worry. I wouldn't say a thing.

"I wish I still had it, but it disappeared in the move. What was it made out of, Denny? You put so much time into that, just to cheer me up."

"You know—just stuff. I think it was pencils and string or something. It's really not important."

"Of course it's important. It's our story," she exclaimed, setting her hand down on his forearm. "Everything matters."

"Straws stuffed with toothpicks," I blurted out. "The poles were straws that I stuffed with toothpicks so they wouldn't bend. The swing's chain was a broken necklace, and I cut the seat from an old shredded bicycle tire I found behind my dad's garage. I painted the grass and flowers on tissue paper and then cut them all out, one by one, before gluing them in place."

"Denny, is that true?" Trudy said. She looked relieved.

I suddenly realized that she'd known all along.

"Is what true?"

"You didn't make that swing set for me—James did?"

Denny took a deep breath before slamming his fists on the table, reminding me of that night after the homecoming dance, the night I decided this was not my town, not my future, and these two were not my entire world.

"Does it matter? I don't think it does. I put that ring on your finger. I sat by your side all of these years. I've fed you. I've put a roof over your head. Does one swing set made of used shit really matter that much to you?"

The silence that lingered was interrupted by Betty returning with our order, sliding porcelain plates over the linoleum tabletop.

Grease pooled underneath the bun of my cheeseburger, and I was oddly satisfied by this slop that would normally turn me off. After leaving for college, I'd found myself wholeheartedly believing my body was a temple; my best stress relief was a good hard run. I wasn't even sure when I'd last tasted beef.

"I put that ring on your finger," he repeated before taking a healthy gulp of his vodka coke.

"And the baby in my belly."

Denny coughed and a small trickle of his half-swallowed drink dribbled from the corner of his mouth. I dropped my burger into a broken mess over the thin fries.

"The what?" he asked. His face was turning a shade past red, into purple territory. "When were you planning to tell me you're knocked up?"

"I've been trying," she said.

"No. No, you haven't. And there is no way that is my child. We are too young. I have too much to do. You know I'm training again and I'm going out as a free agent. You know I'm going to get back in the game and go pro." His furious growl slowly grew to a yell. "I can't believe you'd do this to me. You're a cheap whore! That is not my child, and I'm not taking care of it. Matter of fact, I'm not taking care of you anymore, either. Give me back my ring, and while you're at it, get your stuff out of my house."

"Denny. You can't be serious," she stammered.

"Oh, I'm serious. From the very beginning you have held me back from everything I wanted in my life. You kept me from being the football king who deserved his due. You were late to the game when I hurt my knee. If you'd been on time, I would have been more aware of the game and never would have gotten hurt. I asked you to talk to the dean about letting me stay while I healed and you failed to convince him to hold my scholarship. I asked you to finish my papers, and you didn't. I failed because of you. I am back here in this town because of you. I lost my dreams because of you. And now, when I'm getting closer than ever to getting back on top, you dare to throw this at me. And here? In public?"

"Denny. Please."

"No. No more begging. Get out. Tonight. And you?" he said, glaring at me. "I thought you were my friend. Are you in on this? Is that what this is about? You still want the trashy small-town girl you've been in love with since kindergarten? You're welcome to my sloppy seconds. You two deserve each other. I should never have wasted my time."

Denny stood up from the table and walked out, not looking back. The tires of his oversized truck ground over the gravel, shooting stray rocks across the parking lot as he peeled out of the lot.

I reached over to take Trudy's hand.

"Do you need help packing your things?" I asked, after a long pause, not sure what to say.

"What things, J? What things? I have nothing. I have one pair of shoes, four outfits, and nothing else. I wasn't allowed to work. I wasn't allowed to spend money. I didn't want this baby, either, but when I found out we were having one, I thought he might change. Oh my God. I am so fucking stupid."

The tears started.

I'd never seen Trudy cry. Not when she fell off the swing; not when the rumors started about Denny's appetite for other women; or any of the other times he'd broken her heart. Now she was across from me, large tears flowing into her still-steaming tomato soup.

"I don't want anything from that house. You know what's funny, J?" she asked, looking me straight in the eyes. "I feel free. My heart may be broken—I'm a puzzle without all the pieces—but I feel free, for once."

"Trudy, I only have one semester left in school. Let me graduate, and then I'll take care of you. Move in with me. We can take it slow. Get a two-bedroom. The baby will never know. You can't do this alone. I can do this. I want to do this . . . for you."

She sighed. "I always knew you were the one who made that swing set. Denny never had the heart."

We laughed. She pulled a thin paper napkin from the holder on the edge of the table, dabbed her eyes, blew her nose, and then dropped a large spoonful of hash browns into her tomato soup. With a smile on her face, she eagerly ate the soggy potatoes.

"Just like old times," she said, sliding her left hand across the tabletop to gently hold mine.

"Nothing will ever be like old times again. I'll make sure your future isn't full of pain. I promise you that."

CHAPTER SEVENTEEN

Ava

"This all needs to go," Denny said, throwing a thick roll of industrial trash bags into the master bedroom. It landed with a heavy thud on the floor, settling into the plush carpet with ease.

I sat on their marital bed, a shiver running down my spine. I knew we all had to process these horrible events in our own way, but it felt like it was all so easy for him. He simply turned his face the other way and told his minions to clean up the mess.

Last night I heard him on the phone ordering new tile for the kitchen. My heart broke, foolishly believing the pain of seeing the flowered linoleum once covered with Mom's blood was too much for him to handle. There was already a new chair in the living room, one he spent his evenings sitting in, comatose in front of the television.

I tried not to be too upset at his rudeness this morning. I had agreed to help, to stay here as long as he needed me. He'd have to be a single father until Christopher recuperated and moved on, if he ever could. We still weren't sure what functions he'd recover, if he'd ever resemble the man he used to be. There were some promising movements, like wiggling his toes, blinking, almost saying words we could understand, and asking for food. Small moments we'd always taken for granted that now defined what kind of brother I'd have for the rest of my life.

Only time would tell. And I didn't have time. I had to keep moving forward.

And so did Denny.

I unrolled a heavy black plastic bag and got to work. First: the closet. I opened the doors, unsure of what I'd find. I thought I'd see a good split between his things and hers.

Shock set in when I saw she only had one tiny bar for her belongings, in the upper right-hand corner. Her hangers were precise, each one facing the same way, perfectly spaced. They held a few shirts, two dresses folded over the bottom wooden rod so they didn't graze Denny's haphazardly hung shirts below, and three pairs of jeans. There were two pairs of shoes: one pair of white sneakers and one pair of sensible black heels.

Denny's shirts stuck out the longer I looked at their awkward shape slumped over the cheap plastic hangers. The left side of the closet was impeccably organized, exactly as I would expect his shirts to hang. The rest of the house looked untouched, and he preferred it that way. He didn't want any signs of other people encroaching on his space, and he wasn't shy about this, either. These clothes were perfectly perched on hangers that matched Mom's, making the bottom rack an even bigger anomaly.

I fingered the soft, out-of-place flannel and plaid button-downs. I'd never seen Denny wear any of these, yet they were familiar. The fabric carried the soft scent of the light blue fabric softener I'd loved as a child, another sign these didn't belong. Denny didn't allow for any scents in his laundry, said it was too feminine, weak. I'd never forget the day he came for Mom when she had changed the soap in an effort to liven up a boring chore. The soft red welt on her right cheek made sure this never happened again. She was a prisoner here, unable to have even the most basic of her desires become a reality.

Lost in that thought, and the sorrow over what a sad life my mother had led, I suddenly recognized these shirts. They belonged to James. I shuddered and dropped my hands from the thin fabric. She had kept his shirts in with the same clothes as her husband's, their scent slightly tainting the lower right-hand corner. This was probably why they weren't hung as neatly as the rest of the clothes, and probably why Denny was making me clean out the closet. He couldn't bear to look at the betrayal of his wife and his best friend. Signs of their toxic codependency and inevitable ruin would always surround him. If Mom was with James, she wanted Denny. If she was with Denny, she couldn't let go of James.

All I wanted was to let go of them all. Banish their memories and the corrosive lingering residue from any pieces of my life that weren't already shattered. I wasn't sure how to accomplish this, but I could start right here. The shirts ripped off the hangers with ease, although I didn't care if the hangers came with them or not. As far as I was concerned, this entire house belonged in a trash bag, to be carted out to the curb and sent to rot in the hellacious depths of a landfill—although I was sure even the most desperate maggot would sense the negative energy seething out of the items and would stay away.

I walked through the house with my arms loaded down with textiles, not caring when the scraping of the hangers down the hallway told me

I was leaving marks on the wall. Denny could deal with that on his own time, and if he yelled at me, I'd leave. I'd let him deal with this mess, with his demons, with his drama. He wouldn't say a thing to me and we both knew it; he needed me for the first time in my life. And I'd let him need me, just so he could feel the guilt of being a failed father more deeply than ever.

The back door had been left open so Denny could pop in and out easily. He was busy tearing up the kitchen floor, which struck me as odd since he didn't have the replacement materials yet, and the spot where Mom bled to death would be even more obvious. Bleach was able to remove most of her from the linoleum, but the part that had seeped into the baseboards would forever be a part of this house unless he decided to rip up the entire floor as well. And I didn't want to see that scar.

"What are you doing with those?" he said gruffly, eyeing my hands full of the clothes that belonged to no one living under this roof.

"Burning them. I want to burn it all," I replied, walking outside to drop the clothing on the ground before turning around to go back into the house. I wouldn't give him time to respond or to convince me otherwise. I would burn the house down if given the opportunity.

The rest of Mom's clothes fit into my hands easily. They made no complaints as we made the same journey to the backyard. The clothes were light and seemed eager to meet their fiery death. I know I was eager to see the plain shirts and dresses erupt into bright yellows, oranges, and reds. The flames to come might be the biggest spark ever to hit a part of Mom's life.

"Not those," he said, stumbling over his feet as he tried to stand too quickly. He tumbled back down, the steel toes of his boots catching the debris he'd been piling up.

I smirked as he hit his knees.

I had planned to roll one of the fire barrels over and fill it with Mom's clothing, but in my haste, watching Denny rubbing his knees and finding joy in his objections to burning Mom's pitiful wardrobe, I jumped the gun. I pulled the small container of kerosene out of my back pocket, dousing the pile of discarded items. A quick match strike and the dropping of a small flame sealed their fate. They would be gone in seconds.

He eyed me angrily but made no effort to move toward the flames.

"Those weren't hers to burn."

I rolled my eyes and turned back to the house.

Did he mean I shouldn't have burned those without permission, or that those few pieces of clothing weren't Mom's? If they weren't, why did he already have another woman's clothes in his closet, and where were Mom's?

I returned to the bedroom and hastily pulled open every drawer, dropping the ones to the floor that came out of their tracks too easily. I had to find her. I needed to see what was left, what he wanted gone if there was nothing left. All I could find were traces—a T-shirt here, a bra there, a couple pairs of panties there. Her jewelry box was relatively empty except for a few cheap pairs of earrings and her wedding ring.

I picked the dainty band out of the drawer, running my finger over the floral engraving. This was her ring from James, not Denny.

I fished through the box some more, pulling out the top tray and shaking the humble white box. There wasn't a single rattle. The box was empty. I knew her other ring had to be here somewhere. She wasn't buried with the diamond on her finger. I'd seen her body, thanked the funeral home staff for their hard work on her mangled face, even though the casket would remain closed, and told her good-bye. I had noticed she wasn't wearing her ring and was told it wasn't brought in with her final outfit.

"Must be in evidence still," I whispered, the only logical explanation.

She'd always taken it off whenever she prepared food or washed the dishes, setting it right next to the small fern she kept on the windowsill. No matter how hard she tried, she couldn't keep that damn plant healthy. The edges of the leaves would brown and burn in the sun, she'd overwater it, or knock it over when washing a big pot. I tried to act like I never noticed when a new one was brought in to replace the one she'd devastated. I wished she cared that much about us, about making sure we flourished, or finding ways to repair our broken edges. But we could have withered in front of her and she would have just turned her head the other way, never asking what she could do better the next time around.

I found myself ripping the sheets and blankets off the bed. Denny had said it all had to go, and I was going to make sure that's what happened. Anything they had shared together had to be destroyed. I wanted her memory wiped off the Earth, wiped away from him, and silenced.

As much as I wanted to be upset with James, only a fool would say he had acted alone. His actions were just as much driven by Denny and Mom. They antagonized him, teased him, helped to create the outcome. Deep down, we all knew they got exactly what they wanted. They all knew they couldn't move on until one of them was gone, and the easiest person to remove was Mom. She was always the glue that had held their sick fantasies and need for competition together.

"I'm way too young to have this much resentment," I said to no one in particular.

I bagged up the rest of the sheets and the pillows before ripping off the horrible rust-colored dust ruffle. When it stuck on the corner, I bent down and gave it a tug, pushing my leg against the bottom of the bed for some leverage. The ruffle gave way, bringing with it a V-neck gray T-shirt pocked with blood.

I froze. This wasn't a small amount of blood. This wasn't from a simple accident, but something more intense. Was this what Denny was wearing when he'd found Mom?

I kicked the shirt with my toe, recoiling in disgust. The red stains had heavily soaked through the gray fabric, splattering over the left shoulder.

"No," I whispered in shock, gathering the dust ruffle and shirt quickly to shove them into a bag destined for the makeshift burn pit in the backyard.

I pulled open the drawers of Mom's vanity, tossing out papers, journals, and pens. My hands fell over a stack of sealed cards, their envelopes a mixture of bright pinks, purples, blues, and yellows. They were all addressed to Christopher and me. I knew that writing. The wobble of my legs forced me to roughly fall back, leaning against the tall frame of their king-size bed.

The first envelope's seal popped open quickly and the card slid out, eager to be read after so many years tucked in a drawer. Three wrinkled dollars fell out of my sixteenth birthday card, shaky writing inside telling me how proud he was of me. I turned the card back over. There was no address, no postage. James would have had to drop this off by himself, or else Mom would have met him somewhere.

I looked at the stack of cards, one for every holiday, birthday, or just because. There was no question that some of these had to have come from one of the many times he was in jail, but without any addresses or stamps. That meant he left these before he went in, if he'd had time to plan, or made up for the days he missed as soon as he got out.

He never forgot us.

I quickly shook the memories away, scoffing at how clichéd this moment was. I felt like I was trapped in every sad made-for-TV movie I'd ever seen, discovering a pile of locked-away memories. I should have felt angry that these were kept from me. But I didn't. I felt relieved. Hating him for murdering my mother was easier when I thought he'd abandoned us and didn't care. For all I knew, these cards were as much of a lie as the memory of James being a caring, doting, pure-hearted father, and man.

"Trash," I said, throwing the envelopes into an open bag. I'd burn every letter written by shaky hands driven by alcohol, and every crumpled dollar bill he'd salvaged from begging with outstretched palms. I hoped he'd missed a meal for every dollar he slid into those cards and felt the pangs of anguish as he tried to sleep on a rough sidewalk.

Mom's wedding ring still sat on the edge of her vanity, taunting me with the dainty filigree. I unclasped my simple silver chain that held a wishbone charm and slid the ring onto the thin strand. I never wanted to forget the power, and evil, of love. I never wanted to forget James and what he did. I never wanted to forgive her for the life she put us through and the weakness she had.

I never wanted to forget a thing from this small-town life I hoped to be able to leave behind again soon. The life that right now was dependent on Christopher getting better so I could move on without guilt.

God, I wished he'd been hit just a little bit harder.

"Now what are you doing?" Denny asked, watching as I kicked and tossed the bags of things I'd pulled out of the house toward the slowly dying fire, desperate for more fuel.

"Exactly what you told me to do. Everything has to go," I replied, and opened up the bag loaded with cards. "Did you know these were here? All of this shit and fake apologies, well wishes, and lies?"

He paused, catching my eyes. They held a dark spark that reflected the energy of the fire, like staring into Dante's inferno.

"I thought so," I said. "Well, it's not a big deal. I'm glad you didn't let us know. But she shouldn't have kept them."

"She always held on to things," he replied.

"Even if they weren't part of her burden," I said, shaking the bag out until I was sure every last instance of my name was being turned into ash.

We both knew what I meant with those words.

"I don't know how she did it, keeping herself from moving on and being locked into such an angry life."

"Don't you feel like you do the same?"

I shot him an equally fierce glare, letting him know I was his daughter and had more of him in me than he would ever know. I watched him catch my message and rejoiced in the recognition settling over the deepening lines in his overly tanned forehead. We both went quiet.

Next up was the bag containing the pillows and the duvet. I pulled them out quickly, throwing them into the fire before he could object. He opened his mouth to start but quieted immediately. I had won this round. I watched his lips start to move, looking at the bags with an almost worrying level of curiosity.

"Oh, yes. It's all in there," I said. "Just like you asked."

I pulled out the sheets, wadding them up into a ball and throwing it into the fire to make sure the flames didn't get smothered. I didn't mind when the fine blonde hair on my arms slowly singed and curled into black balls in protest of the heat.

Next came the dust ruffle, balled up onto the other side of the flames. They were now licking higher and higher, picking up heat and burning with anger from the bottom. Years of pain, loneliness, and solitude were released to the sky. I wondered if Denny felt the same, watching years of fake love also go up in flames.

Without fear I pulled out the gray V-neck T-shirt, locking eyes with

Denny. I threw it on top. I wanted to ask him why he'd kept such a sick memento, why he would hold on to pieces of her life that he'd only touched once she was gone. The shirt was the perfect metaphor for their love.

"All of it goes," I said.

He watched the shirt start to burn and looked back at me. He was smirking, the left side of his mouth turned up in pure bliss. I froze when our eyes locked through the waving rays of heat. In the thin billowing smoke he looked like he was rising from the flames himself, a black-hearted phoenix out for destruction, not rebirth. I expected him to crumble from the destruction. Instead, he rose, empowered by a secret I couldn't possibly understand.

CHAPTER EIGHTEEN

Minute Two

"James," the executioner said. "James, I need you to open your eyes. James, can you hear me?" He lightly tapped his fingertips on my cheek like a hungry toddler who'd snuck out of his crib and was trying to pester his parents to wake up.

My body was paralyzed and frustratingly unresponsive. According to their medical reports, hastily scribbled in black ballpoint ink into the file chronicling my death, I had now succumbed to the sodium thiopental. My limbs were numb, my body technically asleep; the next drugs they administered would end my life. Yet somehow at this point, I lingered, somewhere between death and the afterlife. My soul hung in limbo, not sure if it should stay in place and wait to wake up, or if it should fly off to be judged, leaving my mortal body behind.

"I'm still here," I tried to say. My voice didn't sound like my own. The words bounced in my head, slinging off the thick walls of my skull and echoing right back at me. I urged my tongue to move, to make the sounds I wanted them to hear. The heavy muscle sat like a freshly salted slug behind my teeth. My lips were tight and immobile, refusing to part and allow the sound out. But I was here. I was right here.

My eyelids wouldn't budge. I tried. Over the course of my life, I'd opened my eyes millions of times. A simple act requiring no thought, a natural instinct. But no matter how hard I tried, willing them to open, they just wouldn't. They stayed hinged like storm shutters in a hurricane.

All I wanted was one more look. One more glance at the faces of my babies, even though they were contorted with emotion, their eyes glazed and red, swollen from pain and confusion. I just wanted them to see that I loved them so they could leave this room in peace. If the thought of me loving them could bring them peace. Maybe it would only bring more pain and heartache.

I wanted to look Denny in the eyes and feel him look back. I wanted him to know the truth. I wanted to burn him alive with a fury he would carry until his dying day. I wanted Ava to see me as human again. To know I would always be with her and see her as mine. I wanted Christopher to know I believed in him. That he could overcome and regain his life.

There were so many important thoughts rushing toward me in these final seconds that I thought I'd already said, or didn't need to say. But I did. I needed to say it all.

In seconds I was off the frigid table and back on Daytona Beach. I was no longer starting to grow cold from the chill of death; my blood was no longer slowing from the drugs. I was back in a time of warmth. A time when I let myself act my age, have fun, and forget the chains and confines of the hometown I'd never be able to truly escape.

I had never seen the ocean before. When my study group had found out, they insisted I head down with them for spring break. I knew college was supposed to be fun, wild, and full of mischief, but I didn't have parents who were bankrolling me. The slightest extra expense could seriously hinder my future. I knew this. They didn't.

I came up with a million excuses. Each one fell flat. Eventually my roommate Tom caught on and pulled me aside, offering to pay for my trip. I did everything I could to explain that this wasn't the reason I wasn't going. He promised to keep my finances a secret. His parents were loaded, his mother a high-profile corporate lawyer, and his dad, the CEO of a food company. They'd never notice an extra five hundred dollars on his credit card. They never even commented when he'd bought a new Mustang convertible. Money just fell from the sky for them, and life was good.

One day I'd graduate from law school and hopefully life would be good for me, too. But, for now, I knew I would give in and go. There was no other choice, really. Tom and I agreed to tell the others I'd decided to put my research on hold for a week.

"There's no serious James this time," Tom told them. His naturally tanned Italian skin was already shining, and we hadn't even left Pennsylvania yet.

I watched his thick, dark hair rippling in the wind, his perfectly straight and blindingly white teeth shining in the afternoon sun. His slacks were pressed but not creased, the newest style, and the cuffs of his floral shirt were perfectly folded over his biceps.

Subconsciously, I ran my fingers through my lifeless dirty-blond hair.

My tongue felt the slight crooked tilt of my canines. I'd always thought I was pretty good-looking, at least compared to those in my town, but next to Tom I was a Sasquatch.

I promised myself that I'd get my teeth done with my first real paycheck, and only buy clothes that needed to be dry-cleaned. This was the biggest lesson I'd learned in law school so far.

Weeks later we piled into the cars. Five expensive sporty vehicles rolled down the highway to sun, sand, waves, and freedom. In total there were nineteen of us. The morning was full of chatter and thoughts about what the trip would hold. The guys were looking for girls, the girls were looking for guys, and I was hoping to get some peace to sort my thoughts.

What a foolish goal.

Immediately upon entering Daytona Beach I realized I had grossly underestimated spring break. Girls were walking everywhere in tiny bikinis, flaunting their breasts. Thongs were all the rage, and boys ran around like wild dogs, panting and chasing their prey.

"This is crazy," I said, staring out the window. "Is it always like this?"

Tom laughed, slapping his hand against the wood-grain steering wheel.

"This is nothing. Just wait until everyone gets here. Last week's visitors are rolling out. Our week is just getting started."

And he was right. When we woke up the next morning, even finding a spot on the beach was impossible. Radios competed in boxing matches of bass lines, volleyballs flew, beer cans popped, and there was nothing I could do but jump in headfirst.

A beautiful redhead walked by, her hot-pink bikini making her hair seem even more vibrant. She was curvier than the other girls on the beach and didn't hide it with a sarong or shorts. Her roundness was a source of pride, solidified by her highly held head. Her body drove me wild; her hair was like nothing I'd ever seen. I had to meet her.

I stood up to chase her down, unaware of how quickly three beers and a shot of vodka set in under the tropical sun.

"Wait," I slurred.

"Not that one, James," Nick called. Another high-class kid with too much money, a gene-pool lottery win, and the ability to rake in a beauty queen with a single wink. "She's not for us."

"She's for me," I replied, stumbling over my feet.

Nick laughed and slapped the sand next to him. He cracked open another beer and I heard him say, "That's why he doesn't get tail on campus. We don't have any dogs like that around. Who knew the guy didn't have taste?"

A chorus of laughter rang out. Tom said something about beer goggles and they all laughed harder. Someone else said I just needed to get laid, and an easy target like the redhead was the best option to get my confidence up for my first spring break.

I didn't care what they thought. I just wanted to get to know this siren.

I followed her red hair, calling after her as loudly as I could over the busy beach. My words never met her ears, however, and before long I couldn't see her anywhere. The beach seemed to grow and pulse around me. I'd officially lost my fiery femme fatale to the largest party I'd ever seen.

After spinning in circles, desperately pushing people out of my way, I gave up. She was gone. After spinning some more, I realized I had no idea what direction to take to return to my group. With no sign of a familiar face, I threw my hands up in frustration.

"Motherfucker!" I screamed.

Spring break sucked.

"Chill, bro. It's the best week of your life. Here, drink this," an overly tanned and sculpted guy said. His body was adorned with every shade of neon, from his ridiculous folded straight-brim hat to his sunglasses to his thin crinkly swimsuit. He held out a beer, chips of ice dripping off the outside of the chilled can.

It looked delicious.

"Thanks, man. Sorry. I was chasing a chick and she disappeared."

"That's spring break for you," he laughed, holding out his hand. "I'm Alabama Steve. This is North Carolina Suzie, and that's Jersey George."

"I'm Pennsylvania James," I replied, feeling absolutely ridiculous. "And I am so fucking lost."

"You're never lost during spring break. Take a seat and hang with us. You'll find your way eventually."

I looked at the group of random people who had stumbled upon each other. If fate did exist, maybe this was it, and something great would come from today and this chance meeting.

I tilted my head back, downing the cold amber liquid before crushing the can. Alabama Steve threw me another can with a laugh and I plopped down on the blanket.

There's no way of knowing how much I drank that day. All I remember is I never went without. The beer flowed more heavily than the waves. Each pop of an aluminum top made my eyelids heavier and my body slower. Eventually I lay down on the blanket, telling myself to keep my eyes open but unable to make them obey. I could hear laughter around me, feel some pokes, and maybe a few words, but no matter how hard I tried, my eyelids wouldn't stay open.

When I finally came to the next morning, the sun was already beating on my face. A sharp pain was emanating from my back, driven by what I eventually recognized as the thumping from someone's foot against my bare skin.

"Wake up, asshole," a voice called. The foot hitting my back was getting more forceful with each push. "Come on. You had us all worried."

"Not all of us," another voice said.

I instantly recognized it as Tom.

The words I was trying to say didn't come out. Instead a mumbled string of incoherent sounds slipped out as one of my eyes finally popped open. I groaned from the shock of the blinding sun. My head throbbed, my throat was dry, and my skin was burning.

"What time is it?" I managed to grumble.

"Eleven a.m.," he replied. "Get your naked ass up. Looks like you lost your clothes."

"Which would explain how someone got our room key and tried to get in last night, before I punched them in the face."

The gruff baritone voice belonged to Al. He was as wide as a barn door and as tall as the corn before harvest. Intimidating on the outside, he was a massive teddy bear on the inside, and everyone loved him.

"I can't move. Carry me," I said, hoping he'd just pick me up.

"Nah. Your clothes are gone. It's bad enough we have to look at your sunburnt junk. I'm not touching it," he replied.

Laughter erupted, and I realized the whole gang was around me. I heard the click of a camera before I realized what he'd said.

My hands flew down to my sides and he was right. I was definitely missing my shorts. Mustering all of my strength, I managed to open both of my eyes and roll over to shield my body.

"You have a cute ass."

"Thanks, Cathy. I appreciate that. Any comments about the rest of me?"

"No. I've seen better," she laughed.

I couldn't say anything else. Physically, my body just wasn't working.

Everything hurt. Every ounce of my strength went to pushing myself to my knees, which pushed whatever was left inside of my stomach to the surface. I lurched, vomiting a ridiculous amount of liquid all over the sand.

Tom laughed and patted me on the back. "This is going to be the most memorable spring break ever," he said, patting my back as I vomited again. "Get it all out, buddy. Then we'll get you back to the room. There's a raging party tonight at the Cue Bar and we need you to be in top shape. Who knows? Maybe the mysterious red-haired vixen will be there to lure you on another adventure."

No matter how hard I tried to rest that afternoon, sleeping off the night before was impossible. The group went to the party without me, laughing and talking about the legend I was unknowingly about to become.

I spent the rest of the week in bed with sun poisoning, a swollen face, ice on my crotch, and my brain loaded down by shame. I was not able to add any morechapters to my story as the fool of Daytona Beach. Still, my first and only visit to the ocean was hands down one of the best weeks of my life.

"The patient is unresponsive," the executioner called out, making a note on a clipboard.

We were two minutes and forty-three seconds into my execution, and so far, right on track.

"Prepare the second injection."

CHAPTER NINETEEN

Marriage

Elvis walked toward us, tight white jumpsuit snug in all the wrong places, Swarovski crystals sparkling. A disco ball hung from the ceiling, maniacally reflecting the colored lights coming from the wall sconces.

"Is this a wedding chapel or a nightclub?" Trudy asked.

"I think it's a bit of both. Does it bother you? We could ask for a refund and go find Cupid or a casino mobster to do the deed."

"No refunds once the contract is signed and the bill is paid," Elvis replied in his trademark drawl, with a swish of his hips. "Y'all ready to do this? Let's go."

Trudy looked stunning. Over the past three years her hair had softened, and life had returned to her eyes. Her sallow skin was glowing again, and the shakes that had plagued her hands had subsided. Standing next to me was an angel in an off-white silk dress that lightly hugged her body, proudly showing every change that comes from becoming a mother. I loved the way her arms had filled out, the slight thickness under her neck, and the poochy remnants of where she had carried the little girl standing to her left who the courts now allowed me to call my daughter as of yesterday.

Ava was like any two-and-a-half-year-old. She couldn't care less about what we were doing. Her focus was on the balloons bouncing from the thin silver threads tied to her wrist, the way the light played around the room, and the way her dress bounced when she spun in circles. Her laughter made our ceremony take longer than it should have, but every time the balloons bobbed or her dress flew up around her like a flying saucer, her sweet giggles made us all stop in our tracks and laugh with her.

"All right, you two hound dogs, let's close this up. Do you take this woman to be your lawfully wedded wife?"

"I do," I replied. I couldn't stop my smile from erupting.

"I do, I do, I do. I do, too!" Ava chanted, spinning and dancing as "Can't Help Falling in Love" started to play in the background.

"And you, fine lady. Do you take this man to be your lawfully wedded husband?"

"Absolutely. With every inch of my heart and soul."

"All right, you may kiss the bride," Elvis said, gyrating his hips and giving us the trademark Elvis, Uh-huh with a pull of his lips.

We tried to kiss. Every time we got close we would start laughing. Ava would yell for us to kiss again, and the crowd of couples waiting to get married would cheer, and we'd burst into giggles all over again. We managed a toothy peck followed by a long laughter-filled hug between the three of us.

I had waited my entire life for this moment—to embrace Trudy as my wife, to have a family with her, to celebrate our love, and begin our forever, as one. When her hand slipped into mine and we started our walk back down the aisle as husband and wife, I was that little boy on the playground again, lying down in the mulch next to the world's best swinger, feeling my destiny breathing next to me.

"I love you, J," she whispered.

"I've waited my whole life to hear you say those three words. Still feels like I'm hearing them for the first time."

I pulled her hand and spun her in a circle. She landed perfectly against my chest and we were finally able to share our first real kiss as a married couple.

"That right there is a crazy little thing I call love," Elvis sang out from behind us. "Uh-huh. So much love. Good luck to that married couple right there. Next! Step right up and let's get hitched."

Hand in hand the three of us walked out the front door, captivated by the neon ocean known as Las Vegas.

"Well, what should we do now, wifey?" I asked.

"You know what? I could really go for a strawberry milkshake and some tomato soup. Think there's a diner around here?"

"I'd move Heaven and Hell to find you one, if that's what you want."

"How does that sound, Ava? Strawberry shakes?"

"Berry, berry, berry! Shake, shake, shake!"

"I take it that's an affirmative. My little dancing queen. Man, she's so precious," I replied, my heart full.

Trudy leaned in to kiss me again. Every kiss with Trudy showed me what my first, second, and third kiss had been missing. This woman ignited a spark in my soul that made me want to be a better man, a better lover, and a better friend. I wanted every ounce of me to be better so I could be sure I deserved her.

I knew without a doubt that I would die for her.

Our first year or so of marriage was perfect. We bought a house and made sure there was enough room for a piano, even if this meant giving up the formal dining room. We did have a large backyard for Ava to play, which of course meant we had to get a dog.

One Saturday morning we decided there was no better day to expand our family. We piled into our Jeep and headed for the pound. We agreed to adopt a dog someone had given up, a dog that didn't come from a puppy farm, one that would give us love and not merely serve as a status symbol. The most important deciding factor would be how the dog reacted to Ava.

Before we entered the shelter, we had a long talk and agreed that the dog could be the cutest four-legged fur baby in the world, but one snarl, snip, or raised hair on its back and we would move on to the next kennel. We also had an unspoken agreement that we'd not choose a dog that could easily be mistaken for a pony at the off-leash park.

Ava squealed when the kennel attendant opened the heavy metal door to the dog room. Paws hit cage doors, the frantic barks tripled in volume, and our daughter went from running like a toddler to being Flash Gordon's daughter in a matter of seconds.

"Ava! Come back," I yelled, jogging to catch up with her. "Ava, honey. Look at the dogs. Don't you want to look at the dogs?" I was winded; catching an excited four-year-old is not the world's easiest task.

"This one, Daddy! I want this one!"

Those words were music to my ears. For one thing, this meant she'd stopped. For another, maybe this whole endeavor would be easier than we'd anticipated. Trudy and I had both been worried that Ava would want too many dogs. Like her mother, she had an enormously kind soul and a very large heart for animals.

I turned the corner to see Ava squatting in front of a kennel near the back corner. As I approached, I saw a ragged and scruffy black pile of fur in the back of the concrete room. The dog didn't move, wasn't excited, and if the eyes hadn't shifted to the side, I'd have been worried it was dead.

"Why don't we go see another doggie, Ava? This one doesn't seem very friendly."

"No. This one. I want this one."

I turned around to look for the kennel attendant, who rolled her eyes in a huff and walked over.

"You don't want this one. She's been here a little over a year. Won't play. Won't let us give her a bath. Snips when you put food down."

I nodded my head in agreement, placing my hand on Ava's shoulder. We didn't need a meltdown, and I didn't want to be the villain of the day, either.

"Sweetheart, the nice lady who works here says this doggie isn't very nice. Let's find another one. We want a dog to play with, and maybe one that can sleep in bed with you to keep you warm at night."

"This one will. She doesn't like the people here because they don't love her. They want to give her away. Makes her sad. She wants a home."

Ava paused and put her hand against the fence. I wanted to pull her away, to save her precious little fingers, but Trudy laid her hand against my arm and silently told me to remain still.

"I want to give you a home," Ava said to the dog. "You will be my friend forever."

The matted black ball of fur stood up and slowly moved toward the cage door. She kept her head down. When I looked at the dog I could tell her spirit had been absolutely shattered.

"You said she's been here for over a year?"

The dog sniffed Ava's hand, giving it a single lick, and then laid down with her nose peeking out under the gate. Ava sat down, ran her finger over the dog's nose, and then up the bridge of her snout as far as she could go.

Two deep brown eyes that matched Trudy's peered up at me.

"You've been here that long, huh? You want a home?" I said.

The matted tail gave a little wag before falling still again.

"Can we open the door and see what she does?" I asked.

The attendant took a step forward with a simple looped leash in hand, ready to control the dog in case she ended up being a vicious attack dog. Once the silver gate was open, the small black ball of fur rushed out before the leash could be placed over her head.

We jumped, afraid she'd make a run for the door, and then we wouldn't be able to leave until the potential monster had been found and corralled.

This dog had no intention of going anywhere except home with us. Instead of running away, she ran right into Ava's lap where she curled up into a ball between her legs.

"Well, Ava. What should we name her?" Trudy asked.

"Waffles." Her confidence in this name was not surprising in the least.

I bent down and offered the mongrel my hand to sniff. She looked at me with uncertainty, and I knew we'd have some work to do, to gain her trust. It looked like Ava had already done so, which was a good start.

"Do you like the name Waffles?" I asked the dog.

A quick lick and a single tail flop confirmed that Waffles was a name we could all agree on.

"All right. You can come home with us forever, but you're going to have to let us give you a bath as soon as we get there."

The alarm jarred me from a very peaceful night's sleep. Truthfully, I hadn't slept well for weeks. There was some tension between Trudy and me, something unspoken that made her turn away when I tried to hug her, give me her cheek when I tried to kiss her on the lips, and sleep facing away from each other. I had asked her multiple times to talk to me, to tell me what was wrong, but she insisted it was nothing.

I knew better. I knew her better than I knew myself.

She still lay next to me, wrapped up in her blankets like a burrito, breathing deeply in uninterrupted slumber. I was thankful my alarm hadn't woken her. She deserved to rest, even if it was only for one night.

I slipped into the bathroom quietly, taking extra care not to step on the floorboards that creaked.

When I closed the door to turn on the shower, that's when I saw the answer. Right there on top of the trash can was a pregnancy test.

I picked it up and gasped.

Positive.

Trudy was pregnant? Why was this upsetting her? This should have been some of the greatest news of our life together.

I bolted through the door and jumped on the bed, pregnancy test in hand.

"Trudy," I said, gently shaking her tightly wrapped body. "Trudy, sweetheart. Wake up."

"Mmm. What time is it?"

"A little after five-thirty." I laughed, unable to contain my excitement.

I bent down, moved the flaxen strands of her hair away from her forehead, and kissed her subtle wrinkles.

"Why didn't you tell me?"

"Tell you what, J?" she asked, wiping the sleep from her eyes. "What are you on about? It's too early." She pulled the blanket tightly to her chin. Then suddenly her eyes popped open and she held her breath. She slowly moved her eyes to meet mine and I saw tears begin to well up, threatening to spill over.

"Trudy. Why are you crying? Is this true?" I asked, waving the pregnancy test in the air. "We're going to have a baby?"

She shook her head and the first tear dropped.

"Is this why you've been pushing me away?"

She shook her head again.

"Sweetheart, this is great news! Why wouldn't you tell me?"

She pulled the blanket down and sat up. Her hair stayed in the same shape, her eyes were swollen from not getting enough sleep, and she had bad breath.

I loved her dearly.

"Are you going to leave me?" she whispered, pulling her eyes away from mine.

"Leave you? Oh, God, Trudy. No. I wouldn't leave you over something so beautiful. I wouldn't leave you for any reason."

I pulled her close to my chest, stroking her hair. She sobbed heavily against my thin T-shirt, and suddenly the stress of the past week made sense.

"I'm not him, Trudy. I love you. I always have. I always will. We're in this together, okay? I'm so happy."

She cried harder then, and I could feel my shirt dampen with her tears.

"Okay," she choked out, slipping one arm around my waist to pull me closer.

A light scratching followed by a whimper came from the other side of the bedroom door.

"She knows," Trudy said. "That damn dog always knows."

We both laughed. It was true. Waffles was extremely tuned in to our family, our emotions, and our needs.

I kissed Trudy on the head again before opening the door. We both knew the whining would only get louder until Waffles was allowed to investigate the scene.

She bounded through the door, completely ignoring me as she jumped on the bed and sniffed Trudy. Her snout stopped on Trudy's belly. She gave it a lick and settled down next to her, laying her head lightly over Trudy's left thigh.

"She's been doing that a lot lately. She knows."

"She does. And now, so do I. Should we tell Ava?" I asked.

A soft voice answered from behind me in a yawn. "Tell me about the baby?"

I looked at Ava, standing in the doorway.

"You know?"

"Of course. Look at Momma. She's shiny like the sun, and I can hear the heartbeat."

Ava climbed on the bed next to Trudy and Waffles, snuggling into place.

I wished we had film for the camera. I wanted to remember this moment for the rest of my life.

I walked over to the phone and dialed my office.

"What are you doing?" Trudy asked.

"What's important to do today," I replied. "Hello, Barb. I know you aren't in right now, and hopefully you'll check the messages right away. I won't be in today. Please cancel all of my meetings and move them to next week. Any questions, write them down. I prefer to not be interrupted today. Thank you!"

I hung up the phone and crawled back into bed, wrapping myself up in my girls.

CHAPTER TWENTY

Ava

I saw him. He saw me. I expected to feel fury, anger, and uncontrollable rage when I saw his face, but I didn't. I felt pity. He could have had it all. No one made him leave law school. No one made him step up and marry Mom when Denny left. No one made him adopt me. No one pushed him off the cliff of stability. He made those choices himself. He could have left this town but he was too weak. With all the opportunity in the world, he gave up on hard work and decided he couldn't move on in his life without Mom by his side.

I get it. She's a hard woman to leave. When she finds out you love her, she wraps you deeply in her warm tendrils of care. What she doesn't tell you is that at the same time, she quietly injects poison into your veins that leaves you addicted. Your brain slowly rots away, obsessed with the idea of saving her, until the life you once knew is gone and there's no one left to save. Not even yourself. We've all been there. And honestly, I'm shocked it took this long for one of us to crack and kill her.

In all honesty, I always knew she'd end up this way. Leaving the Earth in an overly dramatic and noticeably painful fashion. It's what she wanted. It's what she pushed for every time she overlooked the trickles of blood that cracked out of her lips She was a weak woman. The way she played games and bounced between James and Denny to serve some selfish need was arrogant and foolish. So many nights she'd cry about how no one cared about her dreams or wishes, but she never cared about any of ours, either. Her favorite game was making someone else pay for her suffering—the suffering she created and designed. She was only happy when someone else suckled from her teat of distress.

Leaving for college was the best decision I ever made. And, likewise, the hardest. I worried about what would happen when I left. Mom was unpredictable at best. One day up, one day down. And when she went down, she went to the lowest depths of the Earth, all the way to the magnetized iron core. The housework would pile up, meals would be missed, showers would be a rarity, and we'd all be blamed for her down-fall. Something we did had triggered her, made her feel unappreciated, worthless, useless.

I already knew she would see my leaving as a slap in the face. Comments would slip out, like I wasn't going to college to better myself. I was going away because I was too good for her and what she was able to give me. As much as I said I didn't care, when those words were finally said and they hit my heart, I carried them with me daily as scar tissue.

I had worried Christopher would never get smart enough to leave. He was slipping. College wouldn't be an option soon. If he didn't change, there wouldn't be any opportunity for him at all in this small town. They were already few and far between, as were the number of people who thought he was a decent human being.

I was always worried Denny would snap. His tolerance of Mom's episodes was decreasing every time she fell down into the darkness. The aggression in his e-mails was palpable, and I knew that meant he was also taking all of those feelings out on Mom, only deepening the cycle.

I worried James would finally lose what little grasp he had left on a life outside of her. And he did.

When the phone call came telling me she was murdered, I didn't find the news to be shocking. But to hear that what you've feared for so long has finally happened—it still hits hard. To know she was gone, and taken in such a brutal and heartless way, would always be more difficult than if it had been an accident. If Denny had been drunk and driven them off a cliff, I think it would have been easier. That's something I would have expected.

Truthfully, I'd always thought that if she died, one of those fools would go with her. And I'd never thought James would be the one who would snap. If James had been the one to take her out, I would have assumed it was an accident, part of a much longer, deeper story.

But like anything in else in life, you can't always plan for reality.

Here I sat, in the gallery outside the execution chamber, watching the man I considered to be my father die while my biological father snuck in last minute.

There was always such a stark contrast between the two, even on their last day together. One was bathed in white and lit up like a Christmas pageant; the other, cloaked in a cheap suit, sitting in the shadows.

Denny didn't hide the smirk on his face. There was an odd energy emanating from his twisted lips. His eyes were cavernous, deep pits, his pupils black, the whites, almost gray. He looked possessed.

I eyed him suspiciously. I couldn't question why he was here, especially after spending the last two hours wondering why he wasn't. I assumed watching James get strapped in and prepped would have been too emotional for him. After all, their life together went back to childhood, even if at times they felt like the most toxic friends in the world.

Denny had been oddly stoic during the court proceedings, stone-faced and contemplative.

At first, I'd wanted to know what he was thinking, or if he needed help. But then, the day Christopher took the stand, sealing James's fate, I'd seen an odd, slight smile creep up the right side of Denny's face. I found myself terrified over what exactly he had been contemplating during the previous weeks.

Denny did not like to show any emotion other than dominance and anger. He said emotions were for the weak, and showed how soft one was. Unlike most people, he said, he always showed the real Denny. For that reason alone I'd stopped questioning why he hadn't been present earlier in the gallery.

But now, looking at his face, I couldn't help but be taken back to the courtroom, when I'd thought he was about to run up to Christopher and give him a big hug, or a high five, after his testimony. He had looked happy, in an energetic—not just relieved—kind of way.

There was some sort of weird, fucked-up love between Denny and Mom. Seeing the person who'd murdered the love of your life being forced to pay for his crimes would surely make anyone drop their guard for a moment and let their true thoughts come through. But there was something menacing behind his grin that made my stomach turn.

Now here in the gallery, our eyes locked and a chill ran down my spine. A thousand bolts of unspoken energy driven by distrust shot between us. Every hair on my body stood on end. I couldn't explain the danger I felt, but I instinctively wanted nothing more than to move a few seats away, to get out of his field of vision, to be out of arm's reach. I could tell he loved watching me squirm.

With a fluidity and speed I'd never witnessed, he scooted behind me, crouching like a tiger. His movement was smooth, quiet, and invasive. His spindly fingers snaked over my shoulders. His breath came over my neck like a hot Saharan wind, scorching my skin.

"Did James say any last words?" he whispered.

The question was a little too eager, a little too joyful.

"Did he finally admit to his crimes?"

My shoulders tensed and I tried to lean forward, to break away from his grasp, but he held tight. His nails dug into my skin through the thin layers of my cardigan. I tried my best not to wince, but he knew I was squirming and only clutched me tighter.

"I think so."

"You think so? Either he did or he didn't. It's a pretty simple question."

My stomach lurched. I coughed and stammered out my response. "He said, 'I won.' I don't know what that means, but it sounds like an admission. Right?"

Denny gasped. I felt his hands squeeze tighter and I yelped, positive my collarbone was about to shatter under the immense pressure.

"Denny," I squealed. "Stop. You're hurting me."

His grip continued to tighten, his left index finger pressing on the throbbing vein in my neck.

"Please. I can't breathe."

I heard the screeching of metal on tile as someone nearby jumped to their feet.

Denny released his hands from my neck with a flurry of apologies as the room faded from black to a soft burnt orange and back again.

Someone asked if I was okay, but I wasn't sure. I wasn't sure about anything.

In the background I could hear Denny say that this was just too much for him to handle. I heard him start to cry, the same retching sobs I'd heard him use against my mother when he had faked emotion to make her feel guilty.

I'd always hated that fake crying. Whether she couldn't recognize that it was fake, or she simply chose to ignore it because she was blinded by her feelings for him, I never knew.

"Damn it!" he yelled, walking up toward the glass.

I watched him lift both hands to the gallery window and then furiously drop his balled-up fists against the thin divider.

"What the fuck?" I finally said, rubbing the pulsing vein in my neck.

I turned to look at the faces of those around me: known, not known, familiar, strangers. Everyone was just as confused as I was.

We all knew something big was coming.

CHAPTER TWENTY-ONE

Minute Three

The next drug entered my veins: Pavulon. This one had a single purpose: to paralyze my diaphragm and lungs. I wasn't sure if I would feel the suffocation because I didn't know exactly what I was anymore. Was I a part of my body, or had I broken free of that physical bond, and I just didn't know how to move on yet?

I felt the liquid, cold, heavy, like a trail of army ants, marching inside of my arm. I might have as little as one minute before my body was forced to stop breathing, maybe up to three if I was lucky. Or was that lucky? Perhaps the better option would be for me to just get it over with and suffocate quickly. Then I would get some answers as to who, or what, I was now.

Thinking about the intense fear and pain of not being able to breathe brought back the summer of 1998.

Denny had convinced me to try out for the football team. And with some prodding from Trudy, I'd decided to give it an honest effort. I started running, attending weight-lifting sessions, and even though it was a struggle, the way my body began to feel—strong and purposeful—filled me with pride. I started to understand how Denny got so quickly sucked in to what we had once jokingly called a cult. The slope was slippery, and I was about to go down headfirst.

I changed my diet, becoming more concerned with protein and vitamins than flavor. My nightstand was covered with magazines dedicated to the latest health news, promises for ways to be quicker, to build muscle at a rapid pace, and to increase stamina. Arnold Schwarzenegger became my idol. Nights were spent posing in front of the mirror to see if a new muscle had popped out here, there, or anywhere. They never did, at least not at Schwarzenegger's level. But if a teenager from Austria could come to my country and make it as an icon in Hollywood, there was nothing stopping me from reaching my potential. The only obstacle to my progress was myself.

With two months to go until tryouts, Denny and I were back to being thick as thieves. Life felt right again. After school, we'd go for a run or head to the park to show off our improving physiques by doing chin-ups on the playground. Once a week we'd go to the vitamin shop and chat with the professionals about supplements, trying to find the best new secret before a magazine touted it and the prices quadrupled. If we were at the forefront of nutrition, knowing what worked before anyone else, able to show off our bodies to verify our claims, we would be on the path toward being the next Schwarzenegger or Stallone. They got where they were by their envy-inducing bodies, not their talent. Everyone who sat through one of their movies knew this.

Trudy was on the outside for once, looking in with frustration. She couldn't stand the chest bumps, the obsession over everything going into our bodies. I started to think Denny was right: Women weren't meant to understand a man's dedication to his body and his work. Women were there to support us, lift us up, and keep us on track.

Trudy was slipping, and we let her know. She'd be late to pick us up from training. She'd eat pizza and fried chicken when we were slamming spinach and vegetables. Our magazines would be pulled from our hands and thrown to the far end of the lunch table, or into the trash, or tossed out of car windows. I let Denny make the first comments; he was vicious in ways I'd never be brave enough to attempt.

Burned into my mind was Trudy's face the first time I told her to leave us alone and find her own place. She was twenty minutes late to pick us up, and this really upset me because technically, the car was mine. And because she was late, we would miss the city library again. Peter Tracker's latest exercise set had just been released, the library wouldn't allow reservations, and if we weren't there when the boxes were unpacked and put out, we could be waiting weeks. Weeks. Maybe even months.

Denny and I got in the car, where he forcefully pushed me into the backseat. Because it was cramped and compact, I had no choice but to slide to the center, my head at an awkward angle against the roof. I also had no choice but to watch their typical front-seat shenanigans, the hormonal hijinks I wished involved me instead of him.

His hand went to her thigh and I watched as his fingers slipped under the hem of her skirt. A spark appeared in her eyes, a mischievous grin on her lips, and my stomach tumbled. He was busy yelling at her, demeaning her, telling her how absolutely worthless she was for not being able to follow even the simplest of instructions, yet with one graze of his fingers she opened up to give him everything.

Disgusting.

When Trudy was the girl who stole my heart, she didn't give in to anything. As she got older, it's like everything her brother did was forgotten. Every promise she had made to preserve what little dignity she had left was gone. She gave in to Denny if he batted an eye.

Truthfully, Denny knew about the hushed rumors we'd promised to never speak about. He knew what came out about her brother. He knew how eager she was for freedom, yet he was determined to take it away.

"Get your shit together, Trudy," I said, revealing my thoughts a little too forcefully.

"Excuse me?" she said, slamming on the brakes.

"This is my car. Be careful how you're driving. If you're going to treat it like shit, you can't drive it anymore. Better yet, why don't you just get out right now? Out. Now," I commanded, pushing on the back of her seat.

I don't know what came over me, but an intense, seething anger suddenly boiled forth, and I slammed her seat again. I watched in silent horror as her body slammed into the steering wheel. "I said out—or did you not understand me?"

She gasped. Her hand shook as she pushed open the door. When I popped out of the small backseat and looked her in the eyes, I watched her become submissive. I felt the power Denny felt. I understood him. And I liked him even less now that I knew this feeling was what he craved.

"In the back," I barked. "We haven't got all day. What a shit afternoon."

I don't know why it kept coming, but it did. I couldn't stop the words; they just flew out of my mouth. My mind was possessed, my tongue bewitched.

Denny stayed silent, smirking his crooked smile and delivering a strong slap on my back when I slid behind the wheel of my car.

"I didn't know you had it in you, champ," he said with a deep laugh. "You'll fit in with the team just fine."

That's what I was afraid of.

When tryouts took place six weeks later, I was at an all-time high physically, but an all-time low mentally. I was a monster. I was obsessive. Compulsive. Mentally lazy but loving the attention. Girls noticed me, teachers started taking it easier on me, and rumors flew that I would be the next big thing.

Me. Someone special. Someone seen. Someone celebrated.

The more people talked, the more Denny pushed me. He pushed me to lift harder, throwing on weight limits I shouldn't have been touching. He yelled at me to run faster, until my body collapsed. Every record I broke, the more furious he became. The more he said I needed to live. To party. To drive until my car didn't want to drive anymore. And every time he pushed, I was too afraid to say no. I couldn't help but feel like he was trying to take me out of the picture, either through injury or—dare I even think it—death.

I showed up to tryouts early. Coach knew my name. He didn't make me sign in and I puffed my chest out with pride. In just a few short hours I would be there with Denny. I would be popular. I would be a king. I'd be able to do whatever I wanted.

Just the thought got me high, and I no longer cared about the nagging voice that said this wasn't me. It was. There was no denying it.

We ran three plays that Denny and I had practiced over and over again in the park. He said they were all I needed to know. If I could master these, I'd be on the team.

On the next huddle, he called a play I didn't know, one he hadn't taught me. A book was thrown on the ground to show the play, but I never learned how to read the X's and O's, and the lines just looked like scribbles from a kid who'd gotten hold of Dad's newspaper. I didn't know what I was supposed to do.

I looked at Denny with deep panic and he smiled, that same evil, crooked, "I've got you" type of grin that appeared every time he pulled off a coup.

Within seconds of the whistle being blown his head was in my stomach with the force of a Texas twister. I hit the ground hard, slamming my head. There was no air left in my body, my lungs completely flattened.

Denny jumped up, stomping on my outspread arm as he took off.

My chest burned. I gulped air like a carnival fish in a bowl warming under the hot August sun. There was not enough to fill my lungs, to replace what had been taken.

The sky spun in circles. Pain radiated from the back of my head down my spine and kept me from rolling over, which I was sure would have taken the pressure off my lungs and helped me to refill. No one stopped to help; no one even noticed I was down until Denny called me out as a failure in front of everyone.

"Three-play James," he called me. With one yell, he'd convinced everyone I was a football illiterate who would cost us the championship, all mirrors and no smoke, all show and no game.

I lay there for a good five minutes until I could finally lift myself up. Then the vomiting began, and I felt the warm trickle of blood on my neck from where my helmet had flown off and my bare skull had smacked the ground.

The nurse would send me to the hospital. Three broken ribs, a concussion, twelve stitches in the back of my head. No spot on the team.

For weeks, I convinced myself that Denny was just playing with me in good spirit, that he hadn't said those things to be mean, or cost me my place on the team. The snickers in the hallway followed by his pats on the back with a big smile on his smug face made me think otherwise. Our vitamin shop runs and gym dates slowly dried up. When I went to the school gym by myself, whispers from people I'd thought were my future teammates, and possibly eventual friends, would drive me out as quickly as I entered.

Within weeks I was back to being alone, on the outside, and Trudy was back on the inside. They paraded their cracked facade of a loved-up couple around school, with aggressive displays of public affection pushing the boundaries of what they could get away with in our hallways. Everyone turned a blind eye to the soft bruises occasionally displayed on her porcelain skin, the bruises that slowly turned the same color as the peacock markings Denny had had when he was a child. I no longer envied the marks or found the swirling galaxy of colors to be beautiful.

I would never allow Trudy to drive my car again. Denny would find his own way home from practice. My bedside table would never again be adorned with magazines, and I found that I didn't mind slipping back into my old clothes as my muscles slowly withered back to my usual slender and soft frame.

I often ate my lunch in the library under the guise of studying. This was a place I considered safe, one Denny wouldn't dare enter. Or so I thought. When I wouldn't cave in and be a puppet in his stage show of self-celebration, he started to come looking for me. He'd tear through the library, telling the librarian to fuck off when she asked him to be quiet or leave. I knew the good hiding spots, though. The secret corners that were invisible unless you went all the way down the aisle and found the tiny nook created by two bookshelves not quite meeting. Many times he came close to finding me, but like everything else in his life, if it took too much effort, he'd quit, often when he was right on the edge of completing his task.

In his mind, I was the one who'd betrayed our friendship, left him when times were good out of jealousy, and was now riding the tailwinds of being a sore loser. He'd never admit that he had framed me in order to solidify his own power. By taking his best friend down in front of boys who weren't sure if he was a god or not, he built a pedestal where people would throw themselves at his feet. He couldn't stand the idea that I was able to separate myself and move on. In his mind, I should be indebted to him because now people knew my name, whereas before, I was lower than a nobody, not even recognizable. Now I had a reputation, even if this reputation was as a noticeable failure who couldn't even read a simple football chart.

Now, back in the execution chamber, I felt pain starting to flood my chest. There was an overwhelming need to breathe, a desire to push my lungs until they inflated, to drink in the air. Each push got smaller. Each effort got larger.

I knew my desires were in vain. The air in this cold, stale, heartless room was no longer meant for me.

For the time being, unfortunately, my mind and body were still one.

CHAPTER TWENTY-TWO

The Affair

The heavy front door slammed behind me. I jumped as it smacked against the frame a little louder than I wanted it to, rattling the handle as it settled into place.

My entry needed to be announced. I was furious, and there was no point trying to hide it from anyone. I couldn't believe she'd done this again.

"Trudy!" I yelled, hoping she'd be home.

There was no reply. I sighed and smacked my hand on the counter, wincing when sharp pains shot up my arm.

"Christopher, please go unload the dishwasher and set the table for dinner."

"Am I in trouble, Dad? It's not my fault. I promise."

His face looked worried and my heart hurt. He was too young to be tackling such intense situations, wondering if he should be taking the blame for an adult's actions. I wanted him to still be innocent enough to know that none of this was his fault. A child should never be caught between their parents. At least one of us felt that way.

"I know, buddy. I'm not mad at you, and I'm really sorry you had to wait at school so long. I'm sure Mommy just got her days mixed up. You know she'd never leave you."

"I know," he replied.

His face matched my thoughts. We both knew that Trudy hadn't been herself lately. Forgetting her kids was something she'd started to do. It was starting to feel like par for the course.

I walked up the stairs and down the hallway that was lined with happy family portraits. I traced the frames with my finger.

What was I doing wrong? Was I not loving her right? I was bringing her flowers, cooking dinner, giving her little gifts, sending her on spa days—doing everything I could to let her know I still loved her. Yet day by day, she continued to pull away. She went to bed early. She forgot the kids at school. She ran too many errands for things we didn't need. She seemed scatterbrained, never fully present in our conversations.

Opening the bedroom door, I found it empty. The bed was made, but covered in her clothes. The closet was disheveled, clearly rummaged through. I chuckled, my frustration temporarily slipping away. This was typical Trudy, trying on everything she owned before settling on something she wore frequently. Her makeup was haphazardly strewn over the vanity, and the scent of Opium by YSL hung faintly in the air.

If Trudy had put all of this effort into getting ready, where was she? Why had she forgotten to pick up Chris from his after-school soccer practice?

I looked back to the bed. The clothes didn't make sense. There were jeans, dresses, business wear, and even some of her daintier items. There was a mix of shoes on the floor, some of the plain-colored pumps she called practical, the not-so-practical brightly adorned summer wedges, and a trail of mismatched, beat-up sneakers.

I ran my hands through my hair. Something was very wrong.

I picked up the phone and called her friend Gina. She hadn't heard from Trudy in a week. I called her mother and she assured me that Trudy was probably just shopping off some stress from being a mom to a teenage girl and an overactive ten-year-old boy.

I knew she wasn't at the mall. She'd never touch her nicer dresses or rarely used business suits to go try on new clothes. The rolling pit in my stomach told me her mother didn't believe her lie either.

I made one more call, to the police station.

"Parker Point Police Station. How can I help you?" a female voice answered.

"I need to report a missing person. I think my wife is missing," I replied.

My hands began to shake and the room started spinning.

"How long has she been missing, sir?"

"I don't know," I said. "She didn't pick our son up from school. She never forgets our son," I lied. She'd forgotten both of our children a few times now, but if I wanted the police to find her, I had to make her seem like the perfect mother. "And I can't find her with any of her friends, or her parents. We had breakfast together, and I can still smell her perfume in the bedroom. Maybe a few hours? I don't know. Oh, geez—I don't know."

"Calm down, sir. A person must be missing for twenty-four hours before we can file a report," she replied. "What's your wife's name?"

"Trudy. Trudy Jackson," I replied, frantically.

"Oh, Trudy? She was in here this afternoon, talking to Detective Lloyd."

"She was there? Talking to Denny? Why?" My questions came out a little more aggressively than they should have. I almost apologized, but something told me not to be sorry.

"Well, sir, I'm not sure. She's probably just taking some time away from home. It's hard being a mother, you know?"

Living in a small town was a curse at the best of times and the worst of times. Everyone knew everything. This woman I had seen only in passing and couldn't even name not only knew my wife, but knew she had children. She also knew she was struggling, and that didn't sit right with me.

"Okay . . . I guess. I mean, I don't know. I'll never know how it feels to be a mother, but I try my best to be a father. Anyway, I'll wait. If she comes back to the station for . . . whatever reason, please let her know I'm worried."

"Will do," she said, disconnecting the call.

I sat on the edge of the bed, stunned.

If Trudy was with Denny at the police station, something bad must have happened. She might not have been missing, but she was keeping something from me. The pit in my stomach grew, and I found myself afraid of the possibilities. Had she been hurt? Had someone threatened her? What secrets was she keeping?

The kitchen door clicked open and the hinges squeaked, echoing through the quiet house. I heard Chris call out to his mother, his excitement and love for her covering the loneliness he must have felt when she forgot to pick him up.

I listened carefully. She didn't ask him how he'd gotten home from school. She didn't apologize for forgetting him. Their conversation was normal, as if the day had been completely normal.

I stayed on the edge of the bed, hearing her heels click over the tiles and up the stairs, down the hallway and into our room. Her steps had energy, confidence. They sounded different than the scraping of her pink woolly slippers from this morning.

She gasped. "I didn't know you were up here. You scared me."

"You scared me. You forgot Christopher at school. I came home and the room was an absolute mess. I called everyone and no one knew where you were. What's going on, Trudy? Has someone hurt you? Is that why you were at the police station this afternoon instead of picking up your son?"

"You called the station, too? Geez, J—that's a new low. Are you stalking me?"

Her tone was beyond accusatory, and the implication that I, her husband, could do something like that was stinging.

"Stalking you?" I scoffed. "You forgot to pick up your son! Should I not look for you or be concerned? No one knew where you were. If someone is hurting you, please let me know. I can help you. You don't have to hide anything from me," I whispered. I pulled her hands into mine, wanting to soothe her, to keep her safe. "I can't protect you if I don't know what's going on, my love."

"I don't need to be protected, James. I'm a strong woman."

"I know you are."

She pulled away from me, and I watched as she undressed. The lace panties were new, and paired with the simple gray V-neck T-shirt under her denim jacket, she looked stunning. To this day, she was still my dream.

"You look amazing. Come here," I said, standing up and walking toward her.

I peeled off her shirt, exposing a slinky bralette that matched her panties.

"Is this what you were up to today? Trying to steal my heart again?"

I picked her up and carried her to the bed, ignoring the heavy, woody musk that competed with her perfume.

It was a Friday night.

Friday was always family night. With only a few weekends left before the snow settled in, we decided one more session of mini golf and milkshakes sounded like the perfect way to spend a late-fall night. I loved the times our family spent together, and felt lucky that Ava and Chris were still willing; most kids their age were more interested in hanging out with their friends, and were starting to keep secrets from their parents.

Even though Trudy and I were together, the distance between us was starting to become visible. She actually stepped away from me when I came near. She didn't hold my hand in the car. She turned off our favorite song when it came on the radio or changed the channel when I'd sing along with love songs, serenading her. She didn't snuggle against me on the couch or share popcorn with me, and we hadn't made love in months. I hated to see her drifting away, but everything I tried just seemed to encourage the fissure in our relationship to grow even wider.

The diner was pretty empty, with most of the town at the elementary school for the Fall Festival. We hadn't gone, as we weren't too excited about the warmed-up grocery-store apple cider or the cheap plastic toys they were selling.

Our usual round of milkshakes hit the table. We always had dessert first on family night, just like we three amigos used to do, when our friendship had constituted family.

I couldn't help but feel a little nostalgic every time we came in for milkshakes. I'd see Trudy as a young girl, dipping her cherry into the largest dollop of whipped cream possible, then eating the cream before starting on the shake.

Denny was the opposite. He'd drink the shake in one slurp, get a headache, complain, and then dive in to his whipped cream.

I preferred to mix my cream into the shake and take my time.

"Are y'all ready to order?" the waitress asked. I still called her "new Betty," even though it had been years since she'd taken the original Betty's place.

"We are. The usual, I believe," I said, looking around the table for confirmation.

"No, not for me," Trudy said. "Sometimes change is good. I'd like a patty melt with extra onions, and onion rings, please."

I was shocked. Never in our lives had Trudy ever ordered onions of her own free will, let alone extra. She'd never liked the flavor. She'd also complained about the grease from her favorite hash browns and how the fat would go straight to her hips. Now here she was, dipping into something loaded with butter, cheese, and onions, no less.

Was she pregnant again? Is that why she'd been so off with me lately?

We'd had some challenges during Chris's pregnancy. I'd had to work overtime to convince her I wasn't going to leave. And I haven't. And I won't.

But the thought of going through nine more months of those mental games felt exhausting.

"Well, that's interesting," I said, locking eyes with her.

She opened her mouth to reply, but we were interrupted by an all-too-familiar voice.

"What have we got here?" Denny said, sliding into the booth next to Trudy and pushing Ava against the wall. His hand quickly dropped behind her shoulders. He was way too comfortable embracing my wife, the woman he'd left behind years ago.

We'd always had an unwritten rule that Ava was not to know the truth. When Denny turned to look at her, my stomach dropped. There was something sinister behind his eyes. I kicked his shin under the table and redirected those evil eyes my way.

"Was that necessary, J Boy?"

"You tell me, Denny. This is family night, and we'd like to enjoy our food in peace. What are you doing here?"

My words dripped with venom and were more forceful than I'd intended.

Trudy was visibly shaken, her breath coming in short spurts.

I eyed Denny, the man I no longer knew, the boy who had given up his space at our table. He sat there before me in a black leather jacket, slicked-back hair, and a gray V-neck T-shirt.

"Oh my God," I said. Now it all made sense.

I looked at Trudy, who met my eyes and then turned to look out the window with a deep sigh.

"Dad, what's wrong?" Ava asked, able to feel the tension that clouded our table.

"Nothing, sweetheart," Denny replied, while looking at me with a smile.

I looked at Trudy. Her eyes were dead. Gone. There was nothing behind them that meant anything to me anymore.

"Kids, let's go," I said. I slid out of the booth and looked at Ava expectantly. "I said let's go. Now."

"What about Mom? Why isn't she coming?"

"Mom really likes the diner. It's where all good things come her way," I said, knowing she and Denny would both understand what I was saying.

Ava slid out from underneath the table and I watched Denny's fingers close over Trudy's shoulder. She barely moved. She wasn't warming to his touch, and I wondered if he had forced himself on her, or if she had been willing. How had this started? How had I missed it?

"Now, kids. Mom will be staying with Grandma for a while."

"Or maybe she'll be staying with Uncle Denny, since your dad seems to have some scary anger issues right now," Denny sniped.

"Don't you dare do this in front of my family," I said.

"Part of your family. See you later, sweetheart," he said, looking at a very confused Ava.

"Daddy . . ." she said, turning to me and grabbing my hand.

"Don't listen to him, Ava. Denny isn't your uncle. He isn't a part of our family, and he never will be. Let's go."

The next day I filed for divorce and started packing Trudy's belongings. She never came back to pick anything up.

CHAPTER TWENTY-THREE
Christopher

There's not a single book, pamphlet, or after-school special that could ever prepare you to watch your father die. Of course, nothing could prepare you to find out that your father killed your mother, either.

I would forever carry the guilt of that night on my shoulders. The last thing I said to her was yelled through an open doorway. It was angry, mean—about how noisy she was, cooking dinner. I was always too caught up in everything she did wrong to see what she did right. I never let her know I loved her, and now, I never could.

My nights would forever be haunted by the fuzzy pieces my shattered mind remembered from the day I let her die.

If I could go back in time and do that night over again, I would. I'd go into the kitchen and help her make dinner instead of telling her she was doing it wrong. Instead of lying on the couch, I'd cut vegetables for the salad. I'd offer to put away the dishes. I wouldn't ignore the fact that she was at another low point just because I was tired of seeing her that way. Maybe I'd even try to understand why she chose to help him.

There are pieces I remember. Pieces I don't. Pieces I relearned in the court case.

I wish I had called Denny sooner, maybe even told him the night before that Mom was looking at James a little too long when we drove by his sleeping spot on the way to school. With more advance warning, Denny could have gotten home sooner, or maybe even stopped them while they were out.

If I had told him earlier, maybe she never would have picked James up that day. She'd still be here, I'd still be myself, and even though our lives were twisted, they'd still be ours to continue to mess up.

Who knows? Maybe by now I would have had an awakening and gotten my life together. I guess I'll never know.

What I still couldn't understand about that day was how everyone else in town saw Mom and James together and no one picked up the phone and called Denny. No one else reported seeing them until after she was dead. No one thought it was strange that the scourge of our town was suddenly back in her good graces.

The entire town knew their sordid history—how she'd spent all of his money while he was locked away the first time, the back-and-forth between the two, how James adopted Ava, and of course, the long-standing affair, where Mom just couldn't quit Denny.

They weren't even quiet about their sordid nights together, wining and dining all over town, out in the open, while James toiled away in his office. No one cared about those dates that should have been secret rather than flaunted, because in this town, you do not disrespect the law.

To tell Dad that she was out with Denny would have been backstabbing the town's celebrated show pony.

And years later, when Dad disrespected the law with his fist against Denny's jaw in our front yard, that's all it took to seal his fate. Mom could do no wrong because she was moving up in the world by getting back with Denny, despite the rumors about his temper and the way he maintained order in our house.

And that is exactly why I couldn't understand why no one called Denny to let them know his wife was out with public enemy number one.

Even with my limited memory and my newfound challenges, I could understand that this made no sense. Unless I wasn't the only one to call him that day. But if I wasn't the only one, either Denny didn't care, or he already knew and was watching them. If Denny didn't care, would that mean he'd hoped that James would snap? Or if he was already watching them, tailing them, would that mean he could have stopped James? He would have seen James go inside, and I knew Denny enough to know he would have flipped out, driven mad by thoughts of Mom possibly leaving him again. In his mind, that would have meant he'd lost the game, and that would absolutely not be tolerated.

I shook those thoughts from my head before the throbbing became too intense.

The evidence proved James had committed the murder. The jury had convicted him. The judge had sentenced him to death. Any other thoughts were not important. The right man was lying on the table in front of me, and my mother's death would be atoned for shortly.

Right?

Seeing James spread out on the gurney, his body in the shape of a cross, I found no comfort. I saw no God, no Messiah—no great protector in that room. I saw an odd man I didn't recognize, whose face barely registered understanding of what was happening to him, and whose story I didn't understand.

The court had tried to paint him as a jealous ex, but the fleeting memories I was able to scrape up from photographs, videos, and stories didn't paint him that way at all. I can't remember him ever hurting me, or yelling at me, or lashing out at Mom. Even with my injuries, however, everything I've lost, I can remember Denny doing those things. My therapist said I might be switching Denny with James in an effort to cope with the accident, but no matter how hard I try to believe her, I just can't. Looking at their eyes, both here in this room, I don't believe I would ever confuse them.

The court tried to paint me as someone different, too, though. They said I was lazy, mean, and unappreciative. When I was on the stand, the defense tore me to shreds and made me sound horrible, unreliable—that I was to blame for what happened that day. That I was an accessory. That I'd made the call with malicious intent, to punish my mother and get rid of James, because I held a deep grudge against him. They said that if I could remember making the call, I should be able to remember the face of the person who had struck me. They refused to believe that I could only remember a gray mass, what I think was a sweatshirt, and pale white hands wrapped around an iron poker.

The jury would have a hard time believing I wasn't the person the defense painted me to be. Thanks to my injuries, I would probably always have a permanent scowl on my face, from the partial paralysis. I'd never again know how it feels to really smile, or to laugh; these things were taken from me with one swing of a fireplace poker. And in a courtroom, when you look angry and become frustrated—because struggling to remember the simplest of words sends a trail of drool down your chin—they see the clenching of fists and wringing of hands as signs of aggression, not embarrassment. I could tell they blamed me as much as they blamed James. But still, I took the stand to make sure he got what he deserved. It was worth every embarrassing second.

Looking at him, one half of me, I wondered if I should feel ashamed. If I should worry. Would I have that quiet rage in me? Did I before? Would I always be the unfortunate survivor whose family fell apart in one night?

No. I would never be that boy. My family was never together in the first place. I could tell that from the way people talked, what they didn't say to me, what they hid—or highlighted—in his trial.

The most painful part of this was that I wasn't sure who I was, then or now. I could go off what they told me, or I could try to piece it together, using the little nuggets of information I found around my room. If I could just figure out some of my passwords, I'm sure I'd be able to learn more about the life I once led and who I might have been.

This feeling of strangeness and uncertainty was only heightened as I looked at James sprawled out and secured to the sterile gurney. I was shocked by what I didn't feel when our eyes locked. Fear. Remorse. Anger. I felt none of those things. All I felt was . . .

Nothing.

I tried really hard to go back to that night. Through the clouds in my memory I could remember sounds, but most of all, smells. One in particular haunted me. One I couldn't place. Strong, woodsy, slightly sweet and tender. I've dedicated months to finding this smell, hunting through bottles on perfume counters, smelling every leaflet in magazines, trying to describe what I could remember only to be let down when the scented slip of heavy cardstock didn't match what I was looking for. I was sure this smell held my answers.

I couldn't help but feel like Ava knew more than she was telling me, too. She tried to talk to me, but I could tell her words were fake. There were times I felt she would use my injuries in an attempt to create a family, one we'd never actually had. She'd make snide comments about all the work she was doing for me, or how I was hampering her plans, swiftly followed by the fact that we needed each other more than ever now. She would dodge my questions and roll her eyes when I mentioned a memory that had come back. Sometimes she'd say that wasn't how it happened, or that what I mentioned hadn't actually happened at all.

But I couldn't help but feel that I remembered Denny's hands around my neck while Mom tried to plug a bloody nose with a dishtowel.

I didn't like this awkward relationship budding between us, but I didn't want to tell her too much. She'd left me once before; why should she care now? And what exactly was she hiding? If history was doomed to repeat itself, I had no desire to go through more pain later. My goal was to protect myself, and only myself.

For now, I would sit here and watch my father die. Slowly. The seven most painful minutes of my life—that I could remember.

CHAPTER TWENTY-FOUR

Minute Four

Do you ever think back to the best day of your life and just sit there, wallowing in the memories?

"Best day ever." A phrase we so often throw around, loosely, until we realize one day that there's a very strong chance we've already lived the most wonderful day of our life and nothing great will ever come our way again.

I wondered what my best day was.

Slowly, over the course of this nightmare, the way I define day has changed, along with the way I define best.

I've started to see rubble where I used to see only strong foundations.

Like our wedding day.

I used to remember a sweet, laughing girl, a beautiful bride. But now, as my eyes refuse to open and my limbs are too heavy to move, I remember that Trudy was shaking. I remember the way she stumbled through saying "I do," like it was a challenge, or forced. The way she kept laughing at Ava every time I tried to lean in and kiss my blushing bride after our vows, instead of meeting me halfway, to seal our marriage. And when we finally did have our first kiss as husband and wife, it wasn't the passionate embrace I'd always imagined. Our teeth hit, and where that memory was once cute, now I seemed to remember a grimace on her face.

On our wedding night, after milkshakes, we fell asleep as big spoon and little spoon. We wouldn't consummate our marriage for two weeks. I had always made excuses for this, saying it was because Ava was in our hotel room with us; it was the stress of combining our lives into one.

Even though Trudy had moved in with me years ago, when Ava was on the way, she'd still kept a storage unit full of her own things. Finally, after much begging and pleading, I'd convinced her that we were together—that we'd always be together. She could let those old things from her past go; she didn't need a hidden storage unit filled with things she could use to restart a new life if ours took a wrong turn. Eventually she would move some of those random pieces of flatware, plates, and tacky paintings into our home, and the rest magically disappeared.

There were times when I thought the birth of Christopher was my happiest day. My sweet boy. I cradled him in my arms and marveled at his dark hair, wondering where those thick brown strands came from. Trudy's grandmother was Italian, and this was enough of an explanation.

When I went to kiss Trudy's cheek, to congratulate her and thank her for giving us this beautiful angel, she turned her head. She let me hold her hand for a second before asking me to leave so she could rest. She needed peace, quiet, and darkness. I didn't think twice because I'd seen how hard she'd worked to give us both Ava and Christopher.

But when I walked out of the room and turned off the lights, she clicked on the TV. I heard the volume go up and thought it a really weird way to find peace. She'd never been a fan of Wheel of Fortune before.

Other days I thought Ava's birth was my best day. I had Trudy. She saw I was committed. She trusted me with the bouncing bundle of energy that had spent her final two weeks in the womb salsa-dancing and learning how to kick-box, using Trudy's ribs as the target. Ava came out with a fierce vitality the doctor and nurses claimed they'd never seen before, laughing at how she pumped her fists and kicked her legs. "Our little disco diva," they called her, even though disco was long dead and Ava's generation would never appreciate the simplicity and modesty of a dance like the Hustle.

But as Ava grew up and became more headstrong, more challenging, more outspoken, the frustration over raising a child who only wanted to fight me made those early blissful days fade away. If I'd only known then that Trudy had been taking Ava to meet Denny, starting the affair long before I ever saw the gray T-shirt that broke our hidden problems wide open, I may have been more patient with her.

The cinema of my life slowly rolled past on the backs of my eyelids, each beautiful day passing by at a relaxed pace, exactly as I remembered it, with happiness and pride.

But now, knowing what I know, no longer forcing myself to see only what I wanted to see, they looked all wrong.

Completely wrong. All lies. Nothing but a fable.

There were the days Trudy would be sitting outside on the lounge, drinking lemonade in that white cotton dress I loved so much. She'd be reading a romance novel and talking on the phone. I remember mowing the grass and looking at my queen on her throne, wanting to make the backyard beautiful for her, worthy of my own personal royalty. I waved to let her know I was thinking about her, hoping she noticed the sweat trickling down my brow and over my bare chest as I roasted my skin in the hot summer sun. She would smile her crooked smile as she flipped the pages, lost in the latest saga of a maiden and her pirate lover.

But now I can see the sadness that lingered on her face, her slender fingers turning the pages, dreaming of the lover she desired. The intense longing to fulfill a carnal need.

And when the phone rang and she answered it, she didn't go inside to take the call because the mower was too loud. No. She glanced at me quickly, looking frantic as she slipped inside, pulling the blinds on the back door.

Next came the day I bought her a gently used pearl-white Cadillac for her birthday. I picked out the one in the showroom with the most supple leather seats. I had a cutting-edge CD player installed and gave her a case filled with the music of her favorite singers. Dolly. Aretha. Whitney. Mariah. And even those weird British ones from high school that shouted a little more than they sang over instruments that fought each other.

She told me she loved it. She hugged me, gave me a quick peck on the cheek, and ran her hands over the hood. I always thought she was taking it in, appreciating the beauty of her first nice car. But now I realized I'd seen flickers of guilt behind her eyes. Anguish. Frustration. Questions.

I tried to look away from these scenes, but I had no control. While I was dying, I would just have to lie here and see whatever I was meant to see.

Was I justifying what happened? Was I excusing it? Was I looking for a reason to not love her any longer?

Surely that would be impossible.

In the darkness of my mind I could feel a presence slide in next to me. I knew it was Trudy immediately by her softness, her scent—the way my body reacted to hers.

I didn't know what to say. I felt her soul approach mine and I waited to find out why she was here.

CHAPTER TWENTY-FIVE

The Downward Spiral

I was a fool. I should have known we were too good to be true. Trudy never loved me. She never wanted me. From the moment Denny stepped in and claimed my Secret Santa swing set, she'd thought her heart belonged to him. She had never cut that cord. And like a fool, I'd never cut the cord between us, either.

There have been many nights when I've told myself I shouldn't have asked for a divorce so quickly—especially not in front of Denny. I should have let her get through this phase, to remember Denny didn't love her, and to try to keep our family together. I could have let her suffer, knowing she'd break my heart and tear up her children through a court battle. But I was weak. Too concerned with doing what was right for her and our family. Believing the empty promises to not rip us apart or challenge their place in my life. She was always a liar. He was always a thief.

The only way to cope was to sit myself squarely in the bottom of the bottle I once chastised Denny for lounging in like a second home. Nights where I'd slink into the softening cushions of my couch, staring up at the detail of our popcorn ceiling that was once a gentle white and now slightly resembled dehydrated urine in the corners where water slowly dripped through the roof. I'd have to replace it soon, but repairs didn't really matter when no one came by in the first place.

My kids were so full of anger, blaming me for their mother's decisions to uproot them again. They refused to set foot ever again in the house that had once brought them so much happiness. Instead they stayed in the house that brought them pain and frustration.

Hypocrites. All of them. Holding me prisoner for the mistakes of another. They saw me take care of her, watched as I pampered her daily. Any small wish muttered from her lips was fulfilled. A longing glance at a new pair of shoes would find them in her closet the next day. She never had to ask for a thing. I sacrificed myself for them every second of every day.

The kids felt the same love and nurturing, although I can admit that at their age, I probably came across as overbearing. I wanted to be the present parent—the one they'd never be able to complain wasn't there. School pickups and drop-offs were our regular routine, even though they'd beg to take the bus, which I never understood. Ten minutes in an air-conditioned car versus forty-eight in a stale, smelly, overcrowded tube of metal? What can I say? I'm weak with love. I always thought that love was a never-ending stream of beauty—one that would grow the more you gave away.

But that was a lie.

Life was a lie.

Family was a lie. Promises were lies. Fate was nothing more than the master of deceit.

Deep down I knew Denny loved the growing discord and constant feuding we couldn't hide behind closed doors. Even going to the grocery store would start a nitpicking fight over which brand of macaroni to buy. Me telling her to get what she wanted, her coming back with how I'm not helpful and continuously pushing all the work onto her shoulders. We both knew this was another lie, but those around us didn't.

The competition provided by our failing relationship fed him, whether he wanted to admit it or not. It was only now, immersed in amber liquid and clouded thoughts, that I could see how toxic he was even as a child—how he would do anything to win.

One time he'd pushed Travis Solomon from the top deck of the metal curly slide so he could try to beat the record for the fastest person from bottom to top to bottom. Travis hesitated and Denny's timer— set to measure how long it took him to get up the stairs and down the slide—was ticking. One boy's simple childhood fear led to a concussion, a broken shoulder, and a lifelong fear of heights.

For the other boy, it generated a lifelong love of power.

No one told on Denny. Once they'd seen what he was capable of, they knew he would come for them, too, if they dared to challenge his newfound place as king of the playground. He looked us in the eyes and said it was an accident; Travis was simply bumped during a rush to the front. While the teachers foolishly believed this explanation, we were already scared of what Denny truly was, driven by the dark hold of power in his eyes.

Whether he was taking responsibility for my hard work, stealing the love of my life, seeing how many times he could cheat on Trudy without consequence, how many girls he could get in bed at once, how many touchdowns he could score, how many drunk bar fights he could get out of just because the football team needed him, or how many speeding tickets they'd brush off as just "boys being boys," Denny's biggest high was winning.

Never in my life, though, had I imagined he would go so far as to also try to steal my children.

I started to notice their plan when they'd be a few hours late for pickup or drop-off. He'd always have some snide remark about Ava being his daughter. The main comment he loved to repeat was that they shouldn't even be dropping her off because she wasn't mine by blood, only by an old court paper he promised the judge would gladly overthrow for the town's most cherished keeper of the law.

He knew this got under my skin. He had left her at five weeks in the belly.

I was there through every pre-birth appointment, blood draw, shot, and Lamaze class—for painting the nursery, the delivery, and every single moment from Ava's first breath to the day they came over, announced their engagement, and their decision to file for primary custody of both children.

"Children should be with their mother," she said with a stone-cold glare.

Ava was there in my front room when she heard this announcement, hugging on to the soft fluffy white rabbit I'd given her for her second Easter celebration. Mr. Snuggles, we'd named him, while furiously popping malted chocolate eggs. Mr. Snuggles went everywhere with Ava for years, and my heart crumbled to see her, too old at age seven to find comfort in a stuffed animal, too scared to approach the future without something to put her at ease. Her refuge wasn't her mother, it wasn't me, and thankfully, it wasn't found in Denny. Knowing this was the only positive thing to come out of the burning tinge of failure sinking into my ligaments.

I tried to argue that she'd left the kids with me for fifteen months before she'd decided she wanted them back. We both knew this wasn't her choice. They were merely two more pawns on Denny's chessboard. I could imagine him at night, whispering to her about how great they would be as a family even as he dreaded the outcome if they ever did arrive. He loved having Trudy; he didn't want, or need, the burden of children. He could barely take care of his wife's needs, let alone two kids he'd never even bothered to know.

I argued as fiercely as I could that Denny was an alcoholic, but this only incited the judge, who thought a law school dropout shouldn't be questioning a man of the law. I brought in receipts and spreadsheets used to file taxes and manage our household. They called me petty for tracking our finances and expenses. I suppose part of me had done this subconsciously, foolishly thinking that one day this might come in handy, because deep down I always knew Trudy was not to be trusted.

Their lawyer successfully argued that my obsession over the money spent to raise a child and provide for the basic needs of a wife proved I didn't have the best interests of the family in mind. What father tracks how much their children will cost them? My lawyer argued I was just fiscally responsible, trying to make sure my family got the best, but his raised eyebrows and tightly pursed lips told me this argument was hopeless.

With one swift slam of the gavel and a few words I couldn't process, my family, my dreams, and my future were taken away. I stood in the dark courtroom, surrounded by the echoes of my fate being sealed. People talk about the moment their body goes into shock, but I don't think anything can ever truly prepare you for the sudden and unexpected breakdown of your mind and body.

My knees buckled. My mouth went dry as all of the liquid in my body flooded up to my eyes. My shins met the thinly carpeted floor with a smack that heightened my already loud sobbing.

I woke up in the hospital the next day.

They used this as a sign I was mentally unstable and incapable of managing our children under stress. The judge reduced my visitation to one weekend per month with optional supervision. At first, Denny and Trudy insisted on supervised visits. I knew this was more Denny's idea. Trudy knew I didn't need to be supervised with my children, but the power of telling me when to move, when to speak, and what not to do filled Denny with a sense of satisfaction stronger than any whiskey could provide.

After six months they grew tired of the commitment involved in supervising visits and let me have my time alone. When another year passed, they slowly asked me to take the kids for weekends. Ava was about to graduate high school and she was angry, hard to handle, and aggressive. She pushed her mother to the edge, but pushed Denny even further. No one questioned Ava when she turned up with black eyes or a limp. She was athletic, and it was easier to assume a game of pickup basketball with some college boys had damaged her body than the town's shining star.

We all knew better.

If I dared to question Ava about her injuries or suggest we seek help, she'd yell at me. This was my fault. I'd been a horrible husband to Trudy. I didn't know how to love someone, or she would have stayed. Ava hated me. She said she'd never speak to me again after she graduated. She stuck to that promise, moving away to California to get a fancy degree and make something of herself. I would never talk to her again. I'd only see her again briefly when the drugs started to knock me unconscious as she sat on the other side of the glass, staring at me with hatred for murdering her mother.

After Ava left, Chris started down the same path. He'd answer me with single words, never make eye contact, refuse food, and stay in his room. I'd hear him sneak out the window at night, smell the marijuana that trickled under his door and not out the cracked window on the few nights he'd stay in. One day he questioned if I was really his father or if I'd lied to him like I had to Ava. I wanted to tell him no, I hadn't lied to him. He was mine.

But was he? How long had Trudy and Denny been sleeping together behind my back?

I yelled at him. I said things about his mother I never should have said.

I don't know what he said to Denny, but it was enough. Two days later, Denny showed up at my house. The lights on top of his squad car were blazing, letting everyone know there was trouble behind my front door. He pounded hard enough to knock the stained-glass panel out of place, slightly cracking a hinge.

I opened the door to be greeted with a face full of vodka and a punch. I felt my nose give way and one of my front teeth loosen down to the root.

"Motherfucker!" I yelled. All of the pent-up rage, frustration, and aggression over constantly being wronged boiled forth. "You do not come to my house," I screamed, not getting to finish before another punch landed and successfully knocked the loosened tooth free. Blood splashed my shirt, and my screaming only convinced my neighbors to look out their window and see why lights were flashing.

My neighbors didn't see Denny attack me. They didn't see his second punch. They didn't smell the alcohol on his breath or hear what he was whispering to me. He told me how good he was at making love to Trudy. How she said no one could do it like him. How happy she was now that she was where she belonged. How Ava called him every night. How I was going to lose Christopher soon, too, because he was going to ask the court to revoke all custody rights.

All my neighbors saw as they stealthily peeked out of the corners of tightly pulled drapes was me jump on Denny, grab his hair, and smack the back of his head to the concrete. When the blood started to flow from the slowly spreading crack on his skull, he looked at me with the smile of a mad man.

"I win," he said.

No punch could have dealt the same powerful blow as those words. We both knew what he meant. He didn't care about Trudy, but he had her. He thought she took his life, his high school fame, his college career, and his reputation. She had left him, found solace with me, and in his twisted mind, he'd lost the first half of the game. But not now. Now he had her, and before she realized what a mistake she'd made, before she could run back to safety, the final touchdown was scored. I would never play the game again.

Once my arrest showed up on the nightly news, the paperwork was filed. The bodycam footage had an error, they'd said, but witnesses at five nearby houses corroborated Denny's story about the assault. The judge already hated me. He didn't need any of this evidence to make his decision, but now he didn't need to justify his decision either. He could only give me three months for a first-time offense, and the town was furious. Didn't our town care about their policemen? They screamed that this sentence would encourage other lunatics to take up arms against the good policemen of our city.

Upon my release, I lost my job. Stupidly, I'd never cut Trudy out of our bank accounts, finding some secret joy when I saw I was still taking care of her. Within three months, she'd spent everything I had left.

I was released from jail after seven months to find out I had lost my car, and our once-happy home full of memories and firsts had gone to the first bidder willing to take over payments from the bank. Our neighbors, claiming I was unsafe and a threat to their security, expedited the sale. No one blinked an eye when the house was deemed to be in foreclosure quicker than any other property in town.

I never saw Christopher again.

My life was shattered. Everything I'd worked for was over because of her. I'd left school because of her. I'd given up on my dreams to clean up her mistakes. I'd stood by her when no one else wanted to tarnish their name. I had spent thousands of dollars on Denny's child, and on picking up the pieces of Trudy's broken spirit. I had been nothing but good to them. I was a fool, guided by dreams, blind to truth, ignorant to reality.

They would pay.

With God as my witness, I swore that one day, I would make them all pay.

CHAPTER TWENTY-SIX

Ava

Seeing James strapped down on a medical gurney like a helpless child was more difficult than I'd anticipated. Almost as hard as trying to figure out why he would do this, or better yet, how he could do this.

But at the same time, in some sick way, I think I understood how he could get to the point of taking someone's life. For years he was taken advantage of, forgotten, pushed to the side, and blamed for simply giving his best. I don't think I ever truly believed he attacked Denny, or any of the stories I was told about his supposed nefarious behavior that led to so many arrests. But I can admit it just seemed easier to go along with the stories because hating him was an outlet—and much less dangerous than hating Denny.

There were many times I wished I could get rid of Denny, and God knows I'd had many thoughts about taking his gun that he'd left in his nightstand drawer and solving our problem once and for all. When I stayed at his house, I always slept lightly, waiting to hear the sound of a gunshot after he finally snapped.

Maybe, deep down, I'm not even mad at James. Maybe I never was. But he left me alone, with Denny, with Mom, with their lies, and even worse, with my mind and the monster that slowly grew inside.

To say I was totally alone would be a lie. Christopher was still there, of course, but I felt like I barely even knew him before our lives were somehow ripped apart even more than we already thought they were. How does one start to build a relationship with a complete stranger you've known your whole life? One who isn't even who they were before, and sure as hell doesn't know who they are now? A familiar stranger who wakes up screaming in the middle of the night and who cowers at loud sounds or fast-passing shadows?

My life was on track, my path secure. I couldn't possibly give up everything I'd worked so hard for to become Christopher's caretaker. I didn't have a single maternal instinct, and I knew from firsthand experience how lacking that instinct can fuck up the people you should be caring for. But if I didn't put in the effort, who would step up for the kid? For Denny?

The way Denny had so oddly stepped up lately didn't sit right with me. I know tragedy makes people change their lives, but his eyes always betrayed him. A darkness sat on his soul, a sinister core he couldn't blink away.

I knew this depth well; my own eyes also had black holes within and I'd always see pieces of him staring back in my mirror. The way his movements felt forced when he was helping Christopher walk down the hallway, or the way he'd visibly recoil upon first touch when he had to help Christopher get to his feet couldn't be brushed off.

I have to give him accolades for the amazing show he's been able to put on, though. The folks in town ate it up, and even years later, they still dropped by with dinner, drinks, groceries, or offers to do lawn care. I never understood how so many smart people could have the wool pulled over their eyes by such a monster.

I tried to look at Christopher without him realizing what I was doing. I saw his shoulders tense and the subtle sideways glances he tried to disguise. He was as aware of me as I was of him, our bodies rigid and unwelcoming with each other. Maybe we were even thinking the same thing. What comes next for him? I was fine on my own and he knew this. When the opportunity came for me to get free, I ran, and kept running. He stayed, withered away, and is now a product of that choice. I have no sympathy for the choices he made.

One thing I would never understand is why he stayed. Did he feel responsible for her? Did he feel like her protector? Or was he just a lazy mooch who couldn't get his act together and would now live firmly planted in the regret of being a piece of his mother's murder? If I carried the guilt on my shoulders that no doubt held him down, I would never stay in the same house where my actions had led to the murder of someone I claimed to love.

"Don't think like that," I whispered.

I saw the lady next to me shift uncomfortably in her seat when my words hit her ears. She probably assumed I was thinking about James, the man who raised me, who I trusted, who now lay strapped down to a medical table with poison coursing through his veins.

The thoughts running through my head weren't fair to Christopher when I didn't know all of the information. When we hadn't even talked, I mean really talked, in ages. There was a time in our lives, when we were first ripped from the comfort of our home with James and pushed into the stale cell of Denny's existence, when we'd found solace in each other. We'd read books together at night, talk about our fears, and finally fall asleep surrounded in comfort. And in the mornings, the beating would come. Denny told us it was wrong, but he'd never listen that we weren't doing anything wrong, anything he thought we were doing. But every strap or fist or open palm slowly drove us apart until we only knew each other as pain.

My feelings toward my own flesh and blood stemmed from layers of deep betrayal. Mom had baked me a funfetti cake on the day she decided to tell me James wasn't even my dad—that Denny was. I thought I'd done something special, that she'd noticed how I'd gotten my math grade up and been nominated for class president. Instead, she took a great moment, covered it in sugar and sprinkles, and shattered my identity.

I screamed that James would always be my father, throwing the cake to the floor where it landed at Denny's feet. The smack that hit my jaw sent me across the kitchen. She didn't ask him to stop and didn't step in when another was delivered across my back as I stood up to walk away. Amazingly, they'd always deny that day for years to come, doing everything they could to convince me I only remembered him hitting me because I'd needed to focus on concrete pain to deal with the truth.

Denny was the one who couldn't deal with the truth. He had abandoned me, yes, but he'd left me in the hands of a man who actually wanted me, who could be a father, who could overlook the truth of my nature and love me anyway. James raised me with so much love, so much attention, and if the courts would have listened to me, I would have stayed with him. But they argued that a little girl doesn't know what's best for her, and they argued well.

When they showed up in that big black car and forced me to leave our house, I couldn't even look James in the eye. I didn't say good-bye. I didn't tell him I loved him. I silently walked past him as he held open the front door with outstretched arms, vowing to never talk to him again. In my head, he had failed me. He hadn't fought hard enough. Because he'd given up on me, I'd give up on him.

The transition was hard, and I know I made it harder. I'd cry at anything, and once the tears started, Denny would punish me. He'd call me names. He'd tease me. He'd make me feel worthless. Only babies cried.

Looking at James now, I wondered if my not looking at him on that horrible day helped drive him down this path. After his trial, after seeing and hearing all of the evidence—how he'd felt abandoned and alone, staring at the life that should have been his from the outside as it was constantly thrown in his face—I felt the guilt of my previous years settle in heavily.

Never in a million years would I have imagined he'd murder my mother. But as much as I couldn't understand why he'd done it, I also couldn't deny that I understood how one could be driven to that point. The resentment, the anger, the frustration—the way your world crumbles around you. Had I not left, had I not been smart enough to get out, maybe I would have cracked around the edges, too. Maybe my dreams of watching them all fade from my world would have come true. Maybe James had somehow seen my dreams and thought I was asking him to help me achieve them?

I still never understood Denny even when James was at his lowest. Why any court would look at him and think he deserved custody of children over James was mind-boggling. His power over this town was immense, too big of a reach for a man with such deep shadows. No one questioned his ability to raise Christopher and me when he had the largest arrest record of any law enforcement officer in the county, even though they'd all seen the bruises we tried to hide. There are only so many days you can wear a long-sleeved shirt in the summer before people start to question your home life. According to the courts he kept the streets clean of riffraff, and we'd be better off in the hands of someone capable and community-oriented.

They didn't know, or maybe they didn't want to know. And I couldn't blame them. Everyone wants their town to be safe, and they'd protect those who did so over those who couldn't have that kind of influence.

But Denny wasn't right in the head. He laughed at the wrong things. Loved power and dominance. Loved to inflict pain. Too many of his arrests would come in with major injuries, with stories that didn't make sense. The more power he got, the more bold and brash he became. He wasn't afraid to use his status as a silent threat, and people let him, because that's small-town mentality.

I understood the people in my town. People basically deserve what they get. If you step out of line, you're saying you think you're above the law. I have absolutely no problem with the theory of an eye for an eye. Some people just can't be taught common sense, or decency. They have to be scared, to have order beaten into them. If people won't listen to you, you have to make them. Denny taught me this, and while I wasn't quite ready to test all of his methods, I was growing stronger each and every day.

I suddenly felt thankful for James. For what he did. Yes, I loved my mother. I loved her dearly. And I hated her at the same time. But together with James, she gave me a great childhood. Their actions showed me that I was surrounded by monsters, a whole family of monsters just waiting for an opportunity to shed their human skin and show their truth. Without James, without what he did, I may never have learned that I was a monster, too.

At least now I could prepare for when it's time to shed my skin and step into my own.

I just needed to decide if that next phase would involve Christopher or not. Should I welcome him along the journey, offer to help him, love him, and lead him forward?

Watching him today, I wasn't sure if he'd be strong enough to be there, to walk next to me, to embrace his own truth. In the history of our lives, he was just as guilty as anyone in this room of the events that had led us back together. He could try to hide his role, but we all knew he had darkness in his heart, too.

He knew what he was doing when he called Denny. He knew his phone call wouldn't end well; there'd be pain, tears, blood. He got exactly what he wanted.

Maybe we all did.

CHAPTER TWENTY-SEVEN

Minute Five

I can hear the executioner walking over, checking my pulse and respiration, his latex-gloved hands the same temperature as the cold metal on his stethoscope. My waning body functions are barely registering. My lungs should have stopped by now, paralyzed two minutes ago. I've either willed them on with superhuman strength or my active consciousness thinks they're still working as I lay here slowly dying.

Everything is blurry now, and I'm not sure if I've blocked out the impending pain of death while still clinging to my mortal body. Maybe I should just let go easily and wait for whatever comes next?

Regardless, the potassium chloride that will enter my veins shortly will seal my fate. In seconds the electrical signals telling my heart to pump will be disrupted by the same drug used to treat low levels of potassium.

Life's fragility is both beautiful and tragic. The same compound that could kill you could also keep you moving one more day. Like everything, it depends on the situation and how one uses the gifts from the universe. Water can fuel your body or drown you. Heat can rescue you from the bitterness of cold or suck your body dry until every cell withers and gives up.

And, most importantly, there's time. Every second that ticks past puts you closer to death, like me right now.

Even though I know my life is coming to an end, and even though I've had more troubles than blessings, I can't deny that my life has been well lived. Through all the ups and downs, even as my spirit is in the process of letting go and giving up, way before I found myself bound to a cold metal gurney with people collecting a paycheck to lead me through my final moments, I knew that I would live every single minute all over again if I could. I'm not sure I'd change a thing. Even in this purgatory where I can't figure out if I'm dead or alive, I have no regrets for the choices and actions that led me to this table. Every moment of my life was created for a reason by a power higher than me. It's not my place to question. I chose the path I walked on, both the smooth and the rough.

I can still feel her next to me, not outside, but in here. With me. Her presence is comforting and confusing. She smells the same, but I'm afraid to look for her. I'm afraid she won't be what, or who, I remember—that she'll look like the final photos shoved in front of my face in an effort to make me crumble during the trial. Instead of flowing strands of flaxen hair, she'll have matted dreadlocks of blood and brain matter, a caved-in skull, a missing eye. I don't want to see her like that ever again. Once was hard enough.

She slides closer, gliding on air. I think we're both just two lost souls right now, swimming through our final days while we try to figure out where we belong. We are not ready to give up or concede our beings to the netherworld until we are convinced the right pieces have fallen into place for those we love. Two overly conscious and painfully self-aware people disconnected from our human selves, refusing to leave the life we didn't want to be a part of in the first place.

"Do you remember when I fell off the swing and you came down to lie next to me in the gravel?" she asks.

I feel my body relax as her beautiful voice registers. Her tone is as sweet as the most beautiful songbird's. A gift. With her words, the memory came flooding back. That kindergarten summer, in vivid color. I could smell the sweat of my young body, feel the sharp pricks of the mulch against my skin, the continued itch as the wooden chips embedded into the cotton knit of my navy blue polo shirt. Blood slowly pooled into tiny beads on Trudy's knees, and from tiny cuts on her palms. Her hair was tangled in the same dirt that now kissed her freckled cheeks.

She still looked beautiful to me, covered in dust, dirt, and failure. If I could go back to that day right now, I'd still fall madly in love with her.

I hope she can read my thoughts, see how much I loved her then, and still do now. I want her to see that I will always keep my promise and never give up on her, even when she turned her back on me time and time again. Was I weak? Possibly. Or maybe my love for her is just stronger than anyone would ever know, in life and in death.

"I do remember. I'll always remember that day. It's one of my best memories."

I can't manage to say much more.

"Mine, too." She moves closer. "So why did you do it?"

"Do what?" I ask.

I don't want to play games. She needs to be direct with me, ask precise questions. Get to the point.

We have a lot to talk about, a lot to go over. I don't know how much longer I'll be floating around here, stuck in the head of a dying body, trying to figure out where to go next. Maybe I won't even get to choose the moment when I leave. In a few seconds I could be shooting through the stars, twisting through years of debris and other discarded souls while I confronted the mysteries of the universe.

After a pause, I say, "What exactly are you asking me? Who knows why I did anything, Trudy. Love. Jealousy. Desire. Isn't that what fuels us all? Humans operate on passion. Lord knows I did, often. Sometimes we have to make a choice and do what we think is best, even if it's hard or ends up being wrong."

She digests my words through the mists of her lingering soul before she replies, "Yeah. I guess. Even if those decisions prove to be costlier than you could have imagined."

"Most of the time we pay for our choices in a currency that can't be traded with others," I say.

I imagine she'll hold her breath here, turning her head to the right. When she used to get mad or try to hide her frustration, she'd always look at the wall like it contained an impossible crossword puzzle, nibbling on her lip and furrowing her brow, her eyes twitching with deep thought while her brain considered possible answers.

Life would always be a puzzle to her. I would always be a question that couldn't be answered.

Even now, as we sit in limbo pondering the what-ifs and the why-nots of the life we had both struggled through, neither of us can give the definitive answers the other seeks. Neither of us knows how to ask the right questions, either. Yet somehow we both want the other to find peace.

We sit in silence, our two souls trying to figure out what comes next.

"Do you regret what you did? The choices you made?" she asks.

I know what she's asking. Did I regret her, our children, the way things ended. Honesty is best. While that has always been my policy, I'd always given her what she wanted instead of what she needed.

Now, in these final moments, caged inside this prison, she has to hear what I need to say. Even if it hurts, even if it changes everything, even if it means she will understand that I've lied to her before.

"Some days. I think any sane person would have regrets over bad decisions, tough or life-altering decisions. But today? I don't think so. It's too late for regrets. To be completely honest with you, it's not worth it to spend my last moments of consciousness in rivers of regret. My course was written in the stars from the moment I first saw you. All of this was meant to be, and I think we both know we'd be right here one way or another."

"I think so."

"Just you and me, Trudy. The two of us until the end."

"But this isn't the end, James. It's just limbo."

And with this, I release a breath, feeling the final bubbles of air gurgle like stones up my esophagus, rattling out of my lips. There is no more inside of me. This is my final exhale. I'm dead, lost to my physical form, roaming in my spirit. I will remain here until I decide it's time to go—as long as I don't forget that I can leave.

I had always assumed that ghosts who remained earthbound did so because they had a mission to complete—that they lost their conscious ties as they slowly dissipated into the in-between.

"Will you be there, at the end?" I ask. Hoping she'll say yes. I need her to say yes. I need her to tell me this has all been worth it, that I made the right choices—that her death wasn't in vain.

"I don't know."

The subsequent pause is deafening.

Her voice diminishes, and I feel her start to delicately pull away.

"Don't go just yet—I'm scared," I plead, hoping she'll stay. Hoping if she just remains with me a bit longer, she'll see we were always meant to be. I want her to know I'd give up everything for her. That I had given up everything for her.

"Me, too, James. Me, too. I've been scared for as long as I can remember."

She continues to pull away, but she doesn't leave. I can still smell the soft perfume coming off her hair.

She lingers, shimmering in the dark recesses of my mind. This isn't an invitation to join her, but a reminder that I'll always be a choice she's not sure she can make.

My heartbeat slows, dull thud following dull thud.

My lungs are finished and my life is winding down. It won't be long now. Fractions of a second until the muscle of life realizes there's no more reason to pump.

"Tell it to stop," I say to her, watching her gray form move around the edges of my thoughts like the first rain cloud after a summer heat wave.

"I can't, James," she says. "I can't take your life away, like mine was taken. That wouldn't be fair."

She's right.

That wouldn't be fair at all.

CHAPTER TWENTY-EIGHT

The Last Day

Life on the street wasn't easy. I wasn't made for hardship, either mental or physical. Even in a small town, every night I wondered if I'd wake up the next day or if I'd be seeing the night sky for the last time. I'd wish on every fallen star. If I was smart, I'd have followed one of those stars to a new town and started over. But deep in the marrow of my bones, I believed Trudy and I were meant to be together—that one day she would come to her senses and take me back.

I sat on the same sidewalk every day, knowing Trudy drove past on her way to Christopher's school. He never looked at me, but on occasion, she would. Every day I'd watch her deep red Honda SUV drive past, Christopher's head firmly turned to the left so he wouldn't risk even glancing at me.

Staying there was pointless, an exercise in futility. We all knew this. No one dared give me a cent—the unwritten rule in our town, since I was a brutal cop-beating animal who had abandoned my children. But what a hero Denny was, they'd say, taking in the son of the man who'd tried to end his life!

Every once in a while, Denny would stop and push me, knock me over, pour half-drunk gas station Cokes over me, steal whatever meager possessions I had left just because he could, write meaningless tickets he knew I couldn't pay just to get me locked up again where he could torture me privately to his heart's content. The longer my rap sheet became with petty crimes, the more I wished I could commit something horrible enough to lock me up under that concrete roof, where at least I'd have a shower, toilet, and three meals a day.

One day, after I'd lost track of time—of the number of arrests and nights at the shelter, the bottles of gin and pounds I'd lost from my now-skeletal frame—Trudy stopped on her way back from taking Christopher to school.

I could feel her before she arrived. I smelled the soft powder she sprinkled in her shoes every morning and the slightly metallic hairspray she hoped would set the curls in her hair.

"J," she said firmly. "What are you doing?"

I ignored her.

"I know you can hear me. I saw your eyes move. Enough of this." She kicked the side of my right leg with her foot. "Get up. You're better than this. You're the one who was supposed to get out of this town—make all of our dreams come true. You're not supposed to give up and prove that everyone was right about us." Her voice softened. "C'mon, let's go. I'm taking you to the truck stop for a shower and a haircut, and then we'll get some lunch. Please."

I grunted and shifted. I agreed with everything she'd said. I was supposed to be the one. I felt rage well up inside of me, a rage hotter than any I'd ever felt before. A rage so pure I was scared of what I might be capable of.

"James. Now," she demanded.

I obliged. I followed her to the passenger-side door and cringed when she asked me to wait, laying Waffles' blanket over the seat so I wouldn't have any actual contact with her car.

"I hope you don't mind, but I'm going to have to roll the window down. When's the last time you showered?"

"You could have just left me on the corner, where you put me."

She didn't reply and we drove on in silence. I heard her breath hitch and knew there'd be a single tear running down her delicate, porcelain skin. Only one tear; that's all she would allow herself, and the small droplet would always appear after she'd caught her breath, reminding herself to be strong.

We continued in silence, only speaking when the SUV pulled in to the truck stop parking lot. Trudy informed me that I was to go in and shower, then change into the jeans and T-shirt she had in the back. She promised me they weren't Denny's before I was even able to ask. I hated her and loved her, all at the same time.

I said nothing. I took her $10 bill, booked a shower, got a toothbrush and toothpaste, all-purpose soap, and a Coke. When they called my number I sauntered to the shower room, thankful for the ten minutes of steaming hot water and the privacy I wasn't granted at the shelter, or in jail. I flashed back to our house, our large walk-in shower with the overhead rain option, the scented shampoos, the soapy loofahs, the extended claw-foot tub we would share over a glass of wine with a few candles.

Why had she stopped today? Why was she helping me now? What

good was one shower when I'd be right back on the streets, pulled away from everything because she'd had to run back to Denny?

Anger took hold and I forced it down. I swallowed the lump of envy, confusion, and jealousy that stubbornly stuck in my throat like a honeyed biscuit. The only sensation I wanted to feel was the burn of hot water against my skin.

I watched as the dirt steadily flowed off my body and circled the drain. If only I could wash all the dirt from of my life like this. If only there was something I could do to release all of my struggles and start over. I'd never be able to move forward while they were alive; I'd always be tied to them. I'd always be tied to what they'd done to me, what they'd taken from me. I'd never be able to try and make myself whole until they were six feet underground in reinforced caskets. I knew this. I knew the power they held over me. They knew it, too.

Slipping on the still new clothing felt unbelievable. This was a sensation I'd long since forgotten, one I didn't realize I'd always taken for granted. My life now consisted of discarded articles of clothing, giveaways, pillaging the bins of charity shops, and when times were really desperate, sneaking into laundromats and grabbing clothes from dryers. The best locations were in or next to apartment complexes. People would drop off their goods and then go home, never missing a few pairs of socks or a T-shirt here and there.

I quickly guzzled the rest of my Coke, afraid if I walked out with the bottle of soda I'd disappoint Trudy. She hadn't given me money for treats, and I wasn't sure if she'd expect any change when I returned to her car.

She was waiting for me, the engine running. The door had barely closed before she moved the gearstick to reverse and we started rolling backwards.

"I'm taking you for a haircut and a shave. Real quick at the Clip and

Curl by the diner. No objections, J. You have to pull yourself together. Get out there, get a job, and get back on your feet. Enough is enough. It's not fair to your children to see you like this," she said.

I wanted to tell her that it wasn't my fault. I hadn't taken my children away. I hadn't filled their heads with stories about their horrible worthless father. I hadn't spent all my money, lost my house. I hadn't started the fight that landed me in jail and lost me my job. But Trudy, well, that was a different story. Although she blamed me for causing them more pain and strife, she was not only fraternizing with the enemy, she was warming his bed.

I growled in response. Truthfully, making a noise, even a rough one, was the most respectful response I could think of.

"That's about what I expected," she replied.

We pulled in front of the Clip and Curl. I opened the door and hopped out before the car had even rolled to a stop. I wanted to turn and walk away, to take off down the road and never look back, but I knew a milkshake and a warm meal were at the other end of these clippers. She could chastise me and be a self-serving hypocrite if she wanted. I'd be done with her after today.

The first milkshake went down quickly, the sugar settling in my stomach like a long-lost friend. I didn't have to ask for a second. New Betty brought the thick sip of nostalgia over with a look of pity, pausing at the table before deciding it was probably best not to say anything after all.

I silently thanked her for walking away, for knowing better than to rip open festering wounds that had yet to close and scar over.

"Tomato soup and hash browns, huh?" I said, when our meals hit the table. "Guess your whole life is just back to normal—the good ol' days."

"J, don't start with me. I like what I like, and there's something comforting about tomato soup."

"You like what you like? What about the things you once loved? What about those?" I asked. I tried to keep the venom from my tongue, but it was impossible.

"You know I love you. I'm always going to love you."

"Did you love me when you were sleeping in my bed? Having my child? Did you love me when your husband showed up at my door, jumping me and screaming that he'd won this time, before having me arrested? Did you love me when you spent my money and lost my house? Did you love me when you left me for the man who never loved you, who cheated on you all through high school—who abandoned you when you told him you were having his child?"

My voice was steadily rising, catching the attention of the other diners. Overcome with frustration, I slammed my fist to the table, rattling our porcelain plates against the Formica tabletop.

"Did you ever truly love me, or was I just a convenience? What were we, really?" I demanded.

"J, this isn't fair to me. You know it's not that easy."

"It's not fair to you? I lost everything because of you. Because I loved you. Because I stepped up. You loved him because of the swing set—my swing set. But you know what? You two are meant for each other. I think you need to feel like you're winning by tying him down as much as he needs to win the game of keeping you tied down. You two really do deserve each other," I scoffed. "You took everything away from me. Everything I worked for. Everything I gave you. You're an ungrateful, two-faced . . . I can't say it to your face, but know I'm going to be thinking it every single day for the rest of my life."

Trudy's lips were trembling, her hands shaking.

I felt no remorse. I felt no sadness. I looked at her face and felt only gratitude to see the shock and pure pain etched there.

Before I knew it, she'd smacked me across the face, knocking a cup of coffee to the floor in the process. The breaking porcelain paired with the slap caused everyone in the diner to fall silent.

"You know who you sound like," she snarled, loud enough to be heard by everyone. "Like him. The day he left, when you swore him off, called him worthless, and disrespectful. You sound just like him. You did this to yourself. You and you alone. The answer to your question, James, is simple. No. I never loved you. I never will. Ava never will. Christopher never will."

Trudy slammed a fifty-dollar bill on the counter.

"I suggest you go down to the bus station, buy yourself a one-way ticket to a new town. I'll tell the kids you died. That's all anyone needs to know."

I stared at her in disbelief. The anger I felt grew.

Was I too late to open my case against Denny for assaulting me? To push for the police camera footage? To sue the department for wrongful imprisonment and take them down for theft? I wondered if I could file for fraud if I'd never taken her off my accounts. I did have paperwork filled out to do so; would it be possible to lie and say the bank had messed up? I doubted that would be a possibility. After all, who believes a homeless rule breaker with a record as long as mine when put up against the town's shining detective?

"Well, there it is," I replied, making no attempt to hide the disdain in my voice. "You should have moved to LA, been an actress. You're so damn good at faking everything. By the way, that night at homecoming when you were left all alone at the table, your loving husband was raping Jennifer in the locker room. I could go on and on, naming all the other girls he's been with behind your back, even the one I saw sucking him off in his squad car last week."

I couldn't stop myself, even now, with the look of horror spreading across her face.

"I'll leave this town. But you . . . you're always going to be sad, sorry, forever-the-victim Trudy. You made your bed, and I hope you never get a good night's sleep for the rest of your miserable existence."

We stared at each other, all trace of love or friendship now extinguished.

I wasn't going to be the first to get up and leave. I was going to eat every last morsel of food on this table before I walked down to that bus stop and restarted my life.

Although I'd promised myself that I would never abandon my children, I feared they were too far gone, too immersed in the lies and drama, too haunted by Trudy and Denny's demons.

Finally she gave in, furiously snatching her jacket and stomping out the front door.

I slid my hands across the table, pulling her soup and hash browns toward me. I noticed her credit card still sat there, ready to pay the bill. This small stroke of luck allowed me to order two more cheeseburger platters, a slice of apple pie, a bag of bagels, and a Coke to go.

"You know, I never thought it'd end like this," said new Betty, when she brought the bill. "I really thought you and Trudy would make it forever, James," she said, resting one hand on my bony shoulder. "Truthfully, I'm on your side. She did you dirty, and you're a better man than that. You know, we still have that dishwashing job. It's yours if you want it. I'm sure Earl would even walk you through running the grill. He's getting old and won't last much longer. The man's gotta retire or sell this joint someday."

222

"Thanks, Betty. I appreciate the offer. Trudy's right, though. I lost sight of everything, but I don't have to be down here forever. I need to move on with my life. Restart. How far do you think fifty dollars will get me?"

"Oh, sweetheart. Not very far at all. You might be able to try your luck with hitching. There are a lot of drivers who park here at night. Or . . ." She paused, as we both looked down at Trudy's credit card.

"I don't think I can do that. I may be mad as hell, but I'm not a thief."

"Thief, or debt collector? Seems to me one bus ticket out of here doesn't quite equal what she took from you, if all the rumors are true. I tell you what. I'll go ring in your food to go, get you a hot cup of coffee, and then I'm just going to set the card down on top of this table like I would for any other customer. What happens after I do that is none of my business."

I pursed my lips and nodded. I knew Trudy's finances should be none of my business, but a part of me wondered if she'd left that card on purpose. The same part of me that knew she didn't mean it when she swore she'd never loved me.

One ticket to Santa Fe without so much as a glance at the name on the credit card put me in good spirits. I didn't know what I'd find there, but that ticket was the first bus out, and therefore, the destination for me.

I had two and a half hours before I'd be on my way to freedom, and Trudy's card, stuck in my pocket, just didn't feel right. I was afraid I'd be too tempted to use it again. This was about starting over, not returning to an old pattern.

Denny's house was only half a mile away. I could make it there, put the card in the mailbox, and leave. The ticket would be our little secret when the bill came, payback for the shock I'd felt when I was released the first time and saw my bank statements.

"Calm down," I whispered to myself as I approached Denny's house.

The air was crisp, the sky a beautiful India ink littered with thousands of stars. Each step took me closer, filled my body with a mixture of anger, frustration, sadness, and longing. I hated her deeply, intensely, yet I wanted to feel her again, to touch her again, to lay my lips on hers and feel my hands exploring the soft curves of her frame.

"She's not for you. You deserve more," I reminded myself. "You don't love her. You never did. You get to live."

The porch light was on, illuminating their modest brick ranch. Denny's car was parked haphazardly in front of the mailbox, front wheels digging in to Trudy's carefully laid-out flower bed.

She'd been obsessed with the idea of curb appeal ever since Christopher became more active in after-school activities. She filled her time with early empty nest syndrome, laid up on the couch watching hours of home improvement shows on HGTV. I'd sit outside, in the shadows, and watch. And while she scribbled down notes, I knew that all of her ideas would be shut down at the dinner table.

Sometimes, late at night, I'd get lonely or need to take a long walk to warm up, and I'd walk past their house. Sometimes I'd just get mad and kick a few rocks out of place. One time, I grabbed her early spring flowers with the large yellow heads and pulled them from the ground, bulb and all, leaving them scattered in the middle of the street. I smiled, seeing the damage done to her treasured flower beds.

I knew I should just put the card in the mailbox and walk away, but something told me Chris was home. If I knocked on the door, maybe he'd answer. And I'd be standing there, looking like the father he knew in clean clothes, freshly shaved, with nicely trimmed hair. Maybe he'd recognize me and give me a hug, welcome me back into his life, and we could start to rebuild.

I know that's not what Trudy and I had angrily agreed upon. He was supposed to believe I was dead. Would it be the worst thing in the world if I just told him one more time that I loved him? Would it be better for him if he thought I was dead, or if we made some progress through our angst?

The door knocker hit with a deep thud, echoing through the foyer. I could see Christopher's trademark white socks with the gray heel sticking over the side of the couch. His feet had grown. He always grew uncontrollably, wearing twelve-month clothes by the time he was a few months old. I don't know why his enormous feet took me by surprise now.

I knocked again, but he didn't stir. My stomach twisted. I cupped my hands and looked through the window. No movement. He'd always slept heavily, and because both Denny and Trudy's cars were at the house, I relaxed.

For no reason in particular, I rang the doorbell. Perhaps I hoped I was interrupting something intimate, ruining a tender moment. Once interrupted, getting back into the flow of making love is difficult. If I couldn't reconnect with Chris, at least I could spread my frustration to those behind the locked door.

I laughed, stepped off the front porch, and started my walk back to the bus station. I was on my way to freedom from these emotional ties, somewhere in the dry deserts of New Mexico.

CHAPTER TWENTY-NINE
Minute Six

"Trudy," I call, hearing my voice echo through the cavernous depths of myself.

I'd felt my final heartbeat just a moment ago. It had flickered slowly like a butterfly landing on a flower dusted with poison, wanting to fly but not being able to move, fighting for one more push to grab air and hopefully coast to a safe spot before tumbling off the soft petals to its death. Nature was a beast, even more so when man came into the picture.

"Are you there?" I call again.

I could see her still. She was softer. Her silver waves seemed to spread wider against the shadows of my mind. I could feel her infiltrating the last pieces of my consciousness, just like she had in life. Some things would never change. My love for Trudy would be one of them.

"I'm here," she finally replies, her voice quiet. There is sadness in her words.

I didn't want to die in sadness. I wanted to die knowing there was hope, knowing I'd have eternity with her.

"Do you remember the day Christopher was born?" she asks.

"Of course. You always remember the birth of your first."

I pause, realizing the depth of what I'd just said, how she might interpret my words.

"You know what I mean. I always considered Ava to be mine; I always will. But Christopher—"

"Was your flesh and blood," she interrupts. "I understand. I could see it in your face that day. His birth was different. There was this deep bond that formed from the moment you saw his wrinkly pink body. I remember looking at you and thinking how beautiful you were. I wasn't even concerned with the baby I'd just pushed out, just the glow in your eyes."

"You thought I was beautiful?" I ask.

If my heart had still been beating, this is where it would have jumped a beat. I wished I could stomp on the red tissue and sinew and make it pump just once more.

"I did. And so was he. In all of my living days, that would be one of my favorite memories. I went to it often. I still do when I can't figure out what comes next."

Relief washes over me. She didn't know what came next, either. I wasn't alone. That must be a sign that she's still here for me. We're meant to take our next steps together, to figure out the unknown, as one. I always knew this to be true. She didn't. But now she must.

"I wish I could have given you that day over and over again," I reply.

"I don't."

227

I wince. The response comes so quickly, and shocks me even more than when I'd figured out she was sleeping with Denny.

"I was a bad mom, James. I ruined two children. I didn't need the opportunity to ruin more."

"It takes more than one person to raise a child. We all failed them."

"I failed you. I needed to fail everyone in order for my life to make sense. You were the only one who could have been good for them. We all knew it. You, me, Denny, the kids. I think that's why you failed. Why you went this way."

"That makes no sense," I say. And it doesn't. If we all knew I was the one who was good for us, the one who could provide, lead, and create a family, why had it ended this way? Why was I a mere shell, strapped to a table, slipping away from a cocktail of drugs the State felt I deserved?

She's right in a way, though. We were all a group of cowards. We all acted like we had tough skin, wearing our fears on our sleeves and our truths tucked tightly behind our hearts. We preferred to welcome death rather than life. We chose to walk away from love because chaos felt more comfortable.

I look at her swirling gray mass, flickers of her flaxen hair appearing every now and then. Just as she had in life, she's trying to hold her true self back even now, hiding behind a cloak of darkness.

Perhaps she is the black hole that will consume me in both life and death, waiting for my entry before folding into herself and collapsing for all of eternity.

And I know I'll let her.

After all, I had already died for her.

CHAPTER THIRTY

Christopher

Although James was nonresponsive—almost dead—I knew from personal experience that you could still be present even when your body has already tapped out. There are times I feel myself go back to that day, feel myself slipping back into that couch where I could feel myself slowly breathing in my own blood. The heavy coppery liquid, thick like drying glue, slowly coating my windpipe on its way down.

I shuddered. This was not the place. I shook myself, desperately trying to lose the heavy scent of rubbing alcohol and latex that permeated the air around us. Every visit to the doctor, every trip to physical therapy, every time someone stepped a little too close to me a little too quickly—it all triggered flashes of memories so violent that I'd be ripped from the present and thrown back to those moments I so desperately try to forget.

But Denny was here now, in this room. Here with a slight smile on his face that he was trying to keep hidden. Here to watch his childhood best friend die.

I needed to stay strong, to stay together. He would find too much joy in me crumbling; even the slightest hint that I couldn't handle being here would put an even bigger smile on his face.

Sure, he'd been there for me after the accident, but he'd still been Denny. A hard push here, a string of words blaming me for being a burden there, and a lifetime of using his relationship with me as a way to guilt me into being his whipping boy.

I wouldn't look at him. He didn't deserve my time, and while I knew that my obvious attempts at ignoring him would give him pleasure, I wanted to believe I was getting under his skin, denying him the very thing he craved by denying an emotional display. I'd hold myself together. I'd hide my broken pieces. Even if it was only for today, I'd get myself together.

The beeping of the monitor telling us how much life was left in James was slowing, a sound I hated and didn't want to hear ever again. Each monotonous bell hammered against my head and I winced reflexively while the room spun around me.

"Deep breath," I told myself, trying to avoid a relapse, especially in public.

It didn't work. I swiftly slipped into the abyss.

I heard it again. Steady pounding on the front door. When the first thumps echoed through the open room, I rolled my eyes. Only one person would knock, and I wasn't letting him in to our house. He shouldn't even be here. Not after what he'd done to us.

The knocking intensified, steady and strong. There was a purpose, a force behind each rap. I ignored them. I lay back over the tight couch cushions, dong exactly what I was always told not to do.

"Couches are for sitting on. If you want to lie down, go to bed," Denny would always say. He'd also flip out if he knew I was over my thirty minutes of video-game time. "They rot the brain and make you stupid. Make you violent. You have more important things you could be doing with your nonproductive life." He'd try to drum this into my head, often saying maybe I'd get it if he could just smack it in to me.

Last time he'd tried, I'd met his hand with mine, showing him that making me do anything by force was no longer an option. I should have done it earlier, but I was always afraid he'd take it out on Mom. I preferred he used me. She was too weak, in both body and mind.

Even though Denny was cruel, in some sick, twisted, dangerous way, I knew that he was better for her than James. She found a challenge in Denny, a reason to fight, a reason to push. With James, she found complacency and ease. She fed off the chaos Denny gave her. She needed that pain to feel real. There's no way to explain it other than she was sick.

Our life had been somewhat calm lately. I'd spent most of my time studying, much to their shock and awe, now that I wanted to get out, too. I'd always thought Ava would come running back, realizing that she needed us, that she belonged in our sad, sick, twisted world. But she didn't. She stayed out there, far away from what happened in Parker Point. And when I saw her take those steps, putting the misery of this small town behind her, I knew there was a world outside for me, too. But first, I had to pull myself up by my bootstraps and get my shit together.

High school was too far gone for me to make huge leaps like Ava. First, I'd need to just do well enough to secure a spot at community college. After two years, I could leave with an associate's degree and use that as my ticket out of town. When I looked at the calendar and saw that it would take me three and a half years to get out, to be free, those days felt so long. But when you look back at how fast the last sixteen have gone, three and a half feel like nothing.

Bang. Bang. Bang.

That familiar pounding, the sound of hard metal on soft flesh . . . Why couldn't I place that noise? I thought it was someone knocking on the front door, but no.

Think Christopher, think.

Dinner. Mom is cooking dinner, loudly smacking something in the kitchen that she will no doubt overcook and then find a way to blame us for getting in her way. Her excuses are usually something silly, like she'd just stepped away from the chicken to fold the towels from the dryer, since we wouldn't, and she didn't make it back in time. Ovens have timers for a reason, which apparently everyone knew but her.

The pounding is not just distracting, it's poignant. For some reason, the strength she's putting into it sends a message.

I take a deep breath when the pounding stops.

Suddenly a sharp pain hits my forehead, every nerve from temple to temple registering pain, then the room goes black.

Slowly, I wake. I remember the pounding. The room around me is shrouded in mist, or maybe my eyes are cloudy. I can't tell. The lighting is awkward, red in hue, a color I don't remember seeing in the house before. The air feels tense, strange. Dangerous.

There's something else now, a new sound, like water when it bubbles up through a clogged garbage disposal. A slow gurgling of air struggling to break through a thick mass settled in its way. I realize it's my breath, slipping through a pool of blood that slowly thickens over the couch cushions.

My blood.

There's a scraping to my left. Metal on stone. A deep sigh slipping from a cloaked figure slowly walking toward me.

I struggle to look through the heavy liquid being sprayed over my face with each desperate breath. The figure is wearing a charcoal hoodie pulled tightly over his features. Through the heavy copper smell pushing its way up my nostrils, I catch a light, woodsy smell that reminds me of waking up in the morning with fresh-cut grass after a summer rain. The smell is familiar, but not comforting. There's something odd about the way it makes me feel. Unsettled and aware of potential danger.

The figure pushes to his feet from the edge of the fireplace where blood drips off the end of a black metal rod resting lazily against the brick. That must have been what made the sound of metal scraping on stone, and I would be willing to wager that it's my blood slathered over the end of the rod and lightly sprayed all over the wall.

I watch the figure step closer. My eyes aren't able to focus, and the confusion of trying to make sense of his staccato movements make my stomach retch.

He kneels in front of me. His eyes look like black pools of hatred. I can't see any white around his pupils, just darkness. I feel pressure in my head, and pain shoots through my body as a heavy finger lifts my eyelid. I take a sharp breath in reflex, feeling the heavy syrup of my body welcome itself back inside. The need to cough is uncontrollable, but I'm not strong enough.

He laughs and mutters something.

Think, Christopher. What did he say?

The softness of the chin. The crook in the nose. The hate that floods his eyes. That smell. The gravel in his voice and the smell of his breath as it rains down on you.

Think, Christopher. Think.

The face peering into my eyes slowly moves in and out of focus. The lips become defined, but then I'd lose the nose. If I move to his forehead, I lose the eyes. All I need is for everything to fit, to be clear at once.

He's heavy-handed. Alcohol on his breath. The air conditioner kicks on and he doesn't jump. The sounds of the house are familiar and routine.

Oh my God.

Back in the gallery, my eyes shot open. Beads of sweat dripped down my forehead. The muscles lining my upper back seized into painful knots as my whole body tensed up. The final vision floated through my head: the man who wanted to take my life, leaning over me, nose to nose, finally coming into full view. His laugh as I struggled to breathe through the blood flowing into my mouth rang through my ears.

"It can't be," I whispered.

I looked at James, splayed out in white in front of me. Light. Oddly beautiful. Peaceful. When he'd looked at me earlier, even as his eyes had started to roll around from the drugs coursing through his system, I hadn't felt fear.

But when he walked in, sitting close but just out of reach, I had felt repulsion. It wasn't just hatred. This feeling had followed me for years. Every time he got near, my body would fail, my mind would go blank, my head would sink into layers of pain that rolled with inhumane intensity.

And then I heard it. The pounding.

After realizing the sound wasn't just in my mind, I see him, standing by the glass, pounding, screaming something. I can hear it, but I can't make sense of it. He's in pain, anguished.

I'd seen that look before. Angry. Frustrated. Slighted. Jealous.

Once again, my entire world was about to change.

I have to figure out how I made such an awful mistake.

CHAPTER THIRTY-ONE

The Investigation

"Mr. Jackson, you admit you were at the Lloyds' house the evening of the murder," the tall, chiseled man said as he paced in his three-thousand-dollar tailored suit.

"I wasn't part of the murder," I replied, my hands carefully folded in front of me. My attorney, the short, squat public defender with the stained shirt and thrift store tie, nodded at me while he chewed his bloody fingernails.

"That's not what we're asking. That's up to the judge and jury to decide now, isn't it?" he chuckled.

I cringed when I heard a few chuckles coming from juror number three and juror number eight. Both women. They'd already made up their minds the moment they'd seen the photos of Trudy's dead body, brutally bludgeoned in the kitchen, wearing only her underwear.

"According to previous statements, you were at 1842 Strong Oak Lane on March 28, correct? Remember, Mr. Jackson, you are under oath, and perjury is a crime."

"I was at the house. Correct," I answered, trying to ignore the raised eyebrows and head shakes.

"And why were you at the Lloyds' house on the night of the murder?" He stopped pacing and folded his arms across his chest. His body language was a show of dominance, a power play. We'd been taught the importance of body language in pre-law. He was trying to intimidate me. I wouldn't let him.

"I was returning Trudy's credit card. I was homeless at the time, as you know. She had picked me up, taken me to the truck stop for a shower. Got my hair cut. Took me for dinner. She'd left her credit card at the diner."

I looked out into the courtroom. My eyes met Ava's. Her focus was laser-sharp, watching my every move. Her mind was already made up, too.

Next to her sat Chris. He still walked with a crutch and would forever talk a little slowly, with the hint of a stutter.

That night, when I'd seen his feet hanging over the end of the couch, he wasn't sleeping. He was lying facedown in a pool of his own blood, slowly drowning in it after being hit over the head with a fireplace poker.

"I . . . I had to return her card."

"Trudy is a regular at the diner, correct?"

"Yes, sir."

"Why didn't you leave the card with the waitress?"

"Well, I could have, but that didn't feel right."

I didn't like the way he was backing me into a corner with his rapid-fire questions, while my bumbling lawyer just sat there.

"Or did it not 'feel right' because you'd decided you'd rather take the card and buy a bus ticket to New Mexico, so you could flee the scene of the crime?"

"No!" I shouted.

"No, you didn't flee to New Mexico on a fraudulently purchased ticket? We all know you were found on that bus the next day, still wearing the clothes Trudy had given you the day before."

"I did go to New Mexico, yes, but I wasn't fleeing anything. And yes, I bought the ticket on her credit card. But she had spent plenty of my money after Denny got me falsely locked up the first time. I lost everything because of her. My house, my job, my kids. Everything. That ticket . . . She owed me. And I deserved a fresh start."

I took a deep breath. I never should have said any of this. I was slowly burying myself. I knew it. Both lawyers knew it. And judging by the looks on the jurors' faces, they knew it, too.

"She owed you, you say. Sounds like motive to me, Mr. Jackson. She spent your money, and as you say, caused you to go into foreclosure, losing your house. You assaulted her husband, your childhood best friend, when he came to make custody arrangements, and yet you still blame him. Have you ever been in counseling for anger management, Mr. Jackson?" the sleek-suited lawyer asked.

"No, sir. No. I have not. I've never been in counseling before. Look, Denny assaulted me that day. He jumped on me and just started yelling, 'I win this time, you fucker!' What was I supposed to do? Let him beat me up in my doorway? He was my best friend. My best friend who stole the love of my life because he felt everything was a competition."

"Mr. Jackson, were you going over to the Lloyds' to confront Denny that night? Is it possible he was your real target, and Mrs. Lloyd just got in the way?"

I cringed. Mrs. Lloyd. Trudy never should have been Mrs. Lloyd.

"No. I swear. I knocked on the door. Twice. I looked through the window and saw Chris—I swear I thought he was just sleeping. He's always slept hard. I rang the doorbell, slipped the card through the mail slot, and left."

"The only problem, Mr. Jackson, is that the front door was open and bloody footprints matching the exact size and type of sneaker you were wearing were found right on top of that credit card."

Why wasn't my lawyer objecting to this?

"I was wearing New Balance sneakers that Trudy gave me—probably the same ones Denny wears. And if I did kill her, why didn't I have any blood on me? I was clean."

"Great question, Mr. Jackson. What happened to the clothes you were wearing when Mrs. Lloyd first picked you up from the street on that fateful day?"

I paused. I didn't remember. Did I leave them at the gas station? At the diner?

"I'll tell you what happened to your old clothes. You kept them, and changed back into them before committing the murder. You killed Trudy. You tried to kill your son, but failed. Then you put the new clothes back on, the ones that match all the surveillance footage. Very clever . . . but you weren't quite smart enough to get rid of the old clothes. Perhaps, in a rage-fueled shock, you left those blood-soaked items behind, in the bathtub, where you showered down."

Everyone in the courtroom gasped, including me.

My lawyer threw up his hands.

Photographs were entered into evidence of my bloody clothes in the bathtub. There was no denying they were mine, especially after they added another photo for side-by-side comparison, showing me wearing those items when I'd walked into the truck stop, and then another showing me carrying them with me when I walked out.

Tears ran down my face.

I was done.

The homeless, broken, jealous, enraged ex-husband, betrayed by his best friend. The man I didn't want raising my son. The son who didn't want anything to do with me anymore.

I looked at my lawyer, my poor, pitiful, court-appointed representative. Still chewing his fingernails, his attention was on his laptop. I didn't know if he was looking at his notes or watching Netflix; whatever it was, I'm sure he viewed it as more interesting than saving my life. What was my life worth? Nothing to him; certainly not worth challenging his place in this community.

I looked at Mr. Polished Suit standing before me in his power stance, arms firmly crossed, left eyebrow raised, a slight smirk that told me he'd already won, but wasn't quite finished yet when it came to inflicting pain.

I noticed the jury whispering to each other, giving me the side eye while they nodded their heads in agreement. I'm no lip reader, but I was positive every other word coming through their tightly pursed lips was "Guilty."

"Your Honor, we've finished with this witness," Mr. Suit said to the judge.

"Chance to cross-examine," the judge offered my lawyer, who declined. He couldn't even be bothered to cross-examine his own client, to prove there were flaws in the investigation, to cast even one shadow of a doubt on the investigation. I just needed one juror to hold up the verdict, to pull me from this nightmare.

"Very well, then," the judge said.

"Your Honor, we'd like to call another witness," Mr. Suit said calmly.

There was an audible reaction in the courtroom.

I'd just been destroyed. Who else could they possibly bring forward—and was it really necessary?

"The prosecution calls Christopher Jackson to the witness stand."

The last of my composure crumbled. Christopher? Testifying for the prosecution? If anything could tear my heart out more than burying Trudy, this was it.

"Christopher," I called, standing up at the table. "Don't do this. Please. You know the truth."

I watched him limp past, relying heavily on his crutches. He glared at my weakened form, pure fury driving his walk to the witness stand. I half expected him to spit on me or take a swipe at me with his crutch. I would have welcomed either. At least he was looking at me. For years all I'd seen was the back of his head on his daily drive to school. He was so tall and at the same time, so fragile. He looked like a man in his ill-fitting suit.

"Chris," I cried. "You have to tell the truth!"

The judge banged his gavel three times.

"One more outburst and you'll be held in contempt, Mr. Jackson. I will not have you make a mockery of my courtroom with your begging. Sit down, or I'll have you removed."

I tried to obey him but my legs were like Jell-O. They wobbled and I fell forward, hitting my head against the table. I vaguely remember falling toward the floor before everything went black.

The newspaper headlines made it very clear: I was a wife-murdering, wannabe child killer. Anytime a new one hit the stands, a guard would bring it in, standing by my door to give a public reading. The inmates around me would hoot and holler, egging him on. I was called a monster, a danger to society, an abomination. Both of my children had publicly denounced me, with Ava calling for the death penalty.

Denny was smiling as Ava made this statement. When he placed his arms around my kids' shoulders, declaring he would have Ava's adoption reversed and would be adopting Christopher, I swore I'd kill him if I ever got out of here.

For a month the town rallied against me. They shared stories about how I was always the weird kid, obsessed with death, driving the other two to do things they shouldn't have.

The town had Denny and I mixed up, and no one said a thing or cared to remember who was who. Denny was the one who'd constantly messed around with roadkill, the one obsessed with Halloween, going to see horror movies by himself the day they came out.

And let's not forget the day Trudy's brother killed that girl in the woods. Denny had been extremely eager to see a dead body, practically bounding down the street.

Along with the stories about us being weird kids, they talked about us being a trio of codependent, abused troublemakers. Middle and high school teachers came forward to talk about what a pity it was that we'd all gone in this direction. More stories emerged about us pulling pranks, starting fights, stealing. I was accused of raping a cheerleader after prom. I never went to prom. It felt like the entire town was staring at me down the barrel of a shotgun with a laser sight, creating stories to back me into a corner and push their narrative.

Denny never spoke up. Jennifer Stewart never spoke up. My children certainly didn't speak up. Even new Betty thought I was capable of leaving the diner, smashing a fireplace poker over my son's head and taking a good blow at his spine, almost paralyzing him, before turning on my ex-wife with a meat tenderizer while she prepared dinner.

I tried to plead that this sequence of events didn't make sense. Why would I go for Chris first? Wouldn't his mother hear? He was tall, strong at the time; there would have been a fight, something to grab her attention. Trudy wouldn't have left her son to die in the living room while she pounded on steak in the kitchen. When I spoke up for myself after reading the transcript, my lawyer told me this only made me look guiltier, like I was trying to talk circles of logic around people running the court. The verdict had been delivered. I was guilty. That wouldn't change. We weren't going to appeal something so strongly set in stone. The judge, jury, both lawyers, my flesh and blood, and my entire town were certain I was the murderer. Motive, method, and evidence all pointed my way, and the holy trinity of crime investigation was not to be ignored.

Today was more nerve-racking than any other day of the trial, though. Today would be the day I found out what type of value they placed on my life. What value they put on Trudy, and Chris. I wished I could go into court in a tidy suit, looking like a human, but I was going in these orange jailhouse scrubs, shackled in place like a ravenous wolf.

I was told to prepare a statement. I would be given the opportunity to speak to the judge, and maybe my words could sway him somehow. I looked at that paper. I debated sticking the pen into my jugular. I would start to write something and then scratch it out, start again, and repeat the vicious cycle over and over again until I fell into a sobbing mess, begging for Trudy to come back. The guards leaked this to the press—that I was crying constantly, asking for my wife's forgiveness, and shouting out apologies. The media circus had already doomed my sentencing. Why should I even try to craft a statement for a judge whose mind was made up?

Each step toward the courtroom became more difficult. The leg chains grew in weight. The handcuffs shrank against my wrists. The guard seemed to push me faster, smacking the back of my head every time I'd stumble when the chains didn't give me the ability to take the lengthy steps they wanted.

We entered the hushed courtroom and I was led to my seat. My chains weren't removed. I was not to be seen as human today. I didn't lift my eyes to look for my children, and a hungry reporter took off with this, saying I was too ashamed to look my children in the eyes.

I wasn't ashamed. I was hurt, betrayed, confused, and sad. I loved them. I missed them. The kids and I had taken a vow to always stay together when they were young, pledging our love and support for each other through the good and the bad.

Guess that vow didn't include a murder trial.

CHAPTER THIRTY-TWO

Denny

James lay on the gurney, still and peaceful. I had hoped he would be a little more manic, a bit more frustrated or emotional. But he never was much of a fighter. Even now he'd merely succumbed to the decision of others. Anyone with a little bit of power could rule over him. What a sad, sorry little man.

Sometimes I wondered how we'd been friends for so long. Why had I let him grasp my coattails and ride them so hard? I used to think it was because of Trudy, not James, but that's not true. I would have always had Trudy. She was boring, a useless game. James, he was the real game. Male-on-male dominance, the top of the pack, the strongest king of the jungle.

This town was my jungle. I was the king. James was my prey, and here he was, lying before me, ready to be consumed.

Looking at his soft skin, wired and connected to anonymous people behind the window disguised as a mirror, I couldn't help but wonder if we were ever truly friends. He always needed me more than I needed him. Most of the time he was a thorn in my side. From the beginning he'd acted like my conscience. *That's not right, Denny. Don't do that. You should apologize, Denny; she's not your toy.* But I'm Denny Lloyd. No one tells me what to do. I'm unstoppable. This is my town, and he had to learn that the hard way.

I wanted to feel sorry for him, but I couldn't. The only certainty in life is that you get what you deserve in the end. And lying there, vulnerable, strapped down like a pig going to slaughter, James was getting exactly what he deserved.

Trudy was always mine. She knew it. I knew it. James knew it. Even when I walked away, I knew in my heart she'd come back. She knew she'd come back. But James, he just had to get in the way. He thought he could be her savior. Raise my seed as his own. Slander my name in my town. Make people question me as a man. Even now I'm surprised he expected a different outcome.

The reporter I positioned myself next to said James went peacefully. He didn't fight, but still, he didn't confess. She wouldn't tell me his last words, but she did give me her phone number. All it took was one soft graze against the edge of her ivory knee, delicately exposed under her gray tweed pencil skirt. I saw the slight tremble and clenching of her thighs as she tried to keep her legs together. I'd be with her in no time. Or had I already? It's hard to tell anymore. I couldn't help but wonder if taking her to the bathroom while James died would be viewed as unacceptable, but the sparkle in her eyes told me she didn't think so.

I brushed my hand against the soft bronze curls on her shoulder, perfectly set like a professional woman's hair should be. I missed the days when Trudy fussed over making every inch of herself impeccable. There were days I thought she'd get it back, days when she'd sneak into my office on her way to pick Ava up from day care, but that little girl ruined everything. Even when she found another woman's lace panties in our laundry, she didn't push for herself. I thought for sure knowing I'd been with another woman would encourage her to get herself together. Slowly I learned that I was wrong about her as well. Trophies aren't fun when they quit shining and when no one else wants them. But as long as James wanted her, I'd make sure she stayed high on my shelf. Untouchable. Unobtainable. Mine and only mine.

Ava sat three chairs down from me. I could tell she was trying not to look my way or acknowledge me. Absolutely ungrateful. The weeks after Trudy's death were nice. I thought we'd come together and be a family for once, reunite, continue talking about father–daughter things, and move forward. But that idea quickly faded. Once Trudy was in the ground, her closet cleared out, and her last possessions out of my house, Ava turned away from me again. She couldn't even hang around to help me with Chris, who now needed more help than I cared to give.

The best thing Ava did was convince me to send Chris to his grand-parents. She said I couldn't care for him properly. I could, but I didn't want to. He wasn't my son. He shouldn't be my burden. He shouldn't even be here. Who survives a blunt blow to the head with an iron fire-place poker? Why couldn't he have had that strength and determination before the accident? Because he was his father's son. Well, maybe. That's not for sure, either. Trudy was in my bed long before she went home in my gray T-shirt that blew our affair wide open. I'd convinced her it made me happy to see her wearing my shirt—that he would never notice. I knew he would; I'd just expected it to take longer.

Convincing Ava I was her father after Trudy and James split took a little more time—again, a little more effort than I cared to give. I don't even know why I wanted her under my roof. I didn't raise her. My life was better before children smeared their hands on my windows and left toys over my floors. If I admired James for anything, it was for raising the kids and not killing them.

I turned my head to look at Ava. I wanted her to feel me; to feel the pressure of my eyes against hers. She blinked three times in quick succession. Always a fighter, she refused to turn toward me, but her body language let me know I was in her head.

"Excuse me," I said to the journalist whose name I'd already forgotten.

I started to slip down the row of haphazardly placed chairs, trying my best to put on a friendly smile. Ava finally turned to look at me. Our eyes locked and she froze like a deer staring down the barrel of a gun. I had to stifle a chuckle. She was more like her mother than she thought. That tough exterior and her harsh words didn't fool me. She was weak, and I knew exactly how to break her. She wouldn't even see it coming.

Even though the seat next to Ava was open, I slipped behind her. I wanted her to feel my breath on her neck, to tremble out of fear when my hands slipped close to her windpipe. I wanted her to feel my power, my domination. To let her know that even though she thought our ties were cut, they weren't.

I'd never go away. She'd never be free, and if she didn't change her attitude, she'd be next, leaving Christopher behind as the sole survivor.

The way to get under her skin right away was to make her think about James dying. She loved him, no matter how she acted or what she said. The little thorn in my side would always feel like James was her father. Trudy sleeping with me and breaking their family apart was the ultimate betrayal in her eyes, because it meant James couldn't keep Trudy happy. She'd never forgive him for what Trudy did, and deep down, I loved this about her. She had an innate ability to blame other people for the crimes they hadn't committed.

I wanted to see her squirm, to focus as hard as she could on the final minutes before his eyes rolled back into his head and the executioner declared him unresponsive. Not dead yet, just unresponsive.

"Did James say any last words?" I whispered to her. "Did he finally admit to his crimes?"

I tried not to giggle when she tensed up, but I could hardly contain myself.

All I wanted was for James to finally give in, to concede, to admit he'd failed. I wanted him to lie on that gurney, facing the burning pain of his imminent death, and give the world what they desired: a deathbed confession. He'd always been desperate to please. Why couldn't he do this one last thing?

The murder had made national news. Christopher was a bit of a celebrity afterward, even though he wasn't smart enough to use it to his advantage. Ava had managed to dodge the limelight for the most part, mainly because the press viewed her as lucky, and her pathetic brother made a better story.

I was the grieving widower, the heroic father, and the ace detective who connected the dots to find out my childhood best friend was the one who took everything from me. The country couldn't get enough of the morbid story. I liked being back in the limelight, but it faded way too quickly.

Ava paused before her reply. "He said, 'I won.' "

No. That couldn't be right. There's no way that's what James said. But Ava wasn't smart enough to make that up.

I stumbled back to my seat. The world would see that as a confession, I was sure. But James was wrong. He didn't win. He couldn't win.

The nameless reporter put her hand on my knee and leaned in. She whispered something in my ear, something I didn't hear. I tried to ignore her, hoping she'd go away. She tried again. I couldn't control my thoughts or the rage building up inside of me. I slapped her hard, ignoring the room as it fell into a collection of gasps and confusion.

Bounding from my seat, I threw open the gallery door. The hallway seemed to spin around me as I pushed my way through confused people lining the hallway leading to the execution chamber. They knew me. I was law enforcement. I could go where I needed to go. I'd locked that monster up, and the town was grateful.

Upon reaching the door to the execution chamber, I could see James through a slit in the door. I brought my fists down hard against the door.

"You did not win," I yelled.

"Sir," an oversized guard said, placing his hand on my shoulder.

"Don't touch me."

I reeled around and shoved him. He lost his balance and stumbled, hitting his head against the concrete wall. I watched him go down, knocked out cold. The other officers stayed back, shocked at what they had witnessed. I bent down and grabbed the guard's key card from the springy black plastic cord attaching it to his belt.

"I have to get in there. This execution has to stop," I said, scanning the card and breathing a sigh of relief when the door opened. "Stop!" I screamed. "Stop the execution! This can't go on. There's been a mistake."

"Sheriff Lloyd, you have to exit the room," Warden Stanfield said, his face awash with confusion. "It's too late. The third drug has already been administered. The process has been successful."

"No. No, it can't be," I stammered. "This has to stop."

"I know it's tough. I know this is a lot to go through. But it's done. You can breathe a sigh of relief for a job well done." He patted my arm and tried to turn me around. "Let's go. It's done."

"No," I screamed louder, feeling the veins in my neck start to pop. "This monster did not win! No!"

"I know, Sheriff Lloyd. What he said was horrible. Broke my heart to hear him go out that way. Come on, let's go," Warden Stanfield said, trying to get me to the door.

"He can't die. You have to stop this or save him. Call a medic right now! That man did not win. Not today. He's innocent. I framed him. I set it all up. You're killing an innocent man."

Warden Stanfield fell quiet and dropped his hand from my arm. I looked to the gallery and saw everyone who was watching drop their jaws and look at each other in confusion. Ava's chin trembled. Chris looked at me in horror, recognition finally breaking through the fog of his memories.

"I did it," I said with pride, puffing out my chest. "I killed that bitch when I found his clothes in her trunk. She wasn't going to do me like that. I don't know who she thought she was, going behind my back and helping him. She belonged to me. Only me."

The shocked faces drove my passion. They were hanging on my every word, and I loved it.

"Don't you see? I won. I had her. I kept him from ever getting her again." I pounded my chest. "I won. You have to reverse this! He can't be with her. He doesn't get her for eternity. He deserves to be here with us and live without her. Save him!"

I felt Warden Stanfield push me heavily against the wall.

I turned to look at the kids. Ava was pressed against the gallery window, tears streaming down her cheeks. Christopher was doubled over and rocking. Even now, when I'd once again ripped their world apart, you couldn't deny how different they were. Strong and angry Ava. Weak and useless Christopher. I tried not to laugh as I watched him rock back and forth, but I couldn't help it. His self-soothing always looked absolutely ridiculous. From the time he was a child to this moment, he would crawl inside himself and rock back and forth, knees to his chest. Only now he couldn't quite get his knees up because they still didn't bend all the way, and his spine would threaten to crack under the pressure.

"You should have been there. I'd have taken you out, too," I yelled, looking Ava in the face. "You are nothing to me. You never will be. Live with this for your entire pathetic life. And thank Christopher for calling me to let me know they were together. I should have hit him harder. None of you deserve to be here!"

I didn't want to say that to Christopher's face. He didn't deserve my words, and it would sting so much more to be ignored. He'd spent his preteen and teen years complaining about being ignored. He needed to grow up. I hoped this would encourage him.

A sharp pain hit my skull and the room went black.

CHAPTER THIRTY-THREE

Minute Seven

My time is up. I can no longer fight to stay in a useless body. Nor do I want to. I'm not sure if that's what I was doing earlier. Maybe I was just too aware of what was happening around me for my soul to naturally leave on its own accord.

But now, finally, I find that I'm no longer rattling around inside my old shell like a pinball. I'm soft around the edges, slowly rippling away into a cloud of air slipping out of my now lifeless form.

I lean against the glass divider separating the execution chamber from the gallery. I watch Christopher and Ava hugging, tears running down their cheeks. Ava is telling Chris it's okay—that it's not his fault he can't remember. He just keeps saying that deep down he knew it wasn't my face in his dreams; he'd just been so mad at me that it felt right to convince himself it was.

I want to travel through the glass and let them feel me one more time. But I don't. This is their battle to fight, much as mine was fought in the confines of a small jail cell.

Memories. Time. Things I've always held on to so tightly.

The concept now feels strange, foreign, fleeting. The thoughts in my mind continue to get cloudier with each second I force my soul to stay in this room, quickly dissipating as if they no longer serve me.

Childhood slips away in a swirl of blue clouds. College is off in shades of yellow. Life on the streets dissipates in red smoke, no doubt carrying the rage of betrayal along with it.

But my kids, sitting behind that glass in so much pain, remain.

And she remains.

I press my misty shards against the glass and take in their faces one more time before letting myself slip away and follow the natural course laid out for me, for whatever is to come next.

The whole world is always searching for answers as to what comes after death, and now, I will get to find out. The universe's most sought-after secret will soon be unveiled. And once again, there's no one for me to share this with, unless she is waiting for me on the other side.

I slip through the upper layers of the atmosphere, too quickly to enjoy the view. We always dream of flying, of what it would be like to be a bird, and now, when the powers have given me that gift, it has to go so fast. Too fast. Like life. Here one day, gone the next. A child one day; an adult the next. From freedom to the chains of responsibility, tightly tethered around the cords that keep your heart beating.

And even when you know your death is coming, even when you know exactly the hour, the minute, the precise second you will be taking your last breath, nothing will ever prepare you for what's to come.

My journey has come to an end. I look around. There are no pearly gates, no angels singing, no signs of a golden road to take me home. I am completely alone, a conscious entity that belongs to nothing.

She should be here. I should feel her. Surely she'll come for me. After all, she knows I'm here for her.

"Trudy?" I call into the void.

My eyes trace the expanse, looking for a slight shimmer to let me know she is here. Maybe she moves more slowly than I do, or maybe she's hiding in the corners, waiting for me to get adjusted before she comes to me.

I settle in. I can't feel any wind. The small pieces of myself that were loosely tied together and slowly fading away don't feel pulled by gravity. But the more I sit and wait, the more my old self fades away, the more I realize time is not on my side.

I need to slow things down, but the more I try, the more I slowly roll away. And each piece that slips off is impossible to get back. I can't seem to chase the embers of my life, can't pull the ribbons of myself back.

As pieces of me leave, I wonder if I should simply follow them, in case I don't like what happens when all of me is gone.

"Trudy?" I call again into the void. "Are you here?"

She's not.

I'll just stay right here and wait, then. She'll come. I know she'll come.

CHAPTER THIRTY-FOUR

The Aftermath

The house was a mess. Blood splattered on the kitchen window, the sink, and the steak that I should have at least let Trudy get into the oven before I took my revenge. I didn't even want to look in the living room. Perhaps I was a bit too harsh on Christopher. The kid was so clueless that I could have killed Trudy and slipped out before he'd even bothered to move his lazy ass.

I could have set him up to take the fall easier than James. With James, I really had to find a way to play up his love for Trudy and his reputation in the town. I'd have to do some acting and hope everyone continued to put their blind faith in me. After all, they'd done it multiple times before when I needed to move people out of my way. I could count at least seven people off the top of my head who were sitting in a cell right now, to cover some my tracks. People who got too close to some of my inner secrets and business deals. We couldn't live our life on the modest salary of a small-town sheriff, and those who realized this would have to be dealt with by whatever means necessary. Whether that meant a trail of disappearances or a bag of my prized products dropped into their glove box during a smartly timed traffic stop, I was unstoppable.

A strained breath came from the living room, raspy and struggling.

"Dammit," I said, sighing.

We couldn't have any loose ends. That kid never had an ounce of fight in him, and I found it hard to believe that today would be any different. I'd smacked him pretty hard. That fireplace poker wasn't light, either.

My feet dragged over the carpet that I'd have to replace once the crime scene was cleared. Thankfully I didn't give in to Trudy's constant bitching about updating my home. She had some nerve, acting like she had a say in my house or a right to tell me how to spend my money. Of course, now I'd be forced to do so or live with the remnants of them for the rest of my time here. I suppose she was allowed to have one final "Fuck you" given that I'd just slaughtered her in the very kitchen she hated.

The fireplace poker was perilously perched by my favorite chair. How careless of me. I didn't want to get blood on something irreplaceable, especially not blood from that worthless waste of flesh. I couldn't help but drag the poker down the brick surrounding the fireplace as my head filled with all the ways Christopher had been so ungrateful for the blessings we'd given him. No. The blessings I'd given him.

I sat against the hard brick, looking at him struggle. It was impossible not to smile, watching the bubbles slip from his lips through the heavy red liquid seeping from his skull. Maybe he had more fight in him than either of us realized. But he had to die. There could be no loose ends, no survivors. Only death and closure.

I lifted his eyelid with my thumb. It felt like I was peering deep inside of his soul, suckling on the teat of his recognition that tonight, he'd made a fatal mistake. The fear settling over his eyes filled me with a level of satisfaction I'd never felt before. Sick. Deep. Perfect. I wanted to know what was going through his head, if he recognized me, and if he realized he was slowly taking his last breaths. I wondered if he'd fight back if I pushed his head ever so slightly into the remnants of his life seeping into the couch.

I couldn't risk leaving a mark, though. And I couldn't waste any more time. There was a crime scene to stage, and worst of all, I had absolutely no idea where James was. I had watched them together at the diner, and I'd seen Trudy leave in an animated huff, which unbeknownst to her made my plans easier. That angry meal had ended a little over three hours before. Stupidly, I hadn't tailed him. I was too excited about how every- thing was finally falling into place.

The first step was to put myself anywhere else. I had to be seen, and the most logical place was the station. I walked through, said hello to a few people, and excused myself to go to my office.

There had been a recent influx of meth in town, creating concern that a new dealer had moved to our area. With my stellar record of controlling sudden rises in drug sales, my team would expect me to be hard at work once I'd locked my door and closed my blinds. They'd never remember that I had a back exit, and wouldn't consider that I'd leave my squad car parked out front to make sure the GPS registered I was still there. I'd return as soon as the scene was set, walk right back out the front of the office, and head back home to discover my poor dead wife and stepson.

And now, with one officially dead body and one almost-dead body, there were just a few more pieces to fix.

Trudy thought I wouldn't notice when she took a pair of sneakers from my closet. I always knew exactly what I had at all times. And this would also work in my favor. He'd be on camera wearing those shoes, in multiple locations. I just so happened to have six pairs, because they'd been on sale and I love them.

The clothing James was wearing was in a bag on top of the washing machine. I could smell it from here. Layers of dirt, sweat, and God knows what else tightly soaked into the fabric. The original plan was to wear them in order to get authentic splatter patterns, but I couldn't bear the thought of putting those clothes near my body. I'd have to fake it, but as a trained professional, I could do this well. And leaving them in the bathroom would make sense. All I'd have to say during the investigation is that after cleaning up at the truck stop, he'd had the impulse to take another shower. He obviously didn't want to get his new clothes dirty, and he couldn't stand the sight of his true love's blood on him. After taking a shower, the guilt would be too much and he wouldn't be thinking clearly, in need of another hit. I knew James didn't do drugs, but I'd made the whole town believe he did, and I'd use that to my advantage once again.

Christopher's decision to fight and die slowly would also work to my advantage. The autopsy would show he didn't die from the head wound but from suffocating in his own blood. Investigators would conclude that James couldn't stand the thought of killing his son and had had second thoughts, stopping before he'd completely obliterated the poor kid's skull.

Finally, I'd change my shoes, putting the blood-covered ones carefully in the trash can by the station, taking another pair of my favorite sneakers out of the closet. It had to look like he knew Trudy gave him a pair of my shoes. Of course, since we were childhood friends, he knew my shopping habits. He'd have known that my closet would have multiple pairs in the exact same color and style, just waiting to be unboxed.

For once being a creature of habit would work to my advantage.

I looked back to Christopher, watching the life drain from his eyes. The color was slowly slipping from every inch of his body. He didn't have much time left.

"Sorry, buddy," I said, stroking the hair near the nape of his neck. "You kinda asked for this, though. Couldn't keep your nose out of other people's business. You had to learn the lesson eventually. When you ask for the downfall of other people, you have to be careful not to order your own. But you're just a child. You didn't know any better."

I sighed, looking at his features that continued to grow in a way that mocked my own.

Any feeling of guilt was pushed out immediately. He had a life that he chose not to utilize. I was never a fan of wasted opportunities or potential. People who chose to squander their gifts did not deserve sympathy or apologies. They deserved the cold hard truth, even if that came courtesy of a hard blow to the head.

Time was wasting. I was extremely close to staging the perfect crime scene and I couldn't be sloppy now. Emotions led to mistakes.

I looked at the dark gardening gloves covering my hands. These would have to go, but I wasn't sure where yet. I knew no one would check my squad car. I could tuck them in the spare-tire well and pull them out later after everything had blown over. Getting rid of them right now would be too dangerous, even if I was able to control the crime scene.

I'd do my best to convince my team I wasn't too emotionally distracted, and would mention any instance of incompetence they'd displayed to play off their insecurities. After all, we live in a small town. Murders aren't common. When I tell them they wouldn't be able to handle this, I won't be lying. They're too conditioned to being submissive to fight back and insist they could.

Everything I'd been doing for years had been meticulous and precise, waiting for just the perfect moment. Today was that day.

"Good-bye, Christopher. I hope you'll be more focused in your next life." I leaned down next to his ear. "Oh, and I win," I whispered. A shiver of joy rocked my body as I watched his muscles clench in response. He hated that phrase.

I tried to hide my smile when I walked out of the precinct. I had to look normal. Slightly tired, a heavy case on my mind, and concern for my city. I had to tell the right people to have a good night. No one noticed anything off or felt I was being weird. I was typically pretty reserved and uninterested in the bullshit of other people's inconsequential lives.

As I walked out the front door, I made sure to make eye contact with Sheila. This was a crucial move. I knew she wouldn't forget me being there, or the time I left, because she'd check the clock before excusing herself for a fifteen-minute break.

Sheila knew all of my secrets—the years of affairs, the girls who would come in to "file a report," which meant paying off a ticket in my office, behind closed doors. Secretly, I think she liked it, finding excitement and pleasure in knowing something no one else did. I also knew she wanted to be one of the girls draped over my desk.

I stumbled a little as I left the building from the copious amounts of scotch I'd downed in my office, to calm my nerves, but that was also par for the course. Whenever I was knee-deep in a difficult case, I had been known to tip back a few. There'd be some concerned looks, but no one would follow me, and of course I wouldn't be pulled over.

I slid into my squad car and fingered the worn leather of my steering wheel. When the key turned over, I immediately shut off the radio chatter. Silence was needed.

Time to think was going to be invaluable. I had to start focusing on what a police officer would do and what a grieving husband would do. Somehow I had to separate the two until the time came for me to switch roles.

All I had to do was go home. Slowly. Normally.

My adrenaline was pumping and I wanted to race over the route I knew so well, throw open the front door, and look at my masterpiece. Temptation was high; probably the worst I'd ever felt. The heart palpitations alone were unbearable. I'd felt this flutter of excitement before. This wasn't the first body I'd put in the ground, but the energy coursing through me today was a high no drug had ever given me.

It was dangerous. And I loved every second.

My cell phone rang, the vibrations rattling my already racing heart. The screen said it was the station. I turned my radio back on to hear the call.

My nosy neighbor had called in a report of suspicious behavior at my house. While laying milk out for her cat, she'd seen a man going through the garbage, dressed in dark clothes, a hood pulled tight over his head, and after driving around town, she'd noticed that James wasn't in his usual spot.

I laughed. This couldn't get any better.

I picked up the radio and called back that I was heading over immediately.

A huge smile hit my face as I flicked on the lights and raced toward my house.

And when I pulled in, running over Trudy's haphazard attempt at gardening, I smiled even wider. I hated yellow, and I already knew I wouldn't have to answer to her moaning and complaining about me ruining her hard work.

CHAPTER THIRTY-FIVE

Ava

With the utterance of those final words, "I won," I felt every previous seed of doubt I'd long since swallowed resurface. I knew what those two single syllables meant, but it wasn't until I'd seen Denny's reaction that I finally let myself embrace the truth.

I think deep down we all knew. And once we all realized that we'd been fools, what was there for us to do? We were all together in that gallery, staring at the dead body of an innocent man. Every single person glued to their chairs, shaken to the very core of their beings, had to accept that they had been willing to accept James's fate as the price to pay for the crimes we all swore he had committed. All the while, walking among us in plain sight, was the real monster, the one who'd laughed at us for years as we continued to fool ourselves.

Today was supposed to be closure. Today was supposed to give me peace and open up my future. Instead, I was left with more questions. I knew the coming days would be filled with people calling for interviews, asking their own questions, and no doubt, once again leaving hateful messages, calling me the devil's spawn.

They didn't have to tell me this; I already knew. I already felt it deep in my soul. The urges. The hatred. The anger. It was only now that I fully understood. I hadn't imagined the impulses I'd always hidden. I was born with them.

And now I knew I'd have to spend the rest of my life taming them. I was already prepared for a lifetime of therapy, but with these genetics, with murderous blood running through my veins, seeking help was no longer an option.

If only there was a support group for children of murderers who felt like they were destined to go down the same path, and by admitting this, wouldn't get locked away from society. Every word I uttered from here on out, every single action, would have to be calculated and planned. My outward appearance was now more important than ever.

Denny had just royally fucked my life in more ways than he could ever know. I would never tell him, because I refused to give him the satisfaction. He'd relish it, bathe in it, feed off it. He'd use that knowledge any chance he could. He knew the power of subtle manipulation and would love the chance to explore it further. Give him an inch, he'd take twenty miles, and he'd make you feel like shit for letting him get away with it.

That dark glimmer in his eyes when he tried not to smile—I knew it well. I saw it in my own reflection all the time.

We all knew Denny would never go away, and because of this, we'd never be able to move past what we'd all done to James. The sins we'd all committed were deep and would fascinate experts for years to come.

There'd be made-for-TV movies and streaming mini-series to investigate how this small town had gotten it so wrong, how we'd been blinded by one of our own authority figures. And then of course there'd be the plethora of Internet videos and podcasts from people who considered themselves junior sleuths.

If only this had happened twenty years ago, before the Internet. When I could have simply moved to a new town, changed my name, cut my hair, and found peace behind a nose job. But now, my picture would live on in infamy, unless I could convince someone to give me a complete face transplant.

I looked at Christopher. He was shaking, his body a wave of emotions his injured brain couldn't fully process. I smiled as I wondered whether he'd pissed himself yet. Even when I tried to be nice to him, I always found it humorous that this kid who'd been such a jerk to me his whole life—always power-tripping and knowing he was the favorite, which didn't say much—was now a helpless peon who only recently learned how to wipe his own ass again.

I made a mental note to start looking for facilities where he could live, and to fight for a clause when we sold our story to ensure that a percentage of the royalties would go to that expense. It sure as hell wouldn't be coming out of my pocket. His decision to stay and raise hell was his own choice. His injuries were not my cross to bear.

But as the shaking became more violent and he struggled to breathe through his sobs, I couldn't help but feel a little guilty. He was my flesh and blood—my only remaining family. What he'd gone through was miles beyond what I'd been forced to deal with, tucked away in the safety of my dorm room. When I'd found out what he'd endured, I realized I was happy, overwhelmed with relief that I'd been smart enough to leave.

When he had fits like this, I'd wonder if his struggles to breathe made him feel like he was once again drowning in his own blood, or if he exaggerated these episodes in an effort to not allow anyone to forget.

I looked around, fearful that everyone could read my mind. But no, they were too concerned with what was unfolding with Denny to pay any attention to me.

If only they could see inside my head, hear my thoughts and realize how much like my father I truly was, they'd lock me away as well. But I'd never let them see that side of me. They would never know I was his seed, through and through.

Because if they did, they'd know how happy I was when my mother died. She was finally out of my life for good. I would never have to feel a hint of guilt for hitting cancel on her incoming phone calls. They'd see how relieved I felt when her casket was placed six feet in the ground.

On the day of her funeral, a few people had commented on how I hadn't cried a single tear during the entire service. I told them I was still in shock, overwhelmed by studying for my GRE, watching over my brother's recovery, keeping Denny together, trying to understand my feelings for my father, and planning a funeral because no one else was capable. I told them I hadn't had time to process my grief yet, as I'd been focused on being strong for everyone else. When I had some time to myself, I would find my own way to cope.

They gave me hugs and said they understood, not knowing that when we were chest to chest, I was rolling my eyes behind closed lids and wishing they'd hurry up and move down the line, out of my personal space.

Because our house was still an active crime scene at the time, and would be for months—which I now understood was because Denny had been busy stacking the scene against James—we couldn't hold the traditional post-funeral meal at our house. Instead, we all piled together in a caravan of cars and headed down to the nearest buffet restaurant, where we reminisced and traded stories that were supposed to make us feel good about the days when we'd all loved Trudy and had her with us.

Only I noticed that those who came didn't really know Trudy—or anyone else, for that matter. Their stories all felt forced, like they had to ad-lib the interesting parts to make her feel more endearing. When you listened carefully, it was obvious that most people in the room only wanted to talk about James. They just didn't know how to bring him up.

Then Betty spoke. She was nothing more than a diner waitress, someone who'd met the toxic trio a few times in passing and relied on the stories and memories of others to create her own mental pictures and assumptions about my family. When she talked about meeting them for the first time, James's name slipped out of her lips like hard candy, sweet but shattered, shards of deliciousness waiting to rip into your tongue and make you taste your own blood.

Everyone felt they had the right to share their thoughts about what happened—why James had snapped, Mom's faults, Denny's undying love—revealing themselves as the conniving, drama-seeking parasites they were. I looked at faces that should have been familiar: aunts, uncles, cousins, people claiming to be childhood best friends and coworkers. So many memories thrown out there, webs of lies meant to entrap others into spinning their own.

Eventually the weight of their lies broke my silence. A heavy laugh slipped out and everyone stopped talking, turning to judge me with their newfound powers of righteousness. Some wore looks of shock, others, horror; some had a mixture of morbid curiosity and satisfaction on their faces. I was bound to break eventually, they were thinking.

But like the warrior I am, I didn't allow the crack to spread. There would be no emotional earthquake, no shaking devastation of words spit out to strike people in the heart and make them crumble. I regained my strength and focus, remaining silent, with only my eyes piercing the hearts of those around me.

Right now, in this gallery, I didn't have any thoughts about James. Only myself. And now I had to process the reality that at some point, we would be burying Denny as well.

He might as well have been a cold dead corpse already, he was so removed from my life. Whereas minutes ago I'd been worrying about how to dodge him in the future, to avoid having to take responsibility for my brother, I now felt the relief of potential solitude. For once in my life I'd only have to worry about myself.

I only had to look at Christopher again to realize I still had one more obstacle to overcome.

CHAPTER THIRTY-SIX

Dear Ava

My Dearest Ava:

Sitting down to write you this letter is hard. It's tearing my heart apart. I wish for nothing more than the chance to talk to you face-to-face, to look you in the eyes so you could feel my every desire for your upcoming life. I believe you can do anything, be anything, and conquer any mountain. And I want you to know that from the bottom of my soul, I have always loved you. I will always love you. You are my daughter.

I know your mother's death hurts you even though you try so hard to hide your feelings. I know my role in her murder doesn't make sense, but I also respect the fact that I can't tell you how to process her death. I can't tell you how to handle your emotions, and I can't force you—or even ask you—to think of me in any certain way given what you know from the court proceedings, the trial, and my time in jail.

My darling Ava, there are some things I want you to know. I don't want you to feel manipulated or think that I have any ulterior motives for writing you this letter tonight, on the night before my death. It could be construed that I'm writing to you solely to clear my final thoughts so I can die in peace. If so, I apologize.

First, I need you to know that I loved your mother dearly. I loved her from the moment I first saw her in kindergarten. She was a feisty one. The Trudy you knew had had her light extinguished long before she was given an opportunity to show you and Christopher what made her special.

I truly wish you could have met the girl who spent every single day at recess trying to be the first student to successfully swing over the top bar of the swing set. I always thought she'd do it. No one was more determined to be successful than she was; no one. I only wish she could have kept that fight inside her as the years passed.

I see this part of your mother in you every day, and without a doubt, I adore this side of you. For some reason, it's the side you try to fight against. Once you learn to embrace your stubborn will to rule the world, you may find that some of the barricades you put in your own way will disappear. Ava, maybe I'm overstepping my boundaries, but I hope that one day you will understand how truly powerful and capable you are, if for no other reason than to avoid the destructive path your mother took, giving up on everything that made her great out of fear.

Second, I need you to know that I feel responsible for her decline. I should have spoken up. Loved her more. Fought for her more. Encouraged her to fight for herself. I should have held her hand and shown her that she wasn't dependent on me . . . or him. If I'd been half the man she deserved, I would have spent every day showing her she was capable of doing and being anything she could dream of in this wonderful world.

Instead, I failed her. I spent every day trying to give her everything she wanted, even though I knew that wasn't the life she wanted. I knew presents and possessions weren't what brought her satisfaction. I only wanted her to be happy, and it wasn't until she was gone that I saw all of my errors. Please forgive me for this, because I know it will help you to embrace the parts of your mother's spirit you carry so deeply within you.

And please, for no one other than yourself, keep your spunky fighting spirit, and never let anyone take it away from you. No man. No woman. Whomever you choose to love, let them love you for every inch of who you are, to the point where they understand why you breathe.

Next, my dear Ava, I want you to know that I loved you, too. As I write this, I still love you, even though you detest me. I understand. I took your mother away from you, but not in the way you think. Maybe one day the truth will come out. Setting the truth free isn't up to me. My participation in your mother's death is just as important as the role played by the person who took her life.

Regardless, I need you to know that I loved you. From the moment you were conceived and we made the choice to start our life together, you were mine. You've always been mine. No piece of paper could make you family or take you away.

When you think of me, if you ever think of me, please do not torture yourself thinking of the man you saw on my last day. Maybe it's presumptuous of me to think you'll be coming tomorrow, to watch me splayed out and helpless. I know that won't bring you joy, because that's not who you are.

If you do come, I know it will be because you think there will be peace hidden somewhere in what you're about to witness. But please, do not think of me for the rest of your life as that weak and feeble man who allowed himself to go quietly, without a fight. Think of the happier times, when we would spin around the yard in circles. Think of the autumn days when we'd rake leaves and play hide-and-seek for hours in those towering piles of red, gold, and burnt-orange maple leaves. Think of the road trips where I'd pretend to fight with you over which radio station we'd listen to. I'd always give in, and you always thought you'd won the battle. I wanted to teach you to fight for what you wanted, and to believe in yourself. And you never disappointed me.

Remember me that way, Ava. I know it's a lot to ask, and I know I can't force you to do anything. But for the sake of your heart, please remember me that way.

If I'm honest, I truly hope you won't be coming to see me die. This will be a piece of our history that you'll never be able to forget, a haunting memory to define the end of our relationship. That's a heavy cross for you to carry for the rest of your life. I can tell you from experience that when you see the way someone dies, when you see them without life, that image stays with you. It haunts you. You don't deserve to be haunted. Our family has been haunted enough for one lifetime.

Finally, Ava, I want you to know that I didn't do it. I was not the person who murdered your mother that night. Deep down, I think you already know this. I could never hurt Trudy. She was my everything, my own twisted reason to live.

You may be asking why I didn't fight harder to prove my innocence if I loved all of you so much, and that's a valid question. There's no excuse for why I didn't fight harder, even though we both know the outcome wouldn't have changed. Would you have forgiven me more easily if I'd fought harder, or would that have made the last few years even more difficult?

The truth is, there's always a battle between light and dark, good and evil, in everything we do. Sometimes the light can't fight the oncoming shadows.

I wish I could tell you more, to answer all of your questions, but I simply don't know what you need. I don't know if you'll ever be able to find the truth. We may have to wait for Christopher to come out of his shell, to finally start to remember.

I know what happened in my world the night Trudy was taken from us, the night Christopher's world changed forever. Many nights I've tried to place myself in the house, at the scene of the crime, to try and convince myself I might have blacked out—that I could have killed her. But no matter how mad I was, how frustrated, how betrayed—no matter how many times I had dark thoughts—I never could have hurt any of you.

I have my theories, of course, but theories are just unproven thoughts, and I don't see the sense in fanning the flames without certainty. Not now. The world blames me, and I'm okay with that on my conscience. Truly, I am willing to go because I can't fathom being in this world without her, and I'm hoping she will be waiting for me on the other side.

Maybe the truth will come out one day, and I hope for your sake that it does. I hope it will set you free.

As for now, the only truth I can offer you is that you are unequivocally loved. Even after I'm gone, I will still love you.

Please keep an open heart for your brother. He needs you more than he'll admit, and I know you'll fight me on this, but you need him more than you'll admit, too. All you have now is each other, and the sooner you realize this, the better. Please, Ava. You'll have to make the effort first, but in the long run, it will be worthwhile.

Take care of yourself, and stay on your path.

You deserve the world.

With love,
James Jackson

CHAPTER THIRTY-SEVEN
Christopher

My veins, flooded with anger and frustration, caused my body to shake and betray me to everyone in the room. There was no way to hide the outpouring of emotions that started the moment I smelled Denny's cologne. I was taken back to that night on the couch when his deep, soulless eyes peered into mine as I inhaled the blood seeping out of my skull. If only that memory would have clarified itself sooner, we might have been witnessing a very different outcome.

But it didn't. And that was a burden I would have to hoist upon my now uneven shoulders, forever crooked from the weight of my limp, for the rest of my life. Was it my anger at James that kept Denny's face from my memories? Was it my fear of the truth? Or did I secretly, somewhere deep down in the many layers of my hidden mind, want to rid my life of both of them?

Thoughts barreled through the tracks of my mind, skipping signals to stop and crossing dangerous intersections at rapid pace. When I'd walked into this room, I thought the future was clear. James would die. Ava and I would say good-bye to each other, both of us knowing there was no future where we'd be close, and that our lives would be better that way. I'd go back to Denny's house for just a few more weeks, and like I planned to originally, sneak out with the few bags I could take and head on to my future.

The goal has always been to leave, and I've been saving to that end, spending with caution. The money from Mom's life insurance went into a private savings account that I opened behind Denny's back. Ava said she didn't want a dime, and we both agreed he shouldn't get any. He wasn't on the policy, after all, and we wouldn't allow ourselves to be bullied into turning anything over. This was the one time we actually found ourselves agreeing on something without a fight, except when it came to urging her to take her share. But when she insisted she didn't want any ties to the bad juju Mom carried around, I decided a couple hundred thousand was worth some bad juju for me. I'd had enough for a lifetime, after all.

Now, with my bank account padded and James dead, I should be on my way. I'd been accepted on a scholarship for adult students to a small college in Florida. The warm weather would keep my bones from hurting and the beautiful girls strolling along wearing little to nothing would keep my heart from hurting. I even thought about changing my name, to allow myself to step out of my history. But I could never hide my scars or my limp or my panic attacks.

Although now that I've recognized the truth, maybe I would finally be able to quiet my episodes and step into a life of peace. I hoped for the sake of my future self that I could.

This was my life. One that's thrown me curveballs and hated me as much as I've hated it in return. A life that would always attach a sinker to my dreams and rip the line when I bite hard enough for the bobber to dip below the surface of the water. Freedom was not for me.

I couldn't help but feel like I'd be tied here now, with this new revelation. There'd be another trial. More subpoenas. More interviews. Just when things had settled down and I'd come to accept what was to be, everything had flipped.

As much as I didn't want to cry and waste away in silent screams of "Poor me," I couldn't help but wonder if that was the case.

The room was a blur as the pounding stopped and my shaking subsided. I could barely focus as Denny was cuffed and led away. The sounds of shock and disbelief mixed into a wild and unpredictable orchestra of horror.

"Stay strong," I whispered, trying to keep myself from going over the edge into another attack. "You can get through this. You can get through anything."

A soft hand settled on my shoulder. For a second I thought it might be Ava, coming to comfort me. But of course it wasn't. She was too preoccupied in her own thoughts, lost in her own world. Her eyes were locked straight ahead. They looked dead. Her mouth was twisted in a weird grin. For the first time in our life together, she scared me. And for the first time in my life, I knew I had to be alone. After this, neither of us would ever be the same. Based on the twisted glee spreading over her face, if I wanted to be safe, we needed to be apart.

This should be easy. We were never close to begin with, and she's never been a big part of my life.

The soft velvety hairs on my neck tickled. The person who'd placed a soft hand on my shoulder was whispering, "You can get through anything, Christopher. You are strong. Just breathe."

I looked up to see the blonde reporter from one of those national talk shows. On television she looks regal, beautiful, impeccable. Here she looked like her face was hidden under twenty layers of chipping stucco and sun-faded paint. The powdery fragrance she had poured over her body was overwhelming. The scent even seemed to flow off her tongue with each syllable she pushed out. Flakes of bright pink clung to her lips. Her eyelashes looked like spider legs, clinging to her face because they had nowhere better to go and were terrified of the web woven on top of her head.

Television cameras and lighting do wondrous things for people, I thought to myself.

Looking into her eyes, possibly the only natural part of her face, I saw genuine sympathy, something I wasn't used to experiencing.

"Thank you," I replied. "I'll keep trying."

"Great. So, Christopher, listen. I know it's really crazy right now, but it would be really great if we could get an exclusive with you. Ava, too. That'd be really great. I'd love to get you on camera to share your thoughts and tell your side of the story. What do you say about tomorrow morning, say eight a.m. at the Park Central Hotel?"

I sat in my chair, numb.

"Excuse me?" I stuttered, hoping I'd misheard her and she was back to being the comforting and caring creature who just wanted me to breathe and get better.

"Yes, honey. You can trust me. The other reporters aren't going to take care of your story like I will. I just want to get the truth out so the world can get to know you." She paused and took a deep breath, slightly pinching her eyebrows together in an effort to look concerned. I watched the makeup in between settle into the creases and start to crack like dry desert ground. "You've been through so much and you're so strong, Christopher. It's your time now."

I tried to speak but couldn't. My brain proved to be useless as I stared in complete and utter shock at the monster before me.

"Trust me, Christopher. This is the best move you could make."

"No," I gasped. "No, it's not. You can't even wait for my father's body to be wheeled out of the chamber before you come to me? What is wrong with you?"

My voice started to rise. I had to be careful to keep my heart rate down, to not get too excited so I didn't have a seizure before I said everything I needed to say to this wench.

"How dare you. You slide up to me like you care, trying to act like you're sympathetic, but you just want to make a circus out of me. You know what?" I pushed to my feet, firmly grabbing the top of my walking cane and resisting the urge building inside of me to slam it over her head. "Fuck. You." I took a deep breath as the excitement threatened to topple me over. "Fuck you. No. You won't get my story. You won't ever talk to us, you low-level bloodsucking leech. How dare you. When I do give my story out, if I ever do, I will memorialize this moment in every single interview to make sure everyone knows what a heartless bitch you are."

I looked over to Ava. She was still staring into the chamber at James's dead body. She was so deep in whatever evil thoughts were behind that menacing look that she hadn't heard a single word of what had just happened.

Let the press talk to her. Let her be their whipping boy. This was my time to go. I wanted nothing to do with telling the sob story of my life.

Turning to stumble my way out of the gallery, I didn't look back. I would never look back. I was going to get my bags and I was going to leave this town. Tonight.

CHAPTER THIRTY-EIGHT
Dear Christopher

Dear Christopher:

I'm going to try to write this letter again, but I'm finding it difficult. I don't know why the words just won't come when they are so heavily weighted against my heart. To be honest, this is the eighth time I've tried to start your letter, and it probably won't be the last. At this point, I'm afraid if I keep throwing away the letters, I'll be throwing away my final opportunity to reach out to you.

Oddly, Ava's letter came so much easier. She's always been so hard-headed and such a fighter, I thought I'd have to be much more careful, but the words just flowed. When it comes to yours, I just don't know where to start.

How do I begin to tell you how sorry I am?

I read the transcript of your testimony. Maybe the pain I'm holding on to from what you said is the reason why I can't get this letter started.

In fairness, I understand. Believe me, I do. You went through a harrowing night, experienced something beyond imagination. Deep in your heart you believe that your own father was the one who hurt you. The fog of your memories tells you that I murdered your mother and left you for dead. Christopher, I can't tell you how much this pains me, but I have to accept this until the truth comes out.

I'm thankful I wasn't in the courtroom when you spoke. I probably would have been charged with contempt, like the judge had threatened before I blacked out. Had I been there, I would have yelled louder. I would have begged you to try and rethink what you were saying, what you thought you saw. Maybe I would have fought harder for my rights, for my life, for a clean and honest trial. A trial that wasn't influenced by a town that hated me, without any insight into my situation.

But that's neither here nor there. What I'm putting down here is exactly what's led me to wad up the previous letters and throw them in the trash. I only have so many pieces of paper left, however, and I need to get something to you.

If I had just one wish for you, it's that your life will change and you will no longer be a prisoner of your situation. What has been brought down upon you is not your fault. I know all about survivor's guilt. I watched it destroy your mother and influence Denny's future. I sat with the pain heavily on my heart for years in front of that café.

I know the burden you carry is heavier than the ones we held, but still, I don't want you to follow in our footsteps. We let our lives be run by the actions of others, by the choices of others, and we never fought back and claimed our own truth.

I know releasing your guilt and moving forward will be a challenge, but it's one I pray for, and I'm not a praying man. God and I gave up on each other a long time ago. When I reach the end tomorrow, I will be greeted by one of two people: your mother, or the Devil himself.

But you, Christopher, you have years ahead of you and miles to go before you sleep. There's no reason to continue to invite sadness and remorse to burrow deep into your veins, building nests of grief. Please find your release. I know you are strong enough to do so.

Seeing you struggle has not been easy. You deserved so much more on this Earth. Watching you walk into school with your head low, your shoulders slumped, I couldn't help but feel responsible. If I had been a better father, taken better care of your mother, understood how to love her so that she'd love me in return, I could have kept you.

I would have taught you how to rise up, to stand tall, to be proud of who you are. I would have embraced your quirks and found your passions, helping you to embrace what makes you unique and a force in this world. Instead, I backed away too easily and let the world take your potential from you. I blame myself for every single struggle you've had to endure, long before the events that led us to where we are tonight.

You deserved more from me. As your father, I need you to know that I recognize this, and I ask for your forgiveness. I hope you'll give it to me. Not today, but someday.

I've never been a fighter, Christopher. I've always known what I wanted, but I always let people take it from me. I don't want this for you. It's a difficult path to walk, one where you look around every single day and focus on your faults instead of your greatness. There is so much greatness inside of you, and I know that no one has ever told you that.

If you don't believe me, just look in the mirror. Right now. Go to one and look at yourself. You are still here, Christopher. You fought to keep breathing. You fought to wake up. You fought like hell after the accident, fueled by the dwindling sparks of your soul to live another day.

But you don't see that. You focus on a drooping lip or a bum leg, or a little slur, or a scar on the side of your head. Those are signs of strength placed onto your body to make you see that you are not meant to give up. They aren't ugly. They are beautiful, and they let everyone know you are special; you are a fighter.

There will come a day where you step up and reclaim your life. I'm certain of this because I know you better than you think I do. You can still hate me—you will still hate me—but don't stop pursuing your best life because of the anger you carry toward me. Don't let your frustration with the choices others made keep you from being the best you can be. You've been held down too long, looked over for too long, abandoned and cast aside.

But this is your time. Fuck them, fuck us, fuck the world. All you need is yourself, and hopefully, you'll give Ava another chance as well. She loves you, and you'll need each other. There's something special in the ties of family, something that makes you two unique to each other, even if it's hard work to figure it out. Don't let that go because you don't understand it right now. Rome wasn't built in a day.

I know it's probably frustrating for you when I call it the accident. Truthfully, I don't know what to call it. Your attempted murder? The injury? When I talk about that night, I shake with anger and deep rage because I'm mad at myself. And I know you're mad at me, too, because I should have helped you that day. When I looked in the front window and saw your feet hanging over the end of the couch, I should have known you weren't okay. I am your father, and I should have had the instinct that something wasn't right. But I didn't. And I left.

That guilt is set deep in my heart. I think about it daily. If I had simply come inside, could I have saved your mother? Could I have lessened your injuries? Could I have caught the real killer? Could I have saved my own life and gotten myself together, recognizing I'd been given a second chance?

But that was always my problem, Chris. I never recognized the gifts that were given to me from the universe. I thought the bus ticket was my gift, but Trudy leaving her credit card, driving me back to you two, was my purpose.

I get scared when I think about what was happening when I was ringing that bell. Was your mother already dead? If I'd walked in then, could I have stopped her murder? I didn't enter the house, and my fate was sealed by my cowardice. I imagine if I had persisted, knocked down the door, burst inside, I would have been in more trouble than I already am. Or maybe that's my own self-doubt talking, because like you, I'm afraid to embrace my greatness. You remind me so much of myself. If I can give you one piece of advice, it's this: Don't turn into me.

When the day comes that your memory clears up, when the time comes and you see that day a little more clearly and the faces are no longer blurred, know that I still love you. I'm not mad. I don't blame you. And most of all, I don't hold anything against you. Our minds do funny things under stress, or when confronted with things we don't want to face.

I understand. And I love you. I always have. I always will.

Until we meet again,
Your father

CHAPTER THIRTY-NINE

Denny

The walls feel like they're closing in, choking me, snuffing out the remainder of the days I have left.

I wonder how James remained so calm, so at peace while locked away. I've asked if this was his cell, but they won't tell me. They tell me I'm sick . . . obsessive . . . other choice words. But they're wrong.

I feel him. He comes in at night and sits on the edge of my bed. I feel him looking at me, wanting to ask questions, but the void between us won't allow it. I can't help but hope that he'll find a way to get his revenge and take me out of this world to be with him. But I don't have the same kind of soul that he had. I know we wouldn't end up in the same place.

Days pass at a snail's pace, a repetitive pattern of sleep, shower, shit, sulk. I'm not allowed too much free time, and I'm under guard at all times. After all, I've put quite a few of the inmates here, often with broken bones and bloody noses. I knew when they put me in here that I might not make it to the end of my sentence.

It took a while for the media circus surrounding my case to die down, for the powers that be to decide the proper way to honor James, to compensate the children, and to restructure our department once they'd finished investigating all of my old case files. I know bounties have been placed on my head, and I welcome it. The challenge will make the final days of my jail term interesting at the very least. Gives me a reason to fight, to release some of my aggression, to feel pain and remind myself that I'm human.

The children never visit. I didn't expect them to, but at the very least, seeing their faces might have helped me connect to whatever shards of humanity remain in my soul. With each day that passes, that sliver of humanity slowly shatters more and more until the monster within becomes even hungrier. I've spent my life feeding my impulses under the protection of a badge, and I'll spend eternity feeding my impulses under the watch of another.

Truthfully, I never expected Ava to come. She wouldn't know a blessing or a helping hand if it smacked her over the face. And I'd tried. Many times.

But Christopher; his absence stung a little. No one else was there for him or offered to take him home from the hospital. I even wiped his ass when he was relearning how to be an adult and not a helpless child.

Some might say this was the guilt, but I had none. He should be thankful I showed some restraint. I could have killed him. I thought I had. But I knew if I smashed him too much, they'd never believe James was the culprit. The scene had to be believable, and everyone knew James loved the kids too much to destroy them.

With Trudy, on the other hand, he had a little more leeway. She had manipulated and mentally abused James for years. Wore him down. Tore him to pieces. He would have had deep feelings of revenge against her. There could be a struggle. There could be pain. There could be suffering.

The look of shock on her face when she saw me in the window quickly changed to recognition of what was to come, and I loved every second. She didn't fight, and I knew that would help me to frame James. All I had to say was the lack of a struggle showed she knew her killer and expected what was coming. She was depressed and suicidal, after all, and felt this was her time to go. She welcomed her death at the killer's hands, which wasn't a lie. And this helped convict James. The restraint I showed while taking her life was truly a challenge, almost unprecedented, and worked in my favor, as I'd planned.

I sink down on the hard mattress, feeling the metal links bend and groan in protest. My body is reacting well to the extra attention. The soft roll that was blossoming around my midsection is now gone, the skin instead holding tight over the growing definition. My biceps and triceps have quickly rebounded, showing that I'm a threat. While not exactly the shining return to my glory days, the reshaping of my body makes me feel like the king I used to be. I won't go down easy.

As my eyelids grow heavy, I feel him enter my cell, his familiar weight settling onto the end of my mattress.

I imagine him leaning slightly forward, elbows on his knees, hands on his cheeks. Deep, contemplative, always thoughtful James. Waiting to be spoken to while drowning in his own thoughts.

"Hello, James," I say into the darkness. "Welcome back. I've missed you."

I feel the weight of his spirit shift. His back is now be against the wall, knees pulled up to his chest, feet resting against the cold metal of the bed frame. This was how we'd spend our nights as kids, whispering quietly while promising our parents we were sleeping, hoping they couldn't hear our giggles while we exchanged tall tales and droned on about superheroes.

There would be no giggling tonight, no stories, no monsters in the closet.

"I loved her, you know," I whisper. "I did. Even though she wouldn't really let me. No matter how hard I tried to prove to her she was mine."

I don't feel any shift. I'm sure he wouldn't agree, but what did James know? He wasn't there with us when things were good. He was only there to scoop up the broken pieces when Trudy needed something to put her together again. Alcohol was my choice; James was hers.

"There just wasn't room enough for both of us. You knew this. But I don't understand why you felt like you could slip back in and take her away from me. Christopher called me that day, you know. He didn't want you to take her away, either. You should have just left town, James. Sitting on that corner, making sure everyone saw how pathetic your life was. No one cared. We all pitied you, having every opportunity and just walking away from them for a girl who didn't even love you. None of this would have happened if you would have just left."

I feel the bed lighten. No more pressure.

He's gone.

"Wake up," a rough voice calls, accompanied by a methodic thumping of something hard on metal. "I said, wake up."

I recognize the voice. A slight Southern drawl, even though he tries so hard to add a New York twist for toughness. Sammie.

My blood runs cold. I don't stir.

My body goes rigid when I hear the click of metal and the door starts to slide open.

The light coming through my window is still a soft gray. The rays of the sun are not even warm yet.

"Don't make me say it again," Sammie says, smacking the back of my kneecaps with his club. "Get. Up."

I groan in response, pain shooting up my legs as I try to will myself out of bed.

"Where's Warden Stanfield?" I ask, already knowing the answer.

"Jamaica. You're in my jail now, and this is the third time I've told you to get your no-good ass up."

Another blow settles on my lower back, knocking my body back to the bed.

The only choice I have is to fight through the pain and get to my feet as quickly as possible.

Warden Stanfield would be gone for two weeks. He'd tried to keep his vacation a secret in order to maintain discipline, to not give anyone time to create any devious plans. He knew if shit went down, his vacation would be over.

But word travels fast, and there were a lot of inmates in this jail hungry for revenge.

"Walk," Sammie commands, nightstick firmly pressed into the small of my back.

I bend down to grab my shoes, feeling the stick press harder.

"I said walk. I did not say get dressed."

I obey. The less reason I give him to show force, the higher my chances of getting out of whatever's coming my way.

My bare feet slap against the cold concrete floor.

I'd read the accounts of James's last walk—how he'd asked to go barefoot—and I wonder if this was the hall he walked down.

"This way," Sammie says, pushing me toward the entrance to the yard.

I pause, realizing how quiet it is. No cheering. No yelling. No teasing. I realize it's because no one is in their cells.

"No. It's not time to go to the yard," I say stupidly.

I fall to my knees, my head crashing against the door as the baton comes down hard on my right shoulder.

"It's not time yet. I still need time," I beg.

The door creaks open, and the soft gray sunlight settles over my eyes.

Sammie drags me forward, my feet barely scraping the ground as I try to stand up.

Sammie has a good six inches on me, and a hundred pounds, mostly muscle. I could never take him down, no matter how well I've revamped my body.

"Warden Stanfield will be pissed about this," I say, hoping this would be the one trump card I could play.

"No. He won't. He just asked for an update." Sammie laughs and my blood runs cold.

I notice long shadows slipping over the concrete walkway to the yard, almost reaching my fingertips as I land on my knees with a single shove. I look up to see that the shadows are connected to twenty-five very angry faces—twenty-five faces I'd seen before, when I thought I was untouchable.

"Warden says to leave him alive," Sammie says, turning back toward the door.

I scramble to my feet, looking at him to see if this is some sort of joke.

"Oh, and by the way, Denny, happy fifteenth anniversary."

Sammie smirks and shuts the door.

The words run through my head. I've been in here fifteen years? Time files.

A shadow comes from behind me, and I catch the reflection of a face in the small glass window of the yard door.

When the knife enters between my ribs, softly, right where it will hurt but not kill me, I understand.

"Happy anniversary, Trudy," I say, and wait for the rest to come.

ACKNOWLEDGEMENTS

First and foremost I want to thank everyone at Woodhall Press who took this book and turned it from a NaNoWriMo project into beautiful pages. I'm so happy to be a part of this wonderful family you're building. Chris, Colin, Nathaniel, Matt Jayne, and Miranda: I am so grateful for you, your amazing community of authors and the care you put into every book.

Next I have to thank the amazing authors and writers who make Happy Writing more than an idea, but a community. You gave me the push to turn an abandoned 35k words into a manuscript and the confidence to send it out into the world. To Amie, who started with us when we fit at one table (because it was only the two us), to the first five, to Hannah who helped us expand from one day to two, to Laurel, Marie, the Lauras, Beth, and to those who join us now when we overflow cafés with our words and projects, you mean the world to me.

To Christina, my partner in crime at Happy Writing, I am so thankful for everything you have brought to our community and to my life.

To my MBT and Munich family, thank you for welcoming this little weirdo into your life. Allison, Will, Natalya, Dani, Theo, Kevin, Elliot, Oli, Luce, Marty, Rich, Mai, Roberto, Chris, Jimmy, and the rest, you are the best and you make my life rich beyond belief. To Kyle, who'd always ask how the book was going when I was madly writing in the garage in between tours, sweaty and covered in bicycle grease. To Ryan who let me bounce random ideas for future books off him at the most inopportune times, sometimes knowing what I was doing, sometimes not, but always down to discuss a potential story.

To Debbie Burns who went from a stranger on the internet to a friend, and whose daily email blasts always filled me with shine and glitter, making me believe anything was possible.

To my schoolmates who constantly voted me 'Most Likely to be a Poet or Author' like that was a bad thing, and to the Center Grove school system librarians who fed my book habit and always kept me reading or writing.

To the Pen Name gang: Dori, Leslie, Ralph, Mike, and Scott, thanks for being there in the early days and continuing to trust me to design the covers for your upcoming work. It means the world to me.

And last but not least, to my parents who always bought me copious amounts of books at Scholastic Book Fairs, rebuilt my closet to make sure my clothes didn't get in the way of my reading, who drove me around to meet authors and snagged every new copy of Goosebumps or The Babysitters Club immediately. You're everything.

ABOUT THE AUTHOR

J.D. Wright is the founder of Happy Writing, which celebrates the unique powers of her inspiring community of writers. Wright interviews authors on the Happy Writing Podcast, sharing the joys and challenges of writing without fluff. An award-winning cover designer and lover of authentic, creative living, Wright now lives in Munich, Germany, where she teaches university courses in sustainability, graphic design and branding, editorial design, and social media marketing. She is a Mindfulness in Action Coach and Certified Happiness Coach, focusing her work on helping authors create better writing habits and embrace their authentic, creative selves.

You can connect with Jessica on social media - @imahappywriter and her website, www.imahappywriter.com

7 MINUTES